FOREST OF BONES

CRYMSYN HART

MOCHA MEMOIRS PRESS

Copyright Notice

Cover Art by Lilly Dormishev

Editor: Rie Sheridan Rose

Proofreader: Alexandra Christian

Publisher: Mocha Memoirs Press

OTHER MOCHA MEMOIRS DARK FANTASY TITLES

Dead Heat by Ren Thompson

Nightmarescape by Jonathan Fortin

The Portal Guards by Marcia Colette

I

BONE

CHAPTER ONE

"Y ou shouldn't be out here," Adran scolded her.

Kaya threw him a dark glance. He had worn many labels—friend, one-time lover, traveling companion—the lines had blurred until he became her confidant. "Mother can't keep me cooped up like one of her night birds. The Thralls keep invading our lands and slaughtering our families. I can be helpful."

"She has other scouts to tell her about the Thrall movements. She's doing her best to defend the villages, but the townspeople are nothing more than farmers. Thralls are using silver against her soldiers."

"And it's our job to protect them."

"The Thralls have more *varaz* working for them. Ours are stretched thin along the borders trying to keep everyone safe. Why are you even watching these men? You've been following them for hours."

Kaya gripped the tree branch until it cracked as she perched above the clearing and gazed down at the men below. Everything Adran said was true. Over the last century, the nomadic tribes of the Thralls had pushed further and further into Vyrkola territory. It wasn't until recently they had gotten warlike. The magicians who lived in Vyrkola lands had many jobs to do and, as Adran said, they were stretched thin. Kaya assisted where she could, but her mother didn't want word to spread about Kaya's full abilities.

She pulled the hood closer to hide her face from the stinging light. Clouds cloaked the setting sun, but it still prickled her flesh. Her partial ability to withstand the daylight made her unlike the other Vyrkola.

The men below laughed around the campfire.

"I was scouting the Thrall encampment to see if I could hear anything about their plans. These men infiltrated the camp, killed a couple of the guards, and snuck into the main tent. Their actions piqued my interest. They might have discovered something. I wanted to see where they were going, in case I could get some useful information from them."

"Wonderful. Did it occur to you to turn back when they camped on the outskirts of the haunted forest?"

A loud screech echoed through the night.

"We shouldn't be here." Adran shivered.

The men below stopped chatting. One of them drew his sword and jumped up to face the unseen foe. A few chuckled at the soldier.

"No need to fear, Harish. We're far enough away from the forest's heart that no demon is going to appear. No great beast is going to burst through the trees." A man with light brown hair pulled away from his face threw something into the fire, making the flames jump and shoot sparks into the air. Shadows obscured most of his face so Kaya couldn't see any more detail.

"That's what they want you to think, Stavros. The Shadowed Gods linger in this cursed place," Harish answered him.

The raiders had changed into plain dark-brown tunics and black pants to blend in better with the night. Their horses were tied nearby, where the light from the fire could protect them from the dangers of the wood.

"What of the Vyrks? We're close to their borders. They could be lurking in the shadows waiting to pounce on us. Their lust for blood—"

"Let's not talk of the Vyrks." Stavros's expression hardened at the mention of her people. "Fine. Keep the fire lit—but low. It'll keep away any creatures that venture out of the Bone Forest. Sleep in two hour shifts so you can get a little rest. I want to be out of here before dawn breaks." Their leader leaned back against his pack and closed his eyes.

Kaya stretched out her senses to the world around her. She nearly lost her balance as a strong source of magic enveloped her. The seam of power running through the Bone Forest grated along her spirit like coarse sand. It made her cringe and want to spread her wings and fly back toward the mountains. The magic in the mountains was lighter, almost pure, where this place was murky like a bloody river.

In her mind's eye, she saw a throbbing wound in the thread of power weaving through the forest. This seam was diseased. Pulses of darkness pushed along the vein, widening it to release more sickness into the environment.

"Kaya, did you hear what I said?"

She pulled away from the magical source and focused back on her friend. "Sorry. The magic here is...corrupt."

"Of course, it is. This place is cursed. Vyrkola don't come near here for a reason. Or the *varaz* for that matter. The Bone Forest became uninhabitable after your ancestor—"

A breeze clattered the leaves together. Kaya caught the scent of blood from the distant battles that waged on. "Hush." The wind also brought something else with it: a trace of horses and other men.

"Why are we being quiet?" Adran whispered.

"Something's coming."

"Let them deal with it. You need to come back to the palace."

Kaya jumped from the tree. Her form shrank. Feathers sprouted where skin and clothes had been. The tip of her tail skimmed the top of Adran's head. Even in the tiny body of the grackle, the magic in the area impacted her. The draft fluffed her feathers as she rose above the trees to get a bird's eye view of the land below. A band of ten sped toward the scouting party. An urgent desire to warn the men below gripped her. She couldn't shake it.

It didn't make any rational sense, but something told her she had to try. Kaya dove through the trees and circled the campfire. The fire singed her feet. She pulled them closer to her body as she flew and ignored the brief pain. She darted toward the men to get their attention. They waved their arms and swatted at her. No matter how hard she tried, they only thought her an annoying bird. Frustrated, Kaya pushed back up to Adran and morphed back to human form.

"Let's go. You tried to warn them. Besides, I know you're hungry. The dark circles under your eyes are a dead giveaway."

"I can handle my hunger. They slipped into the Thrall tents for a reason. Their leader—Stavros—came out with a satchel and something he stuffed into his shirt. I couldn't see what it was. They didn't say anything aloud about what they got, so I don't know what it was. They might know something we don't. That information could be useful to us, too."

"I doubt they'll give you whatever intelligence they stole out of the kindness of their hearts," Adran grumbled.

The buzz of his magic flashed over Kaya's skin like a swarm of bees flying at her. She could always tell it was him by the feel of his power.

The pounding of horses' hooves drew closer. A sense of urgency filled her. If the men below *had* stolen secrets from the Thralls, she needed them alive because it might help her mother with the battles the Vyrkola waged with them.

They're going to be massacred and the information lost. If only I could read minds, like the others, my life would be easier.

Adran gathered more power around him. It weighed on her chest.

She glanced back up at him and winked. He opened his mouth to say something, but Kaya dropped from the tree. She pulled her hood down to hide her face and summoned a bit of her own magic, directing the shadows to cloak her so even if the men were close, they wouldn't get a good look at her.

Her landing garnered the attention of the small band. One of his band shook Stavros. He jumped up and grabbed his sword. His men circled around them ready to pounce on her.

"They're coming for you," she warned.

"Who are you?" Stavros held his sword ready to attack.

"Demon." One of their band shouted. He lunged at her.

Kaya waved her hand and, with a little push of magic, sent him back into a tree. The others advanced, but the leader held up his hand to stop them.

"I am no demon."

"If you're no demon, then why are you here, appearing from the darkness and concealing your face?" Stavros asked her.

The others closed in. Kaya pulled back her magic and focused on their leader. "I mean you no harm. If I did, I could've struck you much earlier than this. I'm here to warn you. Gather your weapons. The ones—"

The thump of an arrow at her feet from outside the camp stopped her.

The man who had released the arrow stepped from the shadows. He slipped another into his bow and aimed it at the lead scout.

Kaya kicked the sword aside in a swift move and shoved Stavros to the ground. Intense pain blossomed in her left shoulder and forced her to her knees. Kaya glanced up to see the leader's shocked expression. The rest of his men scrambled to defend themselves against the incoming barrage.

"Need some help?" Adran pushed his white-blond hair from his eyes and gripped the arrow shaft in her shoulder. "I can count to three."

"Just do it." Kaya grimaced.

She pressed her hand to the wound to stop the blood until her body's natural healing ability kicked in. A wave of dizziness passed over her. Her shoulder tingled as it healed. Not feeding had caught up to her. *Adran's right. I need to eat.*

"You should've gone back to the castle," Adran chided her.

A volley of arrows rained around them. One of them glanced off the top of Adran's head. His magic buzzed around her as the invisible energy shield protected them.

"I don't need an 'I told you so' right now." Kaya shook off the wooziness and stood up.

"Good. I suggest we get out of here. We both need our strength to get back to the castle. Let them fight it out. You're healing and my magic is waning. I can't keep the shield around both of us. We need to go."

Kaya was about to agree with him when another arrow hit her left thigh. She crumpled back to the ground.

Adran swore.

The band of men hovered around Stavros. Arrows dropped a couple of them. They couldn't see their enemy in the darkness the way she could. Horses charged into the clearing. One rider forced his horse through the fire. The Thralls surrounded the small band.

"You really know how to push my buttons, don't you?"

Adran asked Kaya, pulling the other arrow from her thigh. This one was deeper than the one in her shoulder. The rush of blood to the new wound made the pain almost unbearable.

"I never told you to come along."

Adran shook his head. A flash of white appeared between his hands as he gathered energy and sharpened it into blades. "You gonna be able to shift to get out of here?"

She nodded. Although she wasn't sure how far she would get. Far enough away she could rest. Knowing Adran, he would give her some of his blood to sustain her until she could get back to the castle.

Kaya took a breath, gathering her strength. The magical shield Adran had erected buzzed stronger as he fed more energy into it and it wrapped around her again like a second skin. A surge of adrenaline hit her as her body repaired itself. Kaya stood up.

Adran threw his blades and hit two of the Thrall riders.

"Get them," Stavros screamed and rallied his men.

A Thrall with a wicked scar slashed across his forehead rushed toward her. Kaya drew her long dagger from its sheath. The slightly curved blade sliced the man across the calf. The explosion of blood scent stirred her hunger. The rider came back at her, but she jumped out of the way. Others came at them on foot.

Adran kept throwing his energy blades.

Stavros fought beside his men with the skill of one trained by a master swordsman.

Kaya cut down another Thrall foot soldier and noted Stavros now fought two different foes at once. If he went down, then so did her chance of learning what he had gleaned from the Thrall encampment.

She raced over to defend him. A sharp slice caught her across the back and made her go to one knee as Adran's magical shield fell away.

Kaya sought out her friend and saw him lying on the ground. Her heart lurched. The clamor of swords hurt her ears. She licked her lips and tried to push her hunger away. It thumped in her ears as the clanging of metal on metal got louder. She pressed her nails into her palms and fought on. She swung at the next man who came at her and killed him. Kaya felled a couple more soldiers until something hard hit her hand, knocking the dagger from her grip. Kaya tried to focus on the man charging toward her. It all got hazy as the pain from her wounds finally overcame her.

She stumbled. Someone grabbed her arm and spun her around.

"My, my, what do we have here?" The man she had been trying to protect had a sword pointed at her throat.

Darkness flickered on the edge of her vision. Her wounds throbbed. Her thoughts flew to Adran and she prayed he would come around. The cold blade touched her throat.

Stavros yanked her hood back exposing her face.

"It would do you best to let me go," she said quietly.

"She wants me to let her go?" He chuckled and looked at his remaining men.

Kaya tried to appeal to the man's rational side. "We both have information we can share to help one another defeat the Thralls."

"How do I know you weren't with them?"

"She took two arrows meant for you and warned you of their approach. I don't think she's working with them, do you?" Adran said behind them.

Her heart lifted, knowing he was okay.

Blood streaked his forehead where he had been hit. One of the soldiers had him in a choke hold with a knife against his throat.

"What do you know, *varaz*?" one of the other soldiers spat. He turned his sword on Adran. "Sire, this could've all been a setup."

"Please," Kaya whispered to Stavros, "we saved you. I'm not working with the Thralls." She swayed as she tried to stay conscious and not give in to her hunger. Cold threaded along her nerves.

He touched her chin. It roused her enough to concentrate on his voice.

"As beautiful as you are, I've never met a magician that didn't have something up their sleeve."

She wanted to answer him, but pain exploded in the back of her head and darkness followed.

CHAPTER TWO

S tavros examined the woman. Something about her caught his eye now that her magic didn't conceal her features as it had before the attack. He didn't think she was a Thrall spy.

She warned us about them and took an arrow meant for me. Both of them are varaz, *that is obvious by their shape-shifting.*

The male elbowed free of his captor and rushed to the fallen woman, hovering over her protectively.

He's her bodyguard. I can use both of them.

He gazed at his troops and the dead Thralls. "Take their horses and see if there are any more coming."

The troops obeyed, giving Stavros a moment alone with the magicians. "Who is she? Why do you protect her?"

The man reached to his side and drew a knife. Stavros was quicker and knocked it from his hand.

"Please, my lord," pleaded the stranger. "I appreciate

you sending your men away. If you desire answers, then you need to let me attend to her."

"Is she ill? I've heard that using too much magic can drain a *varaz*."

The other man lifted his hands and retrieved the dagger.

"Take heed what you do with that blade."

"It's for her. She hasn't exhausted herself from overuse of magic."

"Proceed."

The bodyguard sliced his palm open and brought it to the woman's mouth.

Stavros's heart hardened. He jabbed the tip of his sword into the man's throat. "I should've known. I should take your head and hers. Filthy Vyrks. You're a traitor to other humans."

Stavros kept his eyes glued to her to see when she would awaken. The woman swallowed the blood even though she was knocked out cold. *She'll be on me or one of my men when she revives. I'll have to be quick. Vyrks have lightning reflexes.* The speed with which she'd moved when she kicked the sword from his hand made sense now. Even with magic, he hadn't seen a *varaz* move that quickly before.

"It's not what you think. She's not like the other Vyrkola. She's special."

"We'll see about that."

The beast moaned and opened her eyes.

"That's enough." Stavros pierced the male magician's flesh to enforce the command.

He pulled his hand away. A faint blush returned to the

female's cheeks. Stavros ran his gaze over her womanly form, but knew even with the attractive guise, she was a soulless monster. His guard returned with the Thrall horses.

"Report," Stavros ordered.

"All the Thralls are dead. We should return to the palace in case there's another band behind them. The generals will want reports and—to be honest, Sire—none of the men feel safe in this place."

He understood his men's feelings. The Bone Forest was said to be haunted. No one wanted to travel even on the fridges of the wood where the trees and animals were normal. Stories that told of strange beasts and wood turned to bone had lingered in the kingdom for generations. Some called it a dead forest where the spirits of those who passed on called out for loved ones to join them. The place gave him the chills.

He thought he could use the superstitions to his advantage and hide from the Thralls. But they had come anyway, catching up to them even after they sneaked out of the Thrall camp with vital information that would assist them in the days to come.

"Agreed. Gag the scum." He gestured to the man and unconscious woman. "We don't want them whispering spells to seduce us. Bind this one's hands and let him run behind the horses. Let's see how well he does. The woman comes with me."

Stavros ripped a piece off his shirt and bound the barely conscious woman's hands. He used another strip to gag her. She didn't put up much of a fight, which he thought was rather odd. The blood the *varaz* had given her should have helped heal her.

He kicked the beast in the ribs. "Get up, Vyrk."

Her servant tried to rouse her, but his men slugged him.

The woman tried to rise, but she fell again. On the second attempt, she seemed aware enough to stand.

Stavros mounted his horse.

"Get on the horse."

She struggled to obey. He grabbed her arm and hauled her up in front of him, securing her so she couldn't fall off. His stomach lurched at being so close to this soulless creature who pretended to be a woman, but he wanted answers. Gripping the reins, he focused on the journey back to the castle.

His prisoner slumped over the horse's neck as she passed out again. The steady thunder of hooves and the rhythm of the galloping horse helped ease his mind. *She's far from her lands. Maybe she told the truth. She did save my life.* Stavros shoved the thought away. He hated to think about owing the she-monster a debt. The image of her drinking the blood flashed in his mind. It riled his anger again. He tried to stop the flood of images that followed.

His beloved, dead at his feet. Their son murdered. Both drained of blood. The look on the Vyrk assassin's face before he jumped out of the window when Stavros walked in. Ever since that night, any Vyrkola caught in his kingdom was slaughtered. This one would be next—once he obtained the information he needed. Of course, their extermination wasn't the official word, but he made it known to all of his subjects. He still had to trade with the filth because they provided the silver, gold, and iron his kingdom needed, but it twisted his guts every time he thought about it.

They rode for some time before one of his men came up beside him. "Sire, the male prisoner has fallen and won't rise."

Stavros glanced behind him. "Check to be sure he's dead. I don't need an angry *varaz* on my hands."

He watched as Harish kicked the magician and then stabbed him. He waited a moment, but the fallen man didn't move. Harish indicated that the *varaz* was dead.

Stavros nodded. "Cut him loose."

Must not have been that skilled in magic.

Stavros turned back toward the castle, pushing the horses hard as the moon slid lower into the darkness. He desired to be in his own bed, but there was much to do before he could rest his head. He checked the woman again. She hadn't moved, but she could be feigning weakness.

Probably biding her time until she can find a good moment to strike me down.

Another reason for the fast pace—he didn't want them caught by the sun or she would burn to ash. His chance to interrogate her and find out what the Vyrks were planning as they collaborated with the Thralls would be gone.

When they arrived at the castle, he dismounted his horse, but she remained still. He grabbed a handful of her hair and pulled her down. The Vyrk landed on her feet and stared at him. Her dark brown eyes were shot with silver and held nothing but malice for him.

Stavros took her arm and marched her into the castle. He stuck to the shadows as they headed through an unused part of the castle into an old keep built especially for Vyrkola. He shoved her inside. High walls surrounded them on four sides with no roof. The sky lightened with the coming dawn. A wooden post stood in the center of the keep. Silver manacles hung from a metal loop near the top, untarnished by the elements. He untied her hands and slipped them into the cuffs.

"Don't think you're going to get out of these. They were fashioned long ago out of spell-warded silver so *varaz* can't access their magic. I'm sure the silver will be very uncomfortable for you."

He clicked the last cuff shut and pulled the gag from her mouth. He half expected her to scream—all she did was glare at him. "Tell me what you're planning. Why did you warn me about the Thralls' ambush? The sun will be up in a few hours. It turns this place into an oven. If you don't want to end up dust, then you'll cooperate with me."

"You don't understand," she murmured.

Stavros undid her cloak and threw it on the ground. He ripped open her shirt, exposing the pale skin over her heart. His fingers trailed over her smooth flesh for a moment, entranced by her beauty. He almost released her —then repulsion gripped him as he remembered she was nothing more than a dead thing. "What don't I understand?"

"We saved you."

"Your kind don't save anyone unless they want to turn them or kill them. Is that what you were planning for me? Putting your mark on me the way you did that traitor magician? Maybe scouting me out to seduce me?" His anger at being caught off guard and saved by the creature fueled his irrational rage.

"I'm not what you think I am."

Someone knocked on the door.

"What?" Stavros growled.

A servant boy stepped inside. "Sire, forgive the intrusion. Chancellor Kewskin has requested an audience with you."

Stavros groaned. "Tell him to wait in my private study. After I meet with him, I'm to bed and not to be disturbed." He turned back to his prisoner after the servant left.

She has to pay for her insolence. I'll get a few hours of sleep and then she'll talk. She should last that long before the sun fries her fully. He tore her shirt completely down the middle to expose more flesh. *More skin for the sun to bake.*

The urge to really humiliate her engulfed him, but Kewskin waited. He hated the man's very presence. The quicker he got the meeting over, the better.

"Please, don't do this."

"Good. I like when you beg." He drew his dagger across her cheek to see her bleed, but she didn't scream. "Don't worry. You're all mine. No one is going to rescue you. Your *varaz* is dead."

Stavros left the keep, locking the door on the way out. He grabbed a servant rushing by. "Stay here and guard this door. No one goes inside. Do you understand?"

"Y-yes, my King!" The boy nearly fell over once he was asked to watch the door.

Stavros chuckled as he walked to his private study.

Knowing the Vyrk was secure eased some of his restlessness. After the attack and the race back to the castle, the adrenaline was fading, leaving his limbs heavy and his brain foggy with the need for sleep. In his study, the chancellor hovered by the hearth, warming himself by a newly-built fire.

The older man appeared to be in his mid-fifties, but appearances were deceiving when it came to *varaz*. They could show their true age or use magic to make themselves look younger. The power flowing in their veins aged them slower than normal people. Kewskin had advised his father and helped Stavros in rooting out the Vyrks in his kingdom with his magic along with many other tasks.

"This had better be quick, Kewskin. I wish to find my dreams before I meet with the generals."

The magician turned from the fire. His green eyes flashed in the light. His blue robes swished as he bowed. "Forgive me, I've been watching for your approach. You came into my viewing bowl a couple of hours ago. I saw you had a woman with you. I sensed her power. It's had me curious."

"Why the curiosity?"

Kewskin's lips twitched into a small smile before his expression became unreadable once more. He dragged his nails over the chain of his office. "Only to see what secrets this woman holds. It's clear she's a powerful *varaz*. I didn't realize the Thralls had such magicians on their side. I would love to interrogate her. After you are done with her, of course."

The need for sleep tugged at Stavros, but something about the chancellor's words made him uneasy. "We will see. Assemble the generals for a meeting at the eleventh bell. They have to be brought up to speed on what I have discovered."

"As you wish." Kewskin bowed and left the room.

Stavros thought about the wizard as Kewskin exited his study. He had always been loyal and proved to be powerful when it came to defending the castle. He discovered the manacles that blocked *varaz* magic forgotten under a pile of fallen rubble in some old ruins of the palace no one had explored for generations.

He knew Kewskin kept an eye on him through a viewing bowl that let the chancellor monitor the kingdom. The limited observation didn't stretch to their borders or into the threads of magic that lined the land. He always said there was too much interference. Stavros shook his head at the dynamics of what he knew about *varaz*. The idea of manipulating power the way they did boggled his mind.

What made him seethe were the soulless creatures roaming the land that had killed his wife. One of them was now in the keep. Her face flashed in his mind. The all-consuming anger made him pound his fist against a table. Her death would come...but he needed information first.

She'll get what's coming to her.

Stavros slipped behind a tapestry and made his way up to his room and into bed.

———

Several hours later, the bells in the tower chimed ten. He smelled food and found a tray on the table and a blazing fire. He ate, dressed for his meeting with the generals, and made his way down to the war room. His generals crowded around the long table which held a map of the kingdom and its surrounding neighbors. As he entered, the talking ceased. Kewskin remained at the back of the gaggle of generals watching them all. Their expectant eyes met his as they all began speaking at once.

Stavros held up his hands. "Gentlemen, quiet please."

"Sire, it was against our better judgment that you went into the enemy's camp. We—" one of the generals started.

"Enough! What's done is done. Here is what I know. The Thralls are advancing faster than we anticipated. They're working with the Vyrks. We slipped into their camp and killed a few of their guards. We overheard the Thrall leader talking with a few Vyrkola about their plans to advance further into the kingdom. They've resorted to using *varaz*. I captured one and brought her back with me. The other died on the way here."

"If that's the case, then we're doomed," General Jarik grumbled. He was left over from the regime of Stavros's father. The ancient man creaked as he walked.

"Why would the Vyrks be siding with the Thralls?" Commander Doran leaned on the table as he spoke.

"What else did you hear, Sire? Has this woman said anything? Where is she being kept? I would like to question her," declared General Brop.

"I can't answer why the Vyrks are working with them or where they recruited the *varaz*. Last I knew, the Thralls didn't embrace using magic. Four of our border towns have been burned and ransacked. I've seen the carnage. I didn't want to believe the reports at first. That's why I went there to see what was happening to my people. I also heard the Vyrk mention the ruins in the Forest of Bones. They want something there and have paid the Thralls to get it for them. Once the Vyrks have it, they promised to put all their resources into helping the Thralls expand their grab for land in our kingdom. They'll keep coming unless we stop them." He glanced at the map. If he could set up an ambush for the Thrall raiding parties, then he could push them out of his lands.

"Sire, if I may suggest something?" Kewskin wormed his way through the throng near the king.

"Yes?"

"Maybe they are using these incursions to divert our attention from their real goal?"

"What do you know of military campaigns?" General Chelton growled. "You're nothing more than a two-penny conjurer. Your Majesty, do we have to listen to this drivel?"

"Enough." Stavros pounded his fist on the table. "I don't need you squabbling. Everyone in this room has equal say as to what threatens the kingdom. Continue, Chancellor Kewskin."

The general threw him a look. It was no secret General Chelton didn't get along with Kewskin. They had a rivalry going back even before his father's time. The chancellor reached for one of the wooden soldiers on the map.

"From the king's own lips, the Vyrkola are interested in some ruins in the Forest of Bones. Tales tell us the forest is haunted. Even older stories say the forest used to be a

Vyrkola stronghold. Their king was a great magician who tried to harness the thread of magic which runs underneath the forest. He tapped into the well of energy where it bubbles close to the surface. This king couldn't contain the power. It exploded around him, creating the desolate landscape we know today and turning the trees to bone. Now nothing grows there except on the outskirts where the branches of the thread haven't touched. Dark things linger in the forest."

"Old wives' tales," spat Chelton.

"Not so. I've been to the forest. I didn't make it as far as the ruins because the energy was too...overwhelming...and tried to consume me. Some dark power remains in the heart of that wood. What our gracious king said was that he overheard the Thralls making some agreement with the Vyrks. What if the Thrall advancement is all part of a bigger plan? Stage a few skirmishes. Burn a few villages close to our borders. It draws our attention to defend our towns while they go into the forest. Sire, you captured one of their *varaz*. With a little enticement, she will spill her secrets."

Stavros gritted his teeth. He wasn't about to reveal the woman was also a Vyrk. What Kewskin said made sense. It also brought back the notion he owed his life to the female in the keep. "It's true. We captured one of their spies."

The generals murmured among themselves.

"The female has been in the keep with the sun baking her all day. I'll get some answers out of her. Chelton and Kewskin, find me some men who are brave enough to stare down the shadows in the Forest of Bones. Ten gold pieces each. Kewskin, since you had the idea, you will lead the party, with General Chelton as your escort. Any who survive will receive another ten gold pieces."

Chelton bowed his head. Kewskin smirked. Stavros left the war room thinking about what he was going to do with the woman.

The noon bell rang. She had been in the sun all morning.

She's gotta be pretty close to burned through. Stavros barely noticed those who bowed as he passed. Kewskin caught up with him as he crossed the courtyard heading to the keep.

"What do you want?"

"Forgive me, Sire, but I didn't want to ask in front of the generals..."

"What is it?"

"Is it true the female *varaz* is also a Vyrkola?"

Stavros stopped. The gleam in the man's eyes piqued his curiosity about how much the chancellor actually knew. "What of it?"

Kewskin tented his fingers and clicked his nails together. "When you're done with her, can I keep her to experiment on?"

"Why do you ask?"

"When you brought her in, I sensed her power. Now you say she is also a Vyrk. No Vyrkola can wield magic, not even their queen. If anyone with magic is turned, they lose the ability. This one is special."

Letting the sun take the woman would be a mercy compared to placing her in Kewskin's hands. As much as he hated Vyrks, he didn't want to know what the chancellor would do to her. Kewskin's words only made him want to get to the woman sooner. Her bodyguard had also said she was special, but special how?

Images of the instruments he would use to elicit her cries flipped through his mind. His hands ached to try out some of the new torture mechanisms his blacksmiths had fashioned for him. "Let me question her first. She could be helpful with the expedition into the Bone Forest."

"True. She might know more than we do." Kewskin bowed and left his side.

A tingle of anticipation engulfed him. She should be severely crisped by now. Stavros imagined how she would beg him to release her to go and die in peace.

Sadly, he had plans for her before she expired.

CHAPTER THREE

The sun's rays slowly crept down the sides of the keep until they touched her flesh. Without the protection of her cloak or shadows, her skin reddened. Her body craved sustenance, whether it was food or blood. The blood would heal her faster. Food would satisfy her human hunger. She attempted to free herself from the manacles, but some ancient force cut her off from her magic.

Kaya tried to conserve her energy by meditating and slowing her heart rate. It was obvious Stavros wouldn't believe her. His hatred was evident when he looked at her.

Adran was right. I never should've followed him.

"I thought you'd be a little crispier by now." Her captor entered, carrying a mug.

Kaya licked her cracked lips as her body ached for any kind of liquid. He held a leather bundle underneath his arm. She locked her gaze on the cup.

His brows furrowed. "You want this?"

She nodded.

He set the bag down, brought the rim of the cup to her mouth, and tipped it back. Water passed her lips. She gulped down the few swallows he allowed before he took it away.

"You are a mystery."

"I'm not what you think I am," she forced out.

Stavros smirked. Her death was already written in his eyes. "You're a Vyrkola. I kill all of those who cross my path. Before I take your heart, you're going to tell me what I want to know. My chancellor says you're rare. I don't care if you're a Vyrk with magic or not."

He studied the parcel he had brought with him and pulled out a small silver dagger. He dragged the blade across her skin but didn't cut her. "This has been in my family for centuries."

"Use what you want on me, but I can't bring back whoever you lost."

Anger flashed in his gaze. He slashed her cheek.

Kaya bit her lip from the sharp pain.

"One more thing out of your mouth that isn't an answer to my questions, I'll take your eye. Do you understand? I don't need you in my head."

Unlike her clansmen, she didn't possess the ability to hypnotize others. The sun beat on her back.

Stavros grabbed another implement from the leather bag. He placed the contraption on her chest and positioned the corners over her breasts. Once he found the right spot, he punched the corners into her flesh. With each pound, she winced, until a small cry left her lips. He selected another piece and attached it to the device over her heart.

"You're going to answer questions to my satisfaction or

28

I'm going to use this tool to remove your heart. The blades separate the skin and muscles until I get down to bone. Then I have another piece that cracks your rib cage. After that, I slowly break your ribs until your heart is exposed. If I don't like your answers, I'm going to widen your chest a little bit more each time. Do you understand?"

"Yes." She would die regardless if he took her heart. The only difference he would notice between her and others of her kind was that her heartbeat.

"Good. Why did you warn me about the Thrall raiding party?"

Kaya closed her eyes and drew in a breath. "I saw you and your men kill the Thrall soldiers and sneak into their camp. I was curious. I followed to see what you had learned in the Thrall tents. They're also raiding our villages and killing the people under our protection. The Vyrkola have no love for the Thralls either. I hoped we might share information."

"Liar." He turned a crank on his device.

Searing pain speared her entire body. Kaya screamed.

"You led them to me."

"No."

He wound his mechanism another half turn.

She slumped against the post. She didn't know how long she could endure the pain. Tears slipped down her cheeks. She sent a silent prayer to the dark goddess, Efret, to watch over her.

It went against everything she was taught, but if she revealed herself, then maybe she had a chance. "Please, Majesty. Kill me and you'll start a war you don't want."

"Why is that?"

"Because my mother, the Queen, will send all of our people to invade your lands to avenge me. We have no quarrel with your kingdom. My mother might be gathering the troops now. She'll feel I'm suffering and when I die..." Kaya stared at him and tried to make him realize who she was.

Her attacker stepped back and studied her. "Your mother is queen of the Vyrks? Your kind can't have children. Another lie." He wound the gadget again.

"If you don't believe me, check my back. I carry the family crest. If you know anything about the Vyrkola, then you know we all bear the mark of our bloodlines. It's one way we keep track of how many of us there are. Each is tallied in our registry. Only so many are allowed in the line." Kaya prayed he would believe her.

Stavros tore off the remains of her clothes and twisted her around to examine her back. "Son of a bloodsucking whore beast," he roared. He shoved her back against the post hard enough it knocked the breath out of her. Her captor ripped the contraption from her chest.

She sagged in her chains. *Thank you, Efret. At least I'm saved for now.*

The man grasped her chin. "What is your name, *Princess?*" he seethed.

"Kaya."

He jabbed the tip of the silver knife into her throat. "Not your common name. If you bear a royal crest, then you have another name. Tell me and I'll consider not killing you."

"Kayanna EbonWing, only daughter of Queen Mila EbonWolf."

"Your father?"

"My father's dead."

"Staked no doubt for preying on helpless children. I applaud the ones who carried out the deed."

"My father was human, a mid-level *varaz*. He died before I was born."

"You're the offspring of a human and a female vampire? That's impossible."

"And yet here I am." The sun blistered her exposed skin and blasted on the top of her head. Kaya hadn't noticed before, but the stones inside the keep were highly polished, intensifying the heat and light.

She didn't know how much longer she could withstand the sun in this place. She straightened up the best she could, trying to maintain her composure. Her stomach quivered with fear and pain. Her arms ached from being suspended for so long. Her entire body needed rest. "If you don't believe me, send an envoy. Tell them you're holding me hostage. My mother will pay whatever you want, but you'd get more for me alive. Worth my weight in gold or silver."

He tapped the blade against his palm. "An interesting offer, but what I want from you is worth more than money." He touched her cheek and a sneer tugged on his lips.

The keep's door opened. "Your Majesty!"

"What is it?" he growled.

"A Vyrk messenger has arrived, flying royal colors and demanding an audience with you."

She glared at him.

An exciting thrill went through her. Her mother had

felt her suffering and sent someone to rescue her. "Believe me now?"

"Invite them into the main hall."

The king drew a key from around his neck. He undid a lock on the loop that held the manacles. "You might be free of this keep, but you're not going anywhere." Stavros grabbed the chain connecting her cuffs and pulled her behind him into the castle.

Kaya tried to keep her head high and ignore the guards' stares. He dragged her through a maze of back passages and stairways until he came to a small door and threw her into the room. A servant looked down at her and then back to her master.

"Clean her up and make her presentable. Get her bread and water. She stays fettered at all times."

The woman nodded. Kaya wilted to the floor against the large four-poster bed. The king left the room. The reprieve gave her a moment to realize how close to death she had come. Tears burned her eyes. She wiped them away with the back of her hand. The etchings on the silver chains flashed with a life of their own. The language was ancient, but something she had seen before at the ruins in the Bone Forest.

"Poor child, what did he do to you?" the older servant woman asked.

Kaya glanced down at her chest. Blood still seeped from her wounds. Her skin felt stretched over her frame. The burnt flesh on her back ached. "I'm his prisoner. He'll do whatever he wants with me."

"Before the queen and the young prince were killed,

he was a kind man. After their death, a coldness twisted his heart."

Kaya glanced into the woman's kind blue eyes and saw pity. The servant helped her up and led her into a connected room where she filled a bath. "He'll do anything to see me dead in the end."

CHAPTER FOUR

As he approached the throne room, Stavros caught the court's murmurs. They wondered how a Vyrk had come during the day. None of their kind should be able to withstand the sun. And yet this woman had stood in its direct light. Her skin had reddened and blistered, but she hadn't turned into a burnt cinder. The whispers stopped as he entered the room. All the courtiers bowed as he walked through the throne room and took his place before the throne.

Stavros adjusted the emblem of his office as he waited for the Vyrk messenger to enter. He wasn't sure he had believed Kaya until he saw the crest tattoo on her back. As much as he hated her kind, the kingdom traded with them. All negotiations remained short. He never faced them one on one. If not for the important trade, he would have killed the Vyrk ambassador on sight, even if he was protected by diplomatic immunity.

If this woman is a princess, then she's quite a trophy.

Straightening his robes, Kewskin appeared from the hallway behind the throne room to stand at his side. His stoic expression hid something.

"Let their emissary in. We will see him now," Stavros instructed his guards.

The throne room doors opened. A path cleared for the Vyrk messenger. Stavros steeled himself for what the emissary would give in exchange for the princess. The creature wore a black coat like the princess, with the hood low over its face. No skin was exposed. A short sword and dagger were belted at his waist. He stood before Stavros and went to one knee, but Stavros could feel the Vyrk's eyes underneath the cloak judging him.

"High King Stavros, I have come on behalf of Queen Mila EbonWolf of the Vyrkola."

"Your queen must want something very important to send one of her people out in the daylight," he replied.

The Vyrk raised his head. His eyes shone briefly as the torchlight hit them. "My queen wishes to know if you have decided to announce your betrothal to her daughter, the Princess Kayanna, to the rest of the court. She understands that this is why you brought the princess with you after your last rendezvous—to save her from the Thralls who are invading our country as well."

Stavros nearly let his mouth drop as he heard the emissary's words.

Whispers erupted in the court. His lords and advisors shot him looks. He clutched the arms of his throne and bit back his anger. Kewskin leaned in close to him. The man's breath stank of onions and garlic.

"Sire, I don't think you want to—" Kewskin started.

He waved him away and addressed the Vyrk. "Why don't we continue this discussion in private? I'm sure you're tired from your journey and could use refreshment."

"I appreciate your offer, Your Majesty. Privacy would be preferable so we can discuss the details of your upcoming nuptials."

Stavros left the throne room and walked into an adjoining study. He poured a goblet of wine and downed it. The burn didn't help to ease his anger.

Kewskin and the Vyrk envoy followed. The Vyrkola stayed within the shadows. He pulled his hood back, revealing a square jawline. A single black braid hung over his shoulder decorated with silver ornaments. His dark blue eyes caught Stavros's attention, but he quickly glanced away so he wouldn't be caught by the creature's gaze. It had happened once before and because of it he lost everything. The mistake would not be repeated.

"How could you even suggest I'm betrothed to one of your kind?" Stavros threw his goblet at the monster. The Vyrk didn't flinch as it hit the wall next to him.

"It got your attention and confirmed you'd taken the princess captive." The Vyrk crossed his arms over his chest and looked at him as though he was bored with their conversation.

"How did you even know the princess was here? She could've been captured by the Thralls or held elsewhere?" Kewskin asked.

"Once Queen Mila sensed her daughter was in pain during the Thrall ambush, she could see through her daughter's eyes. My queen saw you. I was dispatched immediately to retrieve the princess or do anything necessary to ensure her safety."

"Sire, how do we even know this filth is telling the truth? Vyrks can't have children. The queen isn't known to have a daughter." Kewskin touched his arm to get his attention.

Stavros rolled the information around in his mind. Queen Mila EbonWolf wanted her daughter back unharmed, but there were too many variables to let her return. He still needed to get information out of her. She knew about the ruins in the Forest of Bones. She could tell him how to invade the Vyrkola lands.

As his wife, she would have to do what he said. The mere thought sickened him—but the potential for a political alliance intrigued him.

"Don't believe everything you hear, *varaz*. If you wish to discuss this matter further, Your Majesty, I suggest telling the wizard to leave."

Stavros looked at his chancellor and then back at the Vyrk. "Out, Kewskin."

"But, Sire—"

"Do I have to tell you twice?"

The chancellor acquiesced and left the room.

Stavros sat at a long table and invited the Vyrk to do the same. The undead creature joined him. Silence stretched between them as he fought the dueling sides of himself.

One said to kill the Vyrkola because all of their kind deserved to die. The rational side told him to hear the creature out because he didn't need to start a war when he already had one going with the Thralls.

"You've made me look a fool before the entire court," Stavros blurted out.

"Again, I did what was necessary to save the princess. You might want to torture her some more, but you're intrigued enough now to keep from slaughtering her. Maybe you'll realize how unique and powerful a woman she is."

Stavros chuckled. "Powerful and unique? I think not. She's a soulless monster. No matter what face you wear, you're all the same. You're walking corpses who hunger for blood and will do anything to get it. I've seen the carnage your kind can bring."

The Vyrk emissary kept his face blank. "Think what you want, Your Majesty, but if I don't get an answer to my queen by nightfall then she will bring her wrath. Then you will know what true carnage is."

"If Queen Mila values her daughter's life so much, then why isn't she here herself? Why send a servant?"

The Vyrk's face went slack. His eyes narrowed as he looked directly at Stavros. "You might be king of this small piece of land, but don't presume you're something special. One day you will return to the earth, and I will still rule. I sent my greatest warrior in my stead. We are also fighting the advancements of the Thralls on all our borders. Don't think I'm not present. I hear and see through my ambassador."

Stavros jumped backward as the female voice came out of the male's mouth. "You are the Vyrk queen?"

"And you are the King of the Pressions, Stavros Frey."

"What sorcery is this?" Stavros looked around the room to see if the vampire queen had somehow appeared to make more of a fool of him. He saw nothing, but she could be concealed in the shadows.

"I am connected to all my subjects. I can cast my consciousness into whom I choose— except my daughter. Our bond is different. Valik offered you Kayanna's hand. I know your reputation with the Vyrkola. You kill those you come across because of your wife's death. You have no love for us. I have told my subjects to leave your lands, but not all obey. We are fighting a common enemy.

"King Stavros, think of this as a union to combine forces and wipe out the Thralls once and for all before they storm your castle then take over my kingdom. Working together would be easier than having me at your door," Queen Mila said through Valik.

Stavros gritted his teeth. He hated being put on the spot, but he had also learned some vital information. They were aware of his vendetta against them. Though, he still didn't believe they were fighting with the Thralls. He had seen with his own eyes that they were working with the invaders. She was keeping secrets. "What do I get if I marry her?"

"Our allegiance. A dowry that could fund your army and kingdom for several generations. Certain things will be earmarked for my daughter. We can discuss the details when my court and I arrive for the wedding."

"I want a show of good faith."

"What do you want?"

"I want you to pull your people from the Thrall encampments and stop aiding them."

Valik's eyes narrowed. "We are *not* aiding the Thralls. If what you say is true, and some of my people have done this, then I will make sure the traitors are executed and deliver their heads. Would that suffice?"

She didn't know she had traitors among her own people. Unless this is all part of her ruse. Interesting.

"I also want you to prove what you're saying about this trove of wealth." If he couldn't get a flesh and blood bride out of the deal, then at least he could get the money and have a concubine on the side. Someone who could produce an heir.

Valik reached into his cloak and threw down a large bag. Gold, jewels and silver spilled along the table. "Will this buy my daughter's life until I arrive with her dowry?"

"Yes. I think that's sufficient." He eyed the wealth. What else were they hiding in their mountain kingdom?

"If you lay another hand on her, then I'll know."

"I swear, from this point on, I won't torture your daughter."

"Good. Valik will remain to watch over her."

Stavros nodded. "I accept that, but I won't be sacrificing any of my people to feed either her demonic hunger or his."

Mila laughed through her servant. "There is much you need to learn about us. We will hammer out the details in two moons time. Expect me during the dark moon with my entourage. Good day."

The Vyrk's eyes focused again. He blinked and glanced at Stavros.

"You and my queen have struck a bargain?"

"Yes."

"Good. I'd like to see the princess, and then be shown my room."

Stavros opened his mouth to object but closed it again. "Of course. Why don't you get settled in? I'll have the princess brought to you so that you can see she is perfectly well." He got up and pulled a cord hidden in the corner. A door opened and a servant entered. "Take our guest to one of the rooms in the tower. Have a maid attend to him."

"No one—"

Stavros shot him a look. "Is my every command to be questioned?"

Valik stood and adjusted the hood of his cloak over his face once more. "If you expect to put me into some old, abandoned part of the castle, then I assume you will put the princess in the next room. I wish to be close so I can make sure no harm befalls her. If you break the deal with the queen and lay hands on Kayanna, I will rip your throat out. I don't care who you are." The Vyrk bared his fangs at Stavros.

Fear erupted in the king's brain and made him back away from the creature before him. "Fine. Boy, set up the suite adjoining mine for the princess. There is a small room off those that our guest can stay in. It's more befitting his station." He turned to Valik. "Why don't you follow him so you can inspect it?"

"And you're coming with me, Your Majesty." Valik laid a hand on his dagger.

The king shot him a dirty look. With one move, the Vyrk could have his head. Stavros straightened but didn't respond. Escorting the monster to a bedroom was beneath him. However, this creature would not be satisfied until he showed him the princess.

Stavros found it difficult to think of the female as a

person, let alone a princess. His generals weren't going to like that he had been bullied into a betrothal with a Vyrk. He shuddered at the idea of being next to her. Sweeping the bag from the table, he returned the spilled contents to the pouch. This had bought her some time. After the wedding, when he'd received the full dowry, he would find a way to make her death look like an accident.

Then I can take a true wife.

"Of course," he forced out. He led Valik through the castle until they arrived at his rooms.

Valik stopped. "She's in here."

He went to open the door, but Stavros grabbed his wrist. "These are my private chambers. I had the servants draw her a bath. Your room is there, off hers." Stavros led him down the hall to a smaller door. He opened it and ushered the Vyrk into the sparse chamber.

Valik nodded at the door in the corner. "That leads to the princess's chamber?"

"It does. Boy, what's your name?" he asked the trailing servant.

"Ben, sire."

"Ben, you're to get anything, or do anything, this man wants. He is your new master for as long as he is here."

The boy looked between them and whimpered. "Sire," the boy leaned into Stavros and whispered, "what if he wants to eat me?"

"You're too young for me. I like my meat more mature. Majesty, this is fine." Valik gave him a small bow and entered the room. "Come here, boy."

"Obey him," Stavros commanded.

Ben rushed into the room. Stavros walked back to his

rooms and found the woman servant drying Kaya off. He got a good look at the princess's backside before the servant realized he was there.

"Majesty, I didn't see you."

"Leave us," he commanded.

The maid bowed. He trailed his finger along the curve of Kaya's shoulder feeling the soft, warm flesh.

It's a trick of the fire. The other one's skin was cold. She's still an undead thing, even if they claim she's not.

Her alabaster skin was pinker than the other Vyrk. Dark brown hair, almost black, fell to the middle of her back. The fire showed red and gold highlights in the strands. Stavros detected the faint aroma of cloves around her.

"Are you going to claim your prize?" Her voice came out in a soft whisper.

He sensed no fear in her. Stavros took in the wounds he had inflicted upon her. They remained angry and scabbed over. He touched the incision along her chest.

She winced.

"Why haven't your wounds healed?"

"I need blood."

"I'm not going to give it to you. None of the servants will either. Don't think you can mesmerize me to get it."

"I couldn't if I wanted. I don't have that power."

"Every Vyrk has that power. I've seen it. I've felt it." He gazed at the fire as the images of his beloved Serena and their son entered his mind. Stavros had stood paralyzed while the Vyrk feasted on them.

Anger welled up. He curled his fist, and when he looked back at Kaya, he didn't see the woman. The beast remained—with claws and teeth that had destroyed his happiness. His fist connected with her jaw. The creature went down to the floor, but he kicked it in the ribs.

"Please, no more." She curled into a ball and put up her hand.

Stavros broke out of his stupor as the fury drained away. He remembered her mother's warning and his promise not to lay a hand on her. He'd broken that.

"You'll never get blood from any of us. You'll have to eat the rats you catch. I'll put on a good show for your mother when she comes with your dowry. After that, I'll put you so deep in the dungeons you'll never see moonlight again." He grabbed the towel and threw it at her. "Cover yourself."

He pulled the key from around his neck and undid the cuffs.

Kaya flashed him a questioning look.

"Don't get any idea of escaping. I'll have your countryman staked out in the sun. You sleep on the floor by the bed. Do you understand?"

Kaya nodded.

He raised his hand and she flinched.

"Do you understand, princess?"

"Yes."

Stavros held the manacles to his chest as he went to consult Kewskin. He needed to know if their ancient magic would remain if they were re-forged.

CHAPTER FIVE

K aya couldn't believe what the king had told her.

Mother wants me to marry him. Why didn't I listen to you, Adran? I should've gone back to the castle, but no.

She wiped her eyes and wrapped the towel around herself, but it did little to cover all of her. She tried to get up, but her legs didn't want to work. Her wounds were great, and her body's reserves used up. She needed blood.

The king's words rang in her ears about another of her kind being in the castle. Kaya closed her eyes and gathered up her strength. She opened her mind and sensed the other Vyrk. Someone she recognized.

Valik, she called mentally.

Princess, what's wrong?

Need blood.

Kaya tried to hold the connection, but her body struggled to keep her alive. She wrapped her arms around herself to stay warm. From the arrows, to the sun, to losing blood, to the torture she'd endured at Stavros's hands, it was all she could to do to remain awake.

Her side hurt when she breathed. When he kicked her, he broke more than her rib. Bile built in the back of her throat. She coughed and tasted blood.

A few minutes later, Valik appeared on the windowsill and jumped into the room. He wore only his pants and his hair was unbound. She had never seen the stoic warrior in such a state. His pale skin glistened in the firelight.

"What have they done to you? Your mother said you were in pain, but this is more than I imagined. I should've expected it of the human." He traced the line over her heart. His fingers came away crimson.

She whimpered at the light touch.

Valik flicked his tongue over the drops. He closed his eyes and quivered at the taste. He stared at her again with something like desire in his dark blue eyes. He cupped her cheek. The coolness of his touch relaxed her some. It was familiar.

"Torture."

"I'd kill him if your mother hadn't already struck a bargain with him."

"Is it true?"

"Shh, princess. Don't think about that now. You need blood. You're lucky I found someone here who didn't mind me feeding from them." Valik pushed his hair aside and angled his neck.

His vein throbbed. Her hunger made her moan. Her fangs lengthened. She licked his throat and tasted his flesh.

Kaya was about to bite when she pulled way. "Are you

sure about this? I've never fed from another Vyrkola. I know the consequences of it. I know it can bind us together."

Valik trailed this thumb along her bottom lip. "Your mother told me to make sure you were kept alive. I am aware of the consequences but feeding from me once shouldn't cement a bond. You need the blood. Drink."

The steady rush of his pulse, quickened from the blood he had drunk, called to her. She licked her lips and sank her teeth into his vein. Life flowed down her throat. Each drop raced to the broken parts of her body. She grunted as the damage repaired itself. Valik touched her neck. The soft caress made her lift her head and peer into his eyes now darkened with a hunger of his own. His mind brushed against hers. She could feel it like the faint stroke of the wind weaving through her feathers when she flew. The sensation made her smile. Her heart raced. She reached out to touch him, but Valik pulled away. Part of her already missed the closeness they had shared. She'd never experienced that type of intimacy with another of her kind before. She already craved to have it again.

"Forgive me, princess. My sharing with you is above my station and not normally acceptable, but I had to be sure you survived."

Kaya put a finger to his lips. "No, Valik. You saved me. I was reckless. I should've listened to Adran and returned to the castle. I know sharing blood between our kind can form a bond maybe even a mate bond. I understand what that means for you...us. You've done your duty. I'm sure the king would reward you if he wasn't such a monster."

"And yet, you are betrothed to him. The monster that

did this to you has other things in store." Valik went to one knee before her and took her hand. "I offer you my service to guard and protect you. To be there when I am needed. You have my loyalty as no other. Whatever bond forms between us, I will act on it accordingly."

"I'm honored by your pledge of fealty. It's good to know I have at least one kinsman here who understands me. At least part of me."

Valik kissed her hand. "The king is coming. I am nearby if you need me." He leapt up onto the windowsill and disappeared outside.

She curled up on her side, drew the towel over herself, and feigned sleeping. Valik's blood pumped in her system and she could feel his mind stronger than before. Kaya tried to push past it and focus on what the king had in store for her.

If they were to be married, he would keep her alive until her mother came and went. She had until after the marriage to find a way out of this madness. Valik would be by her side.

Her thoughts turned to what she knew about him. No one knew how old he was. He always protected the sitting queen. If she was more skilled at the mind powers her kind had, she could bury herself in Valik's memories. All she possessed was telepathy. The way she normally spoke with Adran. Kaya searched for the place he occupied in her mind. After taking in so much of his blood over the years, they had formed a bond the way she and Valik might do if she ingested more quantities of his.

Emptiness greeted her.

He's dead. The cold ache in her heart expanded until it

filled her entire being. She bit her lip and sniffled, trying to keep in her sobs.

The door opened, and the king entered. "I know you're not sleeping. Clothe yourself. I don't want to look at you." He threw something at her.

She took the garment and put it on. The large night-dress itched.

His expression remained cold as he looked at her.

"Thank you."

Kaya tried to get comfortable on the floor. The hatred the king felt shared the space with them as though it were a living being.

He'll never see me for who I am. Adran, because of me, you're dead. Forgive me, my friend.

Adran had taught her to wield her magic after the gift awakened within her. He was the son of the court's *varaz*, a human, and her mother thought it would be good to teach them together. Over the years, she and Adran grew close. When he reached maturity, his aging slowed as it did with all *varaz*. Kaya stopped aging when she reached twenty-seven. They tried to be lovers but discovered they were better friends. He was her mother's eyes when she was sneaking out of the castle. He fed her when she needed it. All of her memories of them together played in her mind as dreams took hold and silent tears carried her into sleep.

———

The next morning Stavros nudged her with his foot. She opened her eyes to swords pointed at her head. "One move toward me and they'll run you through. Do you understand?"

"Yes," she whispered.

He backhanded her hard enough to split her lip. "I didn't hear you."

His guards snickered.

"Yes, Sire," she said more clearly.

He took her wrists and fastened thin silver bracelets over them. As the silver touched her, the heaviness of the magic in them flashed over her flesh. The ancient spells in them bound her powers. He took another heavier collar, secured it around her throat, and pulled it until she gagged. It loosened a moment after he secured the necklace. He held up a key in front of her.

"My blacksmith melted down the silver cuffs and reshaped them for me last night. Luckily for me, he's also a *varaz* who knows how to work with enchanted metal. Kewskin reinforced the spells on them to be sure they remained intact as well." The king looked between her and his soldiers. "You're my prize and mine alone. Men, meet the Vyrk princess. Their greatest possession and my betrothed." Stavros grabbed her wrist and dragged her toward the door.

Her nightdress slipped off her shoulder, revealing her breast. Each guard groped her as she passed. Kaya tried evading them, but they made a game of it to see who could touch her. The king made his way through the castle with her like this. Servants stopped their work and stared. In the throne room, all of the court had been assembled. Kaya glanced around at the men and women, wondering what they were thinking behind their surprised faces. Being around so many warm bodies unnerved her. So many beating hearts in one place made her head hurt.

In her court, all Vyrk hearts were silent. Human servants and magicians came and went, but never were so many gathered in the same room. It made her cringe, along with all the smells of sweat and humanity. She tried to block it out, but the cuffs made it almost impossible for her to call upon any of her abilities.

Valik stood in the shadows. His fury surged across her mind like pounding waves.

"Lords and Ladies, there has been some talk about my marrying the Vyrkola Princess. The rumors of me cavorting with her are greatly exaggerated. You all know I have no love for those filthy creatures after they killed my beloved queen and prince. Don't expect to be seeing much of her. Take a good look at their most *prized* possession," he sneered.

Kaya straightened her back, lifted her head and met the king's eyes. No matter what he said about her, she would keep her dignity. The Vyrkola court never treated her with disrespect, but she wasn't spoiled. Her gaze swept the room once more. Women turned away and men leered at her exposed flesh. This display was to see how she and Valik would react. Stavros wanted her protector to give him a reason to kill them both.

Stavros walked around her as he addressed the nobility.

"Her mother pays us a handsome dowry, so I won't slay

her only daughter. I did not seek out her hand but took her prisoner. The Thralls are attacking our borders. This beauty fell into my hands. I expect her to be treated as the *woman* she is. The queen herself comes in two moons to hammer out the rest of the details."

"But, Great King Stavros, how can you even consider taking this thing as your queen after what her kind did to the prince and your late queen? May they rest in peace," a man stepped forward and asked.

"A good question, Chancellor Kewskin. Our beloved Queen Serena and our son," Stavros paused. His hands balled into fists and his face reddened. He struggled to regain his composure. This wasn't part of the act. A few of the women sobbed.

"You all noticed my absence. I was gathering intelligence for our war council. The Thralls have burned several of our border towns and are planning an invasion. I have seen and heard their plans. We must be ready. The Vyrks are no lovers of the Thralls. Their queen will do anything to keep her daughter alive. I control their queen as long as I have the princess. I indulge you to play along for the time being. You won't see much of her after today. But for now, you will see all of her." Stavros tore the thin nightdress from her body.

Valik stepped out of the shadows ready to defend her.

"No. It's what he wants," she commanded him.

He stopped mid-step. Kaya made no move to cover herself. Many of the court walked around her but didn't touch her. Some spit on her.

"What happens if she uses her evil powers on us?" Kewskin asked.

Stavros held up her wrist and pointed to the silver bracelets and choker. "She's bound with the spelled silver you reinforced for me last night. She is powerless. Let me show you." He took his dagger and sliced a line from her collarbone to her breast. Kaya didn't whimper.

"You see. She bleeds like us and it doesn't heal. She's been tamed. Any other questions against my choices as your king?" His voice grew stern.

Her gaze flicked to Valik. Now she understood his speech. Her mother dispatched Valik with instructions to say anything to keep her alive. The only way to do that was to marry her to the king.

He had to do it before the entire court. They questioned Stavros's leadership. That is why he's doing this?

Valik nodded, indicating he'd heard her thoughts about what happened.

"Good. Bring me a stool," Stavros ordered. The servants returned with a bench. He set it in sight of his throne. "Stand upon your throne, princess."

Kaya stepped up. Stavros touched her leg, but she didn't react. "You'll come to appreciate the freedom I give to you if you behave," he whispered to her.

She glanced down at him. "You're going to kill me after you get what you want from my mother. What does it matter if I do what you want?"

"Oh, it matters. If I see your man approach you again, I'll stake him out in the sun. I know he was in my room last night because you got blood from somewhere. If I see your perfect skin again without my say so, then he's ash. One move to help you while you stand on this, he's dust. Do you understand?"

"Yes."

"Guards, if she falls asleep, whip her. If she moves, whip her again. Keep her there until I say differently. Anyone touches her—whip them. Understand?" Stavros looked at all the court. The guards nodded.

He turned and went back to his throne. He observed her for a while and then grew bored.

———

Time passed. People leered at her as they walked by. Valik remained in the shadows and watched. After a couple of hours, she lost feeling in her legs. Kaya tried to stand steady and not sway even after Stavros turned back to the business of his court. Her stomach growled for food and her throat dried from thirst. The sun crept higher and spilled its rays into the throne room. They crept upon her slowly.

The warmth, combined with standing for so long, made her stumble.

A sharp sting hit her back. The pain jolted her from her stupor. All talk ceased as eyes focused on her.

She cried out as another lash sliced her back. She stood up straight again.

Stavros flashed her a cruel smile.

Kaya squeezed her eyes shut and tried to find a quiet place inside of her mind, but her flesh was her worst enemy. Her legs cramped. Her hunger tugged on her insides. The pain made it difficult for her to focus.

Valik's thoughts brushed across her mind. A sudden surge of strength tightened her heart and gave her the willpower to continue. Whatever his blood had done to her, it was clear their bond was cemented more than she realized.

"Thank you, but you need to be on guard for those who would kill you," she communicated silently.

"If they kill me, the queen sends her army. They aren't prepared for that. Their men are spread too thin along the borders fighting the Thralls. Nor is he really prepared to slaughter you. He talks a good game, but he has other plans. His mind is guarded, as is the magician's. If I find out anything else, I'll let you know."

"He's done this to save face before his people because you put him on the spot."

"I saw what he did to you in his memories. He was going to pull your heart out and make your death a slow process as you baked in the sun."

"I know."

"At the first sign of trouble, I'll kill him and get you out of here. My allegiance is to you alone now."

"What about my mother? You've protected the queens for as long as anyone can remember."

"Yes, I've always sworn to guard the royal line. But I have never shared blood with a queen. All queens have the ability to connect to any bloodline if they choose. When you become queen, the same right will pass to you. You are all that matters to me."

His affection for her rushed into her mind. Kaya gasped and stumbled again. The whip licked her flesh once more. She fell to her knees. The whip cracked again. The sound made her flinch. It came again.

This time she tumbled off the stool. Her knees hit the

hard stone as she tried to find the strength to stand once more. Guards continued to lash her with their whips. The stings of agony rode her flesh.

"Enough."

The pain stopped. Kaya looked up.

A woman had put herself between Kaya and the whip.

She tried to push the woman away. "No. Don't get involved in this."

A guard lifted his whip, but Stavros stopped him with a glare.

"Your Majesty, you said—" the guard protested.

"Not our sister and your sitting queen," Stavros growled. "Get out." He gestured for the whole court to leave the throne room.

Once the room was cleared, the woman laid her cloak over Kaya's back.

She hissed as the material touched her wounds.

"Stavros," chided the woman, "this isn't how you treat people." She reached down and helped Kaya up. "Come with me, child."

Kaya shook her head as she stood up. "I can't. He'll hurt my kinsman."

"He'll hurt no one."

The woman led her out of the hall. Kaya's legs were so stiff, she could barely walk. They climbed up to the second floor and then headed down the hall. A woman opened a door for them. Others rushed in to attend them.

"Go and get a healer. Fetch some broth and draw me a bath."

"Don't go to any trouble." Kaya's vision blurred. Her back was on fire as the woman sat her down on a stool.

A servant came in with a tray laden with water and strips of cloth. The woman dabbed gently at Kaya's back. "My brother is a horse's ass. Having you on display is bad enough, but that whipping." She shook her head in distaste. "He never should've gone that far. I don't care who you are, servant or royalty—and clearly, you're royalty."

"My mother is Queen Mila of the Vyrkola. I'm her natural-born daughter, Kayanna."

"I'm Queen Petra."

"Queen?"

"It's an old tradition. If the king isn't married, it falls back to the next female in line. We are co-rulers. Our mother died right after Stavros was married. His late wife ruled with him until she was murdered. I took over the position. It hasn't happened in three generations. Is it true you're betrothed to my brother?"

Kaya wasn't sure she had a friend in Petra, but she needed someone to trust. "Not by choice. I followed him to the Thrall encampment. I warned him they were coming. He thought I was working with them. I didn't know he was a king. He took me prisoner and killed my friend."

"I'm sorry for your friend. You'll stay here with me. He won't touch you or your countryman."

"You noticed Valik?" The door opened again as the servants brought food and the healer came in. The woman treated her wounds and bandaged them.

There was a moment of blessed peace before the king stalked into the room.

"Petra, what in the gods' names do you think you're doing?" Stavros slammed the door.

59

"Brother, in all of your infinite wisdom, did you ever think about how special this woman is? You can't see past your own hatred."

Kaya glanced at him and then back at his sister.

His gaze remained hard with hatred. "She's twisted you up around her little finger."

"You've bound her in silver. She's powerless. Even you should know she's telling the truth. What color do Vyrks bleed?"

"Dark red. It's almost black."

Petra pointed to the lashes on Kaya's back. "Look at her wounds. She bleeds scarlet like us. Whatever you think, she's human—or mostly human. She's wearing silver. You had her in the sun before the whole court. Her skin didn't blister and burst into flame. Her tears are warm and salty, not bloody. You treat her like a slave when she's your betrothed."

His sister's words appeared to sink past Stavros hatred.

Petra knows more than she's letting on, she thought.

Stavros lifted Kaya's chin. Her eyes burned from fatigue and a tear slipped down her cheek.

He wiped it away with his thumb and tasted it.

"If you're human, then how did your wounds heal so quickly the other night? Now they are barely closing."

The exhaustion made her wobble. "I'm half human. My heart beats. I eat food. I'm resistant to silver. The sun will burn me after a while but not instantly. I need blood to heal and satisfy the hunger all of my kind has, but I'm not driven by it. I don't kill."

"How are you possible?" Petra asked.

Kaya winced as she moved. "As my mother has told me

many times, my father discovered an ancient spell that enabled her to conceive and carry me to term. He gave his life so I could live. I'm a hybrid, the only one of my kind."

"She's a treasure unto herself, Stavros. She needs to be respected, not humiliated," Petra scolded him.

"Fine. Treat her as a human, but the silver stays on. It binds her *varaz* powers," Stavros declared.

"I think that's a fair trade for her freedom to move about the castle."

"I never said that. She sleeps at the end of my bed."

"She isn't your dog. Until the marriage contract is hammered out, technically she is visiting royalty. The princess has every right to demand to be treated better. She stays in the east tower where Serena was secluded before your betrothal. Her man will have access to her. I'll assign a small staff to you, Kaya. You need to be treated befitting your rank."

It relieved her to be as far away from Stavros as she could. "Thank you, Your Majesty. I appreciate your kindness."

"You are more than deserving of it, Princess. My brother should've taken this into account before declaring you his slave." Petra glared at Stavros.

His face turned red and the veins stood out in his temples. "As the king, I have final say. I don't care if we are twins and you declared yourself queen by the ancient laws."

"I don't care if you have final say in all of this or not, *brother* of mine. We're at war with the Thralls. There is unrest in the south over who owns the lands your father-in-law gave to you for Serena's dowry. In the west, the villages closest to the Shadow Pines are talking about something stirring in the forest. Maybe you would know all of this if you weren't so busy trying to find the Vyrks and eradicate them. I have grieved with you for your loss, but it has been six years since Serena died. I've taken up as much of the slack as I can. The court and the people are talking about your state of mind. Your taking initiative with the Thrall situation is good. But now you're making problems by treating the Vyrk princess like she is a dead dog you kicked to get out of your path. We have no official quarrel with them, even though you pronounced open season on all Vyrkola."

Kaya considered the information. It seemed their kingdom was doing far worse than she or her mother knew.

Stavros raked his fingers over his face and took in a breath. "The court isn't going to like this. You're right. I've been neglecting the state of our land and our people."

"Not about the Thralls," she countered.

"No. Not about them."

"Good. You should've brought Kaya to me in the first place. I'm still older than you, even if only by a few minutes. I am your co-ruler until you marry again. Now get out."

"Petra—" Stavros started.

"Out. This woman needs to be treated with kindness and esteem. If she is to be your queen, then she will have to deal with you in all ways and give you an heir." Petra turned her back on Stavros as he walked out the door.

Relief overtook Kaya once the door closed.

"You do have the ability to have children, don't you? Do you bleed?"

Kaya opened her mouth and then closed it. The last time she'd had this conversation was with her nurse when her moon cycle came on her. "Yes. My cycles run every three moons. I guess I have the ability to have a child. I haven't tested the theory, but I'm experienced enough to know how children are conceived. How do you know so much about my kind?"

Petra rummaged through a wardrobe and pulled out a gown. She held it up to Kaya and nodded. "This should fit you. Now to get you healed." She rolled up her sleeve and offered her arm to Kaya. By the inner bend of her elbow were old and new bite mark scars. "Take what you need. I'm no stranger to it."

Kaya let her fangs grow and bit into the woman's flesh. The blood strengthened her. The sting along her back as her flesh healed encouraged her. She drank until her body felt free of injury and her hunger satiated. Kaya pulled away and wiped her mouth.

The door opened as the queen rolled down her sleeve to hide the marks. Questions filled Kaya about the bites. It was clear Petra didn't share her brother's hatred of the Vyrkola.

"Go with Bertha—she's mute, but she communicates well. She will be your maid servant. She has drawn you a bath. Food will be sent to your rooms. Your man has been alerted to your change in apartments. His rooms are off yours. We will talk tomorrow."

Kaya slipped on the gown and followed the serving woman behind a tapestry into a narrow hall. They went up more stairs and along another series of passageways. Bertha led her into a bathroom where a tub stood in the center of the room. She tapped Kaya on the shoulder, showed her the large bolt, and slid it into place. Bertha gestured to Kaya she would be in the other room when Kaya finished with her bath.

"Keep it locked. I understand. Thank you."

Steam curled up from the hot water. Kaya slipped off the dress and stepped into the bath. Hers and the maid's footprints were the only ones disturbing the thick coating of dust on the floor. The gray walls and absence of a window gave the room a lonely feel. After soaking until the water began to cool, she got out of the bath and went into the main room. Another layer of dust blanketed this room. The air had a stale taste. A faded portrait of a blonde woman dressed in a pale blue gown hung over the fireplace.

"Was this the late queen?"

Bertha nodded and looked down. She led Kaya over to the bed and turned down the covers.

Kaya wasn't tired. There was too much to think about.

Another servant brought in a tray. She set it down on a table by the window, curtsied, and left. Bertha inspected the tray and even tasted the broth before she presented it to Kaya.

The princess sat down and sipped at the broth as Bertha left. Kaya studied the bedroom. Whoever had designed it had done it with love. Little details—she assumed things the late queen had liked—were incorporated into the decor. A painting of a seascape took up an entire wall.

Stavros loved this woman. I'm merely a bride of convenience.

Kaya ran her fingers over the collar and the silver cuffs. The power in them raced along her fingertips.

"You won't be able to get them off easily, princess."

Kaya turned and saw the chancellor standing before her. She was annoyed with herself for not bolting the door after Bertha.

Out of habit, she dropped a small curtsy.

His eyes widened, but it only lasted a moment.

Something about him made her step back. "I wasn't planning on taking them off. The magic in them remains powerful even after the re-forging."

"I'm surprised you can feel that. You must be very strong."

"I've been told I am, but I've never explored my limits. Can I help you with something, Chancellor?"

"Forgive me for barging in. I was curious about you. It's my understanding Vyrks aren't capable of wielding magic since the first of your kind created the Bone Forest. In the throne room, I felt the power emanating from you despite the restraints."

He's fishing for information.

Most humans had preconceived notions about her kind. The Vyrkola didn't share their history—or their weaknesses. Kaya didn't want to reveal something she shouldn't.

She chose an answer that should satisfy him and get him out of her room. His presence made her queasy. "The Vyrkola can't. I am an exception. As for the Bone Forest, why are you interested in ghost stories?"

"We know very little of Vyrkola history. As a sorcerer, of course, I have studied what we do know. It's been said your first king tried to tap into the node of magic in the Forest of Bones. The thread of power swelled up from the well, and he couldn't handle it. Somehow, it turned the trees to bone. Ghosts and dark things linger in the shadows. I believe the whole place is cursed. It belongs to the darkness and shadows. I feel it from here. Sometimes people are drawn there for no reason. They are never seen again except as hanging corpses. All these things are merely rumors, of course.

"I'm interested in the power said to be in the forest. I'm sure you feel it calling even with the fetters on. It wants to get out. It wants a vessel. Is that what you were doing so far away from your protective castle? Were you headed there to become this vessel and thus destroy all humans in your path?" His voice rose the closer he got to her.

Kaya backed up until her knees hit the window seat and forced her to sit. Her heartbeat doubled as the cool mask he wore broke. His dark eyes were crazed. The air around him crackled. She went to cast a shield, but then the energy died in her palms where the cuffs absorbed it. Before the chancellor could touch her, a cool breeze entered the room and a sword was at Kewskin's throat.

"You don't want to get too close to my mistress," Valik warned the chancellor.

His energy retreated. "Forgive me. I didn't mean to frighten you, Princess. I was overly excited. Everyone is talking about your upcoming nuptials."

"I'm sure they are," she said under her breath. Kaya put her hand on Valik's arm. He lowered the sword. "I don't have a problem discussing our history, but I think it would be best done with the king and queen present. They must be equally intrigued about my family and my pedigree. Please convey my thanks to them for the exceptional lodgings."

A smile twitched on his lips. "I will let the king know what you've said. Another reason why I have come, His Majesty bids you stay in your room until he comes for you. He wants to be sure you're not hurt. Wouldn't want you to end up dead before the wedding night." Kewskin smiled, bowed, and left the room.

Valik made sure the door was locked before he went back over to her. He rolled up his sleeve and was about to bite into his wrist when Kaya touched his shoulder.

"You don't have to do that."

"But you were whipped. I felt each lash upon you as if it were my own back. I tried to feed you my strength, but with the daylight...I'm sorry I failed you."

She touched his cheek. His warmth brought her a peace she hadn't expected. "You didn't fail me. You gave me what you could and did what I asked, which was to stay alert. Petra—the queen—gave me her blood. She has recent fang marks on her arm. I bet she has a Vyrkola lover somewhere in the castle or close by at least. I took what I needed, and my back healed. All I need now is sleep."

Valik slid his hand over hers. He pulled away when he touched the cuff. "Damn silver."

"I'm sorry I've gotten you into this mess. I should've listened to Adran and turned back. Now I'm a prisoner, he's dead, and we've started something...." Her voice trailed off, and she hung her head.

Valik lifted her chin. He searched her eyes and feelings stretched between them that she couldn't put a name to. "No, Kaya. I've learned over all this time that sometimes fate leads you down paths you can't turn back from. Maybe you wanted to get off this road, but this is where it has brought us. And I wouldn't have chosen any other way. I've noticed you all these years and knew you were special. I've sensed your strength. Even in the shadows, I have seen you." He brushed his lips across hers in a swift kiss before dissolving into mist and floating away.

CHAPTER SIX

S tavros straightened his vest and tugged at his collar. The dinner had been Petra's idea. He wanted nothing to do with the thing who called herself a woman. It didn't matter to him what she was, or what he had learned the other day. Petra had imposed the ancient rules and declared herself queen when Serena died. He had obliged her because it was the old laws, and his generals ignored his sister anyway. She had never gone against how he ruled until it came to this woman. Most of the time he left his twin alone. Kewskin had tried to weasel his way into the dinner, but Stavros forbade him to come.

He glanced at the clock and saw he was running late. Stavros knocked on his sister's door and entered.

The Vyrk woman stood with her back to him. Her long dark hair shimmered in the light. When she turned around, he saw the cuffs and the choker. His eyes flicked to the form-fitting dress and how the firelight accentuated her pale flesh. Her lips had a bit of color to them, but nothing like that of the other ladies in court.

"What's the meaning of this? Where's my sister?"

Kaya curtsied before him. "I don't know, Sire. She wasn't here when I arrived."

"Damn her." He turned to leave.

"Forgive me, Sire, but can we talk? I know that you hate my kind, and I'm not...objecting to how you've treated me. If we are to be married, at least as long as it serves your purposes, do you think we could be cordial with one another? At least, civil? You acknowledge I saved your life if that means anything. You seem to be a man of honor. Your men respect you. You care for your people, and it was a great blow when your wife and son were murdered."

Stavros didn't want to admit she had taken an arrow meant for him, but he couldn't deny it. He was surprised she didn't hold anything against him for torturing and humiliating her in front of the whole court.

It could be another ruse to get out of the cuffs. Then she could use her powers against me.

Stavros felt the familiar fury and walked over to her. He raised his hand, but she looked directly at him, defying him, showing him she was his equal.

"Go ahead and hit me again. Beat me all you want. It's not going to change who or what I am. Your people are going to expect an heir from our union."

"You can't have children."

Her eyes narrowed. "It's quite possible that I can. I *am* part human. You've restrained most of what I am with these cuffs and collar. Being a man of honor, my only request to you is not to throw me away when you're done with me. Don't shove me down in some dungeon or take my head. A life for a life when you've had your fill of me."

Her statement surprised him. He mulled over her proposal. She *had* saved his life. He didn't want to start a war with the Vyrks. The thought of waging battle with them and the Thralls at the same time was not appealing. His kingdom didn't have the resources to deal with both.

He scratched his chin. "I don't want a war with your... people. Your mother's promised us valuable resources against the Thralls, but how do you propose we work this out?"

Kaya pulled out a chair by the table and sat down. "Will you join me?"

Stavros sat across from her and leaned back; a bit intrigued. "What can you offer that's worth me not locking you up until the wedding?"

"You don't want my body so I can't tempt you with flesh. But I can give you information about my people."

"Your strengths and weaknesses?" Learning about them could give him an advantage.

Kaya trailed a finger over her silver cuff and winced. "Yes," she whispered. "I will entrust the information to you, but not your chancellor."

She's hesitant to share that knowledge because she knows I can use it against her even if she says she'll tell me. She's not stupid.

"I can agree to that. What else do you have to bargain?"

"If you take off the silver, then I can share my power."

"That isn't going to be part of the deal."

"I understand. Then what else do you want?"

Stavros stared at her. She *was* fetching and the idea of tasting her flesh did intrigue him. "Submit yourself to me."

She lifted her arms. "Haven't I already? I am your prisoner. You've made that abundantly clear."

Stavros grabbed her hand. "I haven't claimed you. I could throw you down and take you any way I wanted because you're mine. But as a man of honor, I want you to submit yourself to me." He found her flesh to be warm. Her cheeks flushed as he held her wrist. Vyrks didn't do that. They couldn't.

"If that's what you wish."

"Every night."

"Do you still wish me to sleep on the floor and be chained to your bed?"

"Not if you do as asked."

"I don't have a problem being intimate with you every night, but there is something about my kind that happens when we are aroused and I'm no exception."

"What is that?"

"We have a need to bite into our partner. I don't think you'd want to experience that."

Stavros chuckled. "Who said anything about me arousing you? I said you would be servicing me. It would be for my pleasure. If you bite me, I'll rip your teeth out. Does that sound fair?"

He got up and paced. He needed to see her humiliated. Something to pay back her kind for what they had done to him. Nothing he threw her at her made her react the way he expected.

"If that's what you wish. Do you want me on my knees now sucking your cock or do we wait for later?"

Stavros detected a hint of sarcasm. He ached to slap her because the idea made him hard.

"A fine idea. On your knees." Stavros unbuttoned his trousers.

Kaya knelt down before him. He grabbed her hair and pushed himself inside her waiting mouth. Her hands touched his hips.

"No. Just your mouth and tongue. You don't touch me."

Kaya dropped her hands and worked on his shaft. Stavros closed his eyes. His mind wandered back to Serena and the first time he saw her. The sunlight lit her face. He had been a different man then—one who understood love. Now his heart was dead, and hardened until he'd almost forgotten kindness, but he understood honor.

Kaya's tongue wrapped around him. She stroked him faster until he shot his seed down her throat. She pulled away and swallowed a few sips of wine. He buttoned himself back up and sat down feeling a bit more relaxed.

"Dinner looks wonderful. Eat."

Kaya didn't reply but followed his order. He dug into his meat and the wine tasted better than he realized.

"You've had experience. How many of your kind have you whored yourself out to?"

"I'm not a whore," she whispered in cold reply. Anger lit her eyes and her grip on her wine glass tightened.

Stavros saw he had hit a nerve. He took another bite of roast and it tasted even better. "Surely, you had to learn to use that mouth of yours somehow."

Kaya set her glass down and got up from the table.

"I didn't tell you that you could leave."

This time she didn't listen or come back with a witty retort. Instead she stood looking out the window with her fingers pressed into her palms.

He got up, ready to drag her back so they could finish the meal his sister had orchestrated. He spun her around only to see true human tears slipping down her cheeks.

"Is this what you wanted? To see me broken down so you can stomp all over me? Go ahead and hit me. Do whatever you want."

"Why are you crying? Did I hurt your feelings about your whore lovers?"

Kaya turned away from him. Stavros grabbed her chin and forced her to look at him.

"You ordered my best friend killed when you brought me here. He's dead because of your honor. You thought he was a traitor to humanity. We grew up together."

"You loved him. He was your lover?"

"He was my friend, my teacher, my companion. Our relationship was rarely physical. On occasion, we took solace in one another's arms. You wouldn't understand."

He released her as the pain of his own loss overwhelmed him once more. "In this, Princess, I think we are even. Your people took something from me and mine took something from you. I know how the heart works and mine is stone. I will honor our bargain. I will come to you at night and you will service me. When I'm done with you, I'll release you. Good night."

Stavros left the room seeking refuge in his own rooms. Something in him turned at the events of the evening. He still didn't completely trust the Vyrk princess. He didn't see her completely as a woman, but in the brief moment where she spoke of her dead friend, he saw the spark of emotion in her. He recalled what love felt like with his wife. However, he would be true to his word and he would release her. Serena would want him to honor that bargain.

CHAPTER SEVEN

Kaya returned to her own room. She'd tried to appeal to his sense of honor and need for knowledge to secure her life. Most humans knew nothing about her kind except rumors and old wives' tales about them being undead beings who sank their fangs into innocent children's throats. There were good and bad among her kind, as there were among humans. The original Vyrkola made the bloodlines from humans. At least that was the history she'd learned.

People thought there were unlimited numbers of her kind because everyone who was bitten would rise up and become some horrible creature of the night, but that wasn't the case.

Stavros had jumped at the chance to take the information. She had to look past what he had done to her so she could find some common ground with him. Having sex with him would happen eventually. He would either take her by force or, worse, have his men take her. Offering her the choice showed he had some compassion.

It was clear when she went to her knees it would be a one-way relationship. Drinking his seed wasn't as good as his blood, but it gave her strength. She wasn't about to reveal that fact.

When he called her a whore and accused her of having numerous lovers, Adran's face flashed before her eyes. All the emotions and the memories they had shared welled back up. His absence had left her hurt and broken. She'd loved him. Not in the sense of having him for a mate, more like he was another side of herself. When no one else understood her, he did.

"Why are you crying?" Valik's soothing voice came from the shadows.

"I was thinking about Adran. It's nothing." She wiped the tears away and told herself she had to be strong. Whatever Stavros threw her way, she would handle it.

Valik trailed his fingers along her cheeks casting away the remnants of her sadness. "It's not nothing, Princess. He made you cry. I can smell him on you. What did he make you do?"

Kaya told him about her conversation with the king and their agreement.

He slammed his fist against the stone wall.

Kaya could feel the echo of the pain from his broken bones. The bond between them would wind them tighter together the more she shared blood with him and wove her mind with his. She didn't want to go down that road yet. It wasn't something she wanted to deal with when she had to keep her mind focused on staying alive.

"He's turned you into a—"

"Nothing. I agreed to it. I'd rather have a choice instead of him raping me every night. If I could get these cuffs and collar off, then this conversation wouldn't be happening."

Valik's dark eyes smoldered. "I could easily slip into his room and slit his throat. No one would know."

"We'd be the first people they looked for. It would plunge our kingdoms into a war that neither side can afford right now as the Thralls advance on us both."

"Did you tell him this?"

She shook her head. "No. He wouldn't believe me anyway. That's why I left the castle that day—to see what they were doing. There are Thrall camps on the edge of the Bone Forest. Stavros distracted me from following a party into the wood."

"How do you know the Thralls want something in the forest? Humans and our kind avoid it. Only ghosts live there now."

"Because I've seen them digging around at the old ruins."

He took her shoulders and his voice grew stern. "You shouldn't go there. You've been warned by your mother and the other elders to stay away from that forsaken place."

Kaya placed a hand on his chest. A rush of feelings hit her and she stumbled backward. They were so jumbled she couldn't sort them out. All she could process was sadness, anger, regret and self-loathing for something. Valik came toward her again, but she put up her hand. The emotions passed and she could think again.

"I know. I don't need another lecture. Sometimes I can't help it. There's a presence in the forest that calls to me. It terrifies me. Some nights it whispers my name. I hear it even among the minds of our people. When it happens, I go to the ruins. I've confronted it, but it never answers me. After that I get a slight reprieve."

"Have you gone into the ruins?"

"No. I don't dare, no matter how much I'm tempted. Whatever our ancestor called up that night and trapped, it's awake. That's what the Thralls are going after."

"How do you know that? Why didn't you tell your mother about the Thralls going into the woods?"

"I tried. She told me the same thing you did. No one goes into the forest because it's for the dead, but she doesn't know the thing in the ruins has told me things. That's how I know our ancestor summoned it up and trapped it. It never goes into too much detail, because it wants to get me back there any way it can."

Kaya thought about the ruins. The last time she'd gone, the seductive darkness that lured her there had promised her things. Her fear had kicked in and broken the hold the darkness held on her. She never lingered in the forest. Spirits flocked to her, but the only company she had were the vultures that feasted on the flesh of those poor souls who breathed their last in the barren landscape.

"Do you think the Thralls will release the dark spirit underneath the ruins?"

"No. I think it requires a specific type of person to free it. Can we not talk about this anymore?"

"Of course, my lady. Is there anything else I can do for

you?" His tone hardened and she felt the distance through their bond. He bowed curtly and left the room.

Kaya wanted to go after him, but he sealed the connection between them, and she was all alone. She sat on the bed and drew her knees up to her chest. She closed her eyes and tried to clear her mind, but the emptiness in her thoughts from losing Adran, and now Valik turning away from her brought her sadness that tore her spirit apart.

———

D ays bled into nights. She spent her time talking with Petra or in her room. Valik remained distant. Stavros came to her room every night for her to service him. He never stayed and never asked her any questions. Each night, she did her duty; he treated her like a thing. Each night she tried not to cry because she realized how alone she was.

Kaya's hunger for blood grew. The nourishment she received from Stavros's seed didn't quench her thirst. She couldn't bring herself to ask Valik again. As much as she wanted to, she didn't want to strengthen the bond between them—but she also needed the connection to him. The longer she found herself without the taste of him, the more she craved him. The conundrum twisted her heart and ate away at her soul. She fought the urge to call out to him. Her feelings for him grew even though she barely knew anything of him.

Her mother wouldn't be at court for another month, so she couldn't ask her. The telepathic link they shared didn't stretch far enough, or maybe it was the magic in the silver.

She didn't know and was tired of trying. She had no friends in the castle, though Petra loaned her books.

Kewskin pressed her for more information on her magic and the Bone Forest. She gave him vague answers and told him to leave.

The full moon stared at her while she paced her room. The night called to her hunger. The silver burned against her skin. Kaya felt strained in her flesh. Her magic needed an outlet. She needed to stretch her wings and fly. She closed her eyes and extended her senses, but they were dulled from the silver.

A moan escaped her lips as she thought about Valik. The way his lips brushed hers and how he smelled. She didn't know if she could endure this...absence.

The longing got under her skin. It was an itch she couldn't scratch. She needed the connection. It had never been like this with Adran or any other donor she drank from. She knew sharing with another Vyrk could result in forging a deeper bond than with humans. Kaya tried to get past it, but it needled at her. She yearned for his cool touch. Her heart had threaded around him even though it seemed impossible.

"Valik." She prayed he would respond.

Kaya pressed her forehead to her knees and tried to focus on something else before she crawled out of her skin. A cool breeze wound through the room. It did little to calm her.

A light touch roused her. Kaya looked up and saw the outline of a woman by the bed. A white light emitted from her, creating an aura around her. Kaya studied her sad expression and realized who she must be.

"Queen Serena."

The woman nodded and motioned for her to follow. Kaya walked into the sitting room as Serena floated through the wall. Bricks popped out in the outline of a doorway. She pulled it open and found a set of stairs wreathed in cobwebs. Serena moved up the stairs.

Kaya followed the spirit and came to another closed door that opened to more stairs. At the very top was a room filled with ancient tomes and furniture that had seen better days. Serena drifted into the center of the room and pointed to a chest. Kaya cleared books off the top of it and opened the trunk. Inside was a stack of old maps, books, dresses, and then, underneath all of it, a smaller box. Kaya pulled it out and held it up to Serena.

"Is this what you wanted me to find?"

The dead queen nodded.

Kaya opened the small box and discovered a ring made of onyx and silver. Carved into the stone was the same royal crest of her Vyrkola house she wore on her back. "I don't understand. What does this mean?"

Serena floated over to another side of the room and waved her hand. Scrolls moved out of the way to reveal a large locked book. The lock appeared to be the same size and shape as the ring.

Kaya pressed the ring into the impression and the lock opened. The pages were made of thin silver and the writing on them was in blood. The energy that came off the pages was magic—old magic. Kaya trailed her fingers over the writing and her flesh tingled from the power.

"The truth about the darkness that lies in the Bone Forest. The truth about your ancestor, the Thralls, and

Stavros's people." The apparition's voice was like whispered wind.

"Why show me this?"

"It can't happen again. Don't let Stavros go into the Bone Forest."

"He won't listen to me. He doesn't even see me as human. I'm just..." She shook her head and hated to think about it.

The ghost's cool touch made her look into the soft light. "His heart's been torn out and replaced with a stone. I've seen what he's done to you. It's one reason I've come back. I know you love another, but you have a big heart. Some things can be worked out."

"How am I going to get him to change his mind?"

Serena took off the necklace she wore. It became solid once it hit Kaya's hand. The pendant was strands of silver and gold woven together around a small sapphire. "Tomorrow night, go all the way down the stairs. They lead to a covered gate into the back garden I used to tend. Stavros cultivates the flowers now to calm himself and be close to me. Go there before he comes to you."

"He'll be angry if he has to search for me."

"Wear the necklace. He will not strike you."

"Thank you...I think. Why don't you go to him?"

Serena's eyes filled with spectral tears. "I've tried, but with his cold heart he can't see or feel me. You have awakened something in him which has given me hope. I found this place when I first came to the castle. I discovered the book and the ring right before I was killed. Read the tome here. This place is shielded by ancient magic. No one remembers it. Keep the ring with the book. It's the only way to open it."

"Thank you. Do you want me to give Stavros a message?"

"To gain his trust tell him 'Your light will never die as long as I live.' He whispered it in my ear while I lingered close to my body. If you need something, I will be here."

"Thank you."

Serena faded as Kaya opened the first page of the volume and trailed her fingers over the name on the page:

T his is the true accounting of Alerik Vyrkolas Krystos, king of the Osin. My tale should begin in darkness, but it really started in the light. I was born like all others with a predilection for magic. I learned to control my power but heard the whispers of the ancient beings who dwelled in the darkness. Some were called gods, but they were not the gods I knew. I tried to not listen to them, but I grew weak. And the shadows were my downfall...

S omething about the book drew her in. It had an energy to it that pulled at her as though to place her in the events of his life—as if she witnessed them as they happened to Alerik. Kaya rubbed her eyes. She could feel the night waning. Whatever spell ruled over the book, she couldn't let herself get sucked into it further right now, even though there was more to read.

Her need for Valik remained. Her hunger had grown.

She closed the manuscript, took the necklace, and returned to her quarters.

"Hello, Princess."

She jumped at Valik's voice. He was dressed in a loose black tunic and leather pants. His hair was down, and his pale skin glowed in the moonlight.

"Valik." She rushed over but stopped only a few inches before him. She could feel the draw between them. Kaya tried to ignore the chasm that had formed at their last meeting, the tug on her soul winning out. She laid her hand on his cheek.

He stepped away from her.

"No." she whispered. The coldness froze her heart. Her emotions hitched in her throat as she tried to sort them out.

"Your hunger grows. I can find a human for you to feed from."

"My hunger isn't for a human," Kaya admitted. "I need you. I need..." She shook her head not sure she could explain it.

He wound his fingers around hers. Even the small connection with his flesh eased the ache. "I've stayed away because I didn't want this to happen. It's as you said. Bonds are formed when our kind share blood. I've felt your longing for me. It's been infecting me too. The thought of you with the king—watching you with him—infuriates me."

"Why let me suffer?"

"Because I'm weak. Dealing with these emotions isn't something I'm used to. I can't protect you if I feel these things for you."

Kaya pressed her lips to his.

Valik returned the kiss, then bellowed and jerked away. A red mark seared his cheek.

"Damn these cuffs and collar," she snarled, as her fangs grew. She had to stay focused.

Valik tore pieces from his shirt and wrapped them around the silver bracelets. He took another and draped it over the collar. "This isn't going to stop me from claiming you. I thought it would. Even though I've tasted only a couple of drops from you, it's bound us together."

"All the time you've been around, you've never had this with anyone?"

"I've never shared my blood with anyone. I've only taken. It was the choice I made to protect our people and the queens I served. I chose not to have a mate and live a life of solitude so I could stay focused on protecting the queen."

Valik claimed her lips in a delicate kiss that made her moan. "But your mother sent me as soon as she sensed your pain. It was either watch you die or make the decision."

It hit Kaya what kind of sacrifice he'd made by giving her blood. "I'm sorry. I didn't realize what the sharing meant for you."

"What it also means for you. You are to marry the king. The bond that grows between us will only strengthen the more I share with you—the more I taste you—until we are wound so tight together, we are almost one." He shook his head and sighed. "I fear I might not have the discipline to stay away from you if the king hurts you again."

She hung her head. Her hand had been offered. Her mother was on the way. There was no getting around it.

"I'm going to be his wife. I might end up having his child. How can we be together if all that happens?"

"You can conceive?"

She shrugged. "I think so. I bleed. But how can we make this work?" Her voice broke as she thought about the future and the emotions growing for Valik in her heart. Kaya barely knew the man, but when she looked into his blue eyes, the well of feelings she saw there only made her want to explore the bond more.

Valik must have sensed her trying to ease into his mind and brought a wall down between them.

Kaya pulled back and blinked.

He smoothed the hair from her face. "Forgive me. I'm not used to having anyone in my mind. I'm not ready to share. Give me some time."

"I am sorry."

"No need to be sorry. Listen, Kaya, there are ways we can be together. I can come to you at night in your dreams —we can share minds. It's not the same as merging our flesh, but...with the situation the way it is, it's all I can offer you right now. It's something I've thought hard about while I've stayed away. Because the thread between us has formed, I can see into your mind as well. Whatever this turns into, we must ignore the pull. I must be the warrior and you must be betrothed to the king. I know that's contradictory, but I can't let anything happen to you. When there is a chance—when you have married the king —then we can claim one another fully. I leave that to you." Valik knelt before her and threaded his fingers through hers.

A mate bond. It was the highest form of intimacy her

kind could share with one another. That or turning someone. She would never experience the latter, since she was half-human. Although some felt, if she died, she might be reborn a full Vyrkola.

Kaya heard what Valik said, but what if the king married her and then decided to kill her after all? She wanted someone to be on her side. She knelt before Valik and took his face in her hands. She looked into his eyes and brushed her mind along his. He nearly pulled away, but his barrier remained intact.

"What are you doing?"

"What if I don't want to wait? The pull between us is more than just this bond we have started. I can't explain it. After all these years you could've had anyone, but you chose me. Whether it was for duty or something else. I want to know if what you feel is real. I need to see. If it's real, I don't want to wait. If it's not, then...we can do as you suggested and work through it."

"I'm not sure this is a good idea,"

She kissed him a little harder. "Please."

Kaya couldn't explain it, but something told her they were bound even tighter than either of them realized.

Valik searched her eyes. Finally, he nodded.

She closed her eyes and the barricade around his mind lessened. Her mind was flooded with flashes of memory and emotion, but it was their shared feelings she locked onto. "So much pain." Kaya winced.

"I've lived a long life, but you don't need to see that. Look only at what binds us." Valik's fingers slid over hers.

She found those emotions and they passed over the pain she had sensed like a cool breeze and soothed the ache. The well of feelings he had for her was overwhelming.

He admired her for all she had endured. He saw her as strong and courageous and he cared for her. He'd been in the shadows since she was born and always felt protective of her, but even watching from afar he yearned to be closer because he thought she was a miracle.

The past few days he had been away, he couldn't deny the link growing between them. He wanted her in ways he hadn't even thought of before. Valik craved her attention. He angered when she was with Stavros. He wanted to rip her from the king's arms, protect her, and show her what it meant to be with someone who could love her.

Even with all those feelings, there wasn't a burning love. His desire to be with her threaded around her heart. He needed her in the same way she needed him. The craving to be together lived within him as well.

Kaya felt the same way and yet, if she didn't cement their bond, she felt something would slip between her fingers that she couldn't explain. She pressed her forehead against his and pulled her mind away as well.

"I know what I want. I don't want to wait. With Stavros, I don't know how long I have. I want someone who will stand by me. I feel in you the potential for what this could be. You're respected in the kingdom. It wouldn't be a bad match."

"No, it wouldn't. As this bond grows so do the emotions, as I said before. We are drawn closer together."

"Then, I definitely know what I want."

Valik took her hands. "I swear to be yours and I will

follow you into death. I submit myself to you, as is our way." He moved his hair aside and bared his throat.

Kaya couldn't believe what was happening. She was completing a mating ritual. She traced his throat and understood the significance of the gesture. The Vyrkola were a matriarchal society. Each queen was handpicked from the noble houses and elevated. Many assumed she would take up the mantle after her mother decided to abdicate. Her fangs grew once more.

She bit into her wrist above the cuffs and offered it to Valik. "I claim you for my mate. I offer you my blood to weave our lives together."

Valik took her wrist and kept his gaze locked with hers.

A rush of pleasure raced through her. Kaya felt their connection tighten. She needed more of him. She bit the side of his throat. Valik groaned. He wrapped one arm around her and drew her close. For a few moments, their hearts synced as they drank until Valik broke away.

She lifted her head and stared at him as their bond flared to life and entwined them even closer together.

Valik ran his thumb over her bottom lip. "I can taste your power. You don't know how strong you are. You're magnificent, my love."

Kaya blushed. She could taste his strength in his blood. "You're older than you let on. There was a woman—a human—Betha. You loved her."

Valik's expression paled. "How did you...?"

"You were thinking about her for a fleeting moment." Kaya felt the barrier around his thoughts slam down once more until she was completely shut out. He didn't want her knowing any more about that part of his life. She understood and knew there was time to explore one another. "I'm sorry. It caught in my mind. I shouldn't have..."

He smiled. "No. It's okay. You took me by surprise. Yes, I loved her. She died a long time ago because of something senseless that I did. Can we not talk about her?"

"Forgive me. I'm not used to being this close to someone except Adran."

"I know you miss him. Let's think of happier things." Valik kissed her again.

This time he didn't hold back. Kaya felt his hunger and desire coupled with her own. She wrapped her arms around his neck and pressed herself against him.

He broke the kiss and nipped her cheek and neck with his teeth.

She raked her fingers down his back and struggled to get underneath his tunic to his flesh.

Valik took her hands and held them. He yelped from the touch of the metal.

"Why did you stop?" she whispered brokenly.

"We need a full night to enjoy one another. I don't want anyone to interrupt us, Kaya."

She agreed with him. The night was waning. She needed sleep and then must do what Serena had asked her to do with Stavros the next night. "You're right. There's so much I want to experience with you."

Valik bit into his wrist and offered it to her. "Drink love. You need the strength."

Kaya took his wrist and drank. It wasn't as rich as human blood, but it sated her hunger. She no longer felt as though she was crawling out of her skin. She closed her eyes and listened to his slow heartbeat caused by her blood. It would stop again once it worked its way through his system.

Valik's hand slid along her neck and his palm rested over her chest, feeling her own heartbeat. A small jolt of desire raced along her nerves, making her drop his wrist.

She arched her back. It felt as though his lips were on her throat moving lower with his tongue. His hands smoothed over her flesh. She wanted more—but he stopped.

Kaya opened her eyes and saw he was gone.

"Forgive me, my love," he said through their bond. *"We both want more, but this is all for tonight."*

She sighed.

CHAPTER EIGHT

S tavros examined the war reports. The Thralls had sacked another town. He had mustered soldiers and prepared his people for battle. He had given the generals a plan of attack and told them to bring him one of the Thralls alive so he could interrogate them.

Kewskin tried to use his magical abilities to discern what they were doing in the Bone Forest. If there was anything going on, he hadn't been able to find it. The ancient magic in the wood blocked his power, or so he said. Stavros had lost trust in the chancellor since the princess's arrival. All his conversations steered toward Kaya so he could divine any little tidbit of information about her.

He rubbed his eyes and glanced at the clock. A small smile twitched at the corner of his mouth. Stavros got hard merely thinking about Kaya's mouth on him. It felt good to have her suck his cock. He set the reports down and headed off to see Kaya.

He entered her room, but she was nowhere to be found.

Stavros searched the entire suite and still couldn't find her. A wave of anger hit him. He grabbed he nearest thing he could find and threw it at the wall. Shards of pottery and water bled down the wall. It did little to cool his rage. She had to be somewhere. He would locate her and lock her away for not adhering to their bargain. *She found a way to hide from me. When I find her, I'm going to tie her up and keep her locked up until the sun fries her!*

He needed a moment to cool off before he scoured the castle looking for her. He went down the back stairs and out into the garden. Only there could he find the solace he sought.

Serena had planted everything within it, and after she died, he kept it up. It was the last connection he had to her. All were forbidden to enter except him. The comfort of the night calmed him.

He stared up at the silver crescent of moon above him and tried to feel the presence of his wife. He often hoped if he kept the garden alive, she would appear to him.

"Serena, I wish you could hear me."

"She can."

Stavros felt the blood drain from his body. He turned around and saw Kaya standing by a fountain. She wore a white dress, with her cuffs and collar intact. Another necklace hung around her neck.

"W-where did you get that?" He nearly tore it from her.

"Serena gave it to me."

"Lies. She was buried with it."

"How could I be lying? I don't have any access to my magic. I'm no thief who would resort to grave robbing and I don't even know where she's buried."

Stavros stared into her dark eyes. "Then how did you get it? How did you get down here at all?"

"Serena told me about the stairs. She came to me in my room. She's been trying to reach you, but your heart's closed, so she can't make herself known. Her spirit gave me the necklace as proof that what I'm telling you is real. She said the only way you would believe me is to tell you something. The night she died, you said something to her. 'Your light will never die as long as I live.' You whispered it in her ear even though the life had already left her so no one would hear it."

Stavros stumbled backward against the fountain wall and sat down on the bench surrounding it. The words he'd spoken were only for Serena. No one should have known them, but this *thing* knew them.

"Is she here with us now?" he whispered.

Kaya looked at an empty space beside her. "Yes."

"Why can't I see her?"

"She says she will appear if you take off my silver."

"If I take it off, you'll kill me the first chance you get."

Kaya cocked her head as if listening. "Take off the collar then, and she will materialize for a moment. She needs my energy and I can't give it to her with this binding me."

He weighed the consequences and took out the key. If what she said was true, then he would see his beloved once more. If this was all a charade, then it would only prove Kaya's deception. Then he would have grounds to execute her. One glance would be all it took.

If she's telling me the truth, then maybe... He didn't know what he was expecting. She offered him hope and it had been so very long since he had even an inkling of something so precious. He hung his head and sighed. Stavros struggled with his feelings, but in the end, he unlocked the collar and took it off. "It's off."

Kaya sighed and rolled her shoulders. A faint orb of light appeared next to Kaya. It stretched and grew until it formed into a human shape. He recognized it after a moment. The collar fell from his grasp. "Serena..."

"Yes." Her voice was dim, but he heard her.

"Why beloved? Why choose this...creature to appear to and not me?"

Her spectral fingers slid over his cheek. "Darkness waits for the right moment. Kaya is not your enemy. Vyrks did not kill me or our son. You were made to believe that."

"But I saw them as they attacked you. I killed one of them."

"You killed a Thrall and were made to believe it was a Vyrk."

Stavros didn't understand. Serena's form began to fade.

"Wait. There's so much I need to tell you."

"I've heard all you've said." She brushed her lips against his and laid her hand on his heart. "I live here always." She looked back at Kaya.

The Vyrkola's fists were clenched and sweat dripped

down her temples. The veins in her neck throbbed, and she was paler than normal.

"Will I see you again?" Tears gathered in his eyes.

"In time. This woman shouldn't need to give me her energy so I can appear to you. She deserves better than how you've been treating her. That's not the man I love. Give her a chance. Open your heart. If you can do that, then you *will* see me again." Serena touched his cheek once more then faded away completely.

Once she vanished, Kaya crumpled to the ground.

Stavros panicked. He rushed to her—the one link he had to his wife—and touched her skin. It felt flushed. Her breathing was shallow. He patted her cheeks. Serena's words rang in his ears. He scooped her up in his arms and returned Kaya to her bedroom. He deposited the princess on the bed, took a cloth from the stack next to the basin, wet it, and placed it on her forehead. Mixed emotions tugged on his insides. He had heard what Serena said to him but, after all this time, his hatred for the Vyrks had walled up his heart.

Kaya moaned and her eyes fluttered. She raised her hands as though to ward off an attacker.

She whimpered. "No. Get away."

"Kaya." Stavros shook her.

Her eyes opened. For a second, she fought against him until her gaze cleared.

"Sire, what happened?"

"You gave your energy to Serena so she could speak, even though the silver partially bound your powers. Then you passed out and were muttering like you were fighting against something or someone. Do you remember what happened?"

Her brow furrowed. "Darkness. It called to me, promising me things...but I couldn't understand what it wanted. It's never been this strong." She shook her head and was visibly shaken. "I don't know how it found me here."

"What are you referring to?"

"Why do you suddenly care? You've made it perfectly clear how you feel about me. I'm just some repository for your seed and nothing more."

Stavros traced his fingers over her cheek. Seeing his beloved wife had softened his heart. It also proved that the princess hadn't been lying to him.

"You brought my Serena back to me—if only for a moment. The least I can do is give you the respect you deserve."

"If you want to show me some respect, then take these off." Kaya held out her wrists to show him the silver bracelets shackling her.

"Not yet. I think we have many things to discuss before I do. Tell me first about this darkness. You did promise to answer all my questions." Stavros got a mug of water and then brought her one as well.

She sat up and sipped it. The color hadn't fully returned to her cheeks.

He wondered if she needed blood. *How has she been getting blood to sustain her?*

She ran her fingers over her throat and held her head up. "Are you going to put the collar back on me?"

"I don't think that will be necessary. Tell me about this

darkness you mentioned. You said you've heard it before. What is it? What did it say?"

She raked her fingers over her face. "It's this force, or creature, trapped in the ruins of the Bone Forest. I can't always tell what it's saying. What I heard just now was garbled, but I could hear it."

"You mean where the Vyrkola—where your people—came from? I thought some dark magic that a Vyrk king tried to channel exploded around him. He couldn't handle the power, so it killed him and turned the whole forest to bone, draining the life from everything it touched."

"That's what I thought too and what most of our people believe. When I was ten, I started having night-mares about some*thing* living in the dark. I couldn't put a name to it. As I got older, the presence grew more powerful as I did. At times I'd find myself drawn to the ruins. I'd fly to the forest and listen to this dark being tell me things. While it whispered to me, I was safe from the shadows within the trees that grow and take on lives of their own, morphing into monsters. Sometimes I think it's waiting for me."

"Have you ever gone into the ruins themselves?"

"No. I'm afraid. Whatever is trapped in there wants out. It can never get out. That's why I followed you that day. I had shifted into my bird form and saw the Thralls coming out of the forest with shovels. I was trailing them back to their camp and saw you sneaking into the encamp-ment. You know the rest."

Stavros found her story interesting and plausible. It fit together with reports they had gotten about the Thralls going into the Bone Forest. If they were digging around, then they were looking for something. This darkness Kaya spoke about didn't sit well with him, either.

Kewskin was chomping at the bit to get into the forest, but Stavros had insisted he merely peer into the wood using his magic the best he could. The king's thoughts turned back to the afternoon when Kaya and her companion saved him.

"Why did you rescue me?"

"You weren't Thralls. I smelled the blood on your clothes, and I thought you might have some information we could share. The Thralls are encroaching on our villages, too. My mother is doing the best she can, but even our resources are stretched thin." She stopped and glanced up at him. "At the time, I thought I sensed something different about you. We have humans in our kingdom, but none of them have ever been appealing to me."

"What about the man you were with?"

Kaya drew her knees up to her chest and rested her chin on them. "Adran was my friend. When I was a child, he was supposed to be my meal. Instead, he zapped me with magic. We learned to hone our powers together. His father was one of my mother's trusted *varaz*. We've been lovers in the past, but he's always been more like a brother to me. A companion. We understand one another. You...." She blushed and looked away. "It doesn't matter now, does it?"

"It does to me. You saved my life when you could've just let the arrows fall. Why?"

"Because I couldn't see you dead. You had information I needed to bring back to my mother. Besides, I found you handsome, but looks aren't everything, right?" Her voice grew cold.

Stavros understood how she felt. He had misjudged her in more ways than one and treated her worse. Part of him remained furious at her for not conforming to his rules and for being a Vyrk. He realized that he had enjoyed dominating her, but she was the key to seeing Serena. She had leverage over him now. He had to rethink his feelings about her.

"I shouldn't have done what I did to you. You are a Vyrkola. It flashed me back to Serena being killed in front of me and I was helpless to do anything about it. The hatred burns like bile in the back of my throat. Even now, I want you on your knees. Seeing you like that makes it feel like I am getting back at them in some small way."

"I know. You don't have any other outlet for your rage. Even when your sister told you I was only half Vyrk, you still didn't want to see it. Do you see it now?" Kaya asked him.

To admit he was wrong would undermine all he harbored in his heart, but Serena's words lingered. If he didn't change his ways, then he would never see her again. *I have to see her again. Kaya is the only one Serena has reached out to. All this time, she's been right here, and I've never seen her. I have to be good to Kaya. Serena said it wasn't the Vyrks who had killed her. It was the Thralls. Someone made me think it was a Vyrk. Who? Why?*

He sighed. Stavros tried to look upon Kaya as if it were the first time they met.

Nearly black hair fell down to the center of her back. The firelight caught the gold and crimson highlights in the strands. Her brown eyes were flecked with silver. Her skin was pale and yet it had a rosy hue to it. Her form was pleasing. He could see her decked out in jewels and all the other finery his kingdom could offer.

"I see you." Stavros got up. He had had all he could handle for one night.

He stopped at the door before he left. "Goodnight, Kaya."

CHAPTER NINE

After their discussion, Kaya waited for Stavros to return the next night and the next, but he didn't. He left her alone.

Valik returned to her mother so they could prepare for the queen's coming. If she needed him, all she had to do was reach out along their connection. It was comforting to know, but she hadn't told him what had happened with her and Stavros. He wouldn't understand.

On the third night, when Stavros still didn't come, she went up into the tower. Having the collar off gave her a better awareness of the night, but her senses remained dull. She couldn't feel the magic and energy of the night the way she should. As she walked up to the tower and passed through the second barrier, a tingle of power passed over her. It vibrated her bones and made the silver bracelets glow white in the darkness.

She set her candle on the old desk and slipped on the

signet ring. Once she pressed it to the lock, the book opened.

Her fingers tingled when she touched the pages. Her cuffs glowed brighter. The book was written by someone of power and that energy lingered even after thousands of years. Kaya scanned a few pages and felt the magic of it taking hold of her again. This time she let herself get sucked into the story about the ancient king.

———

Alerik battled with local invading tribes who wanted his land for themselves. He used his magic to drive them back.

One day in the forest, he came upon an injured woman. He tried to help her, but she was frightened of him. They didn't speak the same language, but he sensed her magic. The king calmed her down and healed her. She brought him back to her encampment where he learned that she was the daughter of the chieftain the nomads had chosen as their leader. Her father almost killed him, but the woman threw herself between them and told him what happened.

They came to an agreement. Alerik would marry his daughter, Eloise, and the fighting would cease. The king and the chieftain carved out part of the kingdom east of the mountain ranges for the tribes. Peace settled over the land.

Eloise shared her knowledge of the ancient spirits and gods she believed in. The king followed her into the woods where she paid homage to her gods. She showed him how to tap into the power of nature—into the nodes of energy in the forest—so he didn't pull upon his own when he wove spells.

All was happy until Alerik desired more. Because of this craving, every moon they ventured into the woods. As Eloise did her rites, calling to her gods, the king heard something else reaching out to him in the darkness.

His wife warned him not to listen to the voice in the darkness because it came from an evil place–a dark part of the wood she never went into. She told him stories of the gods of light who had once driven the dark ones into the shadows. Under no circumstances should he listen to the shadows or try and tap into their energy.

One day everything changed.

His beloved Eloise grew ill. He and their people prayed to all the gods they believed in. Nothing worked. Not magic or herbs. She kept getting weaker. One night, as he tended to her, Alerik heard a voice in the darkness. At first, he didn't listen, thinking it was only his imagination.

How could it reach the castle when I've only heard it in the woods before?

"You hear me only in the trees because I wish it so."

The king looked around for the speaker. The shock of seeing his own form slumped over his wife's bed made him take a step back. Another chuckle wafted through the shadows. Alerik squinted and made out a lurking shape, with burning gold eyes, standing in the darkness. It had the outline of a man, but Alerik felt the evil emanating from it. "What do you want?"

The beast chuckled. "We can help one another."

"Why do you say that?"

"Your beloved is dying, and nothing can save her.

You've tried magic, herbs, praying to beings long-forgotten —sun gods who don't care about this world anymore. What's wrong with her is bound to her flesh. To heal her, you'd have to accomplish it from the inside out."

Alerik glanced back at Eloise.

Her suffering had been a knife in his heart. He would do anything to cure her after all she had endured. She was his light. Eloise kept the darkness away when it threatened to drag him under. She kept him just and kind. She was his heart—and right now that heart was dying.

Eloise had always told him to ignore the whispers in the wood, but here was a being offering to restore her. *She'll understand. It's the only choice I have to save her. She's lingered along the twilight veils for so long that each breath carries her a little farther away from me. If I can ease her suffering, even for a moment, then I have to take this thing's offer.*

He turned his gaze back to the dark entity. "What do you want from me?"

The creature chuckled once more. The sound grated over his bones. "Fixing her has to be done from the inside. I need a way in."

"What kind of a way in?"

"Come to the forest at night—into the darkest part, where you've never ventured before. I'll clear a path for you. A small pond covers the entrance to my domain. The old ones banished us there and sealed us away, but over time, the portal has splintered, like tiny fractures in ice. A bit of us has seeped through. However, we are still confined by the wood and the power running through it.

Scoop up a flask of water and bring it back to your beloved. All she has to do is drink it."

"This will heal her? What do you get out of it?"

"Take my offer or not. You wife will open her eyes and she will recognize you. It will take a few days for her to return to her old self as the healing spreads through her body."

"What's your price for giving me this cure?"

"Freedom."

Alerik snapped awake.

The demon's words filled his mind as he looked around and saw the curtains fluttering in the breeze.

His wife moaned. Eloise opened her eyes, but they were clouded with pain. He touched her forehead with a cool cloth. Her lips moved as she tried to form words.

"Shh, love. You need to rest."

She shook her head and tried to grab onto his arm. Her eyes rolled back into her head and her limbs contorted as another one of her fits came on her.

Alerik had just enough time to grab the leather piece he put in her mouth to bite down on instead of her tongue as her body went rigid. Tears slipped down his cheeks as he held her and tried to keep her from hurting herself. Once the fit passed, he pressed his face into the sheets and cried, knowing what he had to do.

By the time the dark moon rolled around, his wife wasn't even opening her eyes. Her skin had turned gray and her breathing labored. Death would soon take her if he didn't act. He'd agonized over what the creature said, weighing the consequences, but he couldn't lose the woman he loved. She was all he had.

The kingdom didn't matter. His magic didn't matter. He would give up his soul to keep Eloise alive.

Alerik grabbed his cloak and wrapped it close as he slipped out a side entrance of the castle, saddled a horse under a sleeping groom's nose, and headed to the wood. He ventured into the woods as far as the horse could take him but, after a time, it would go no further. He tied it to a tree and went the rest of the way on foot, already deeper into the forest than he'd ever trekked.

The dark energy of the entity woven into the fabric of the landscape pulsated along his flesh. The hairs stood up on his body and keep his senses alert as he felt eyes on him. When he stepped deeper into the darkness, the trees cracked and shivered, moving aside and clearing a path for him.

The air around him grew colder. He could see his breath, and heard things slithering around in the under-brush. Alerik kept his gaze forward until he came to a small pool. Skeletons of animals and men lay scattered around it. He knelt by the water's edge and took out his flask— then noticed his reflection, or lack thereof. Instead, a creature stared back up at him.

Alerik dropped the flask into the brackish water.

"Leukos's balls," he muttered.

Laughter erupted around him. He steadied his hand to fish the container out of the pool. Instead, the creature's long talons broke the surface holding the flask.

"Take it. It's what you came for."

He recognized the voice of the being who had spoken to him. Alerik hesitated. If he didn't take it, then his wife would wander into twilight soon, and she would never wake again.

Or he could bring her back to him.

Alerik snatched the flask from the creature's hand. Its nails scraped the side and left grooves in the metal. One of those claws touched his palm. He gazed back into the water and saw the creature's reflection fading. Its eyes still burned gold, but its smile was all sharp teeth.

He ran from the shadowed woods, mounted his horse, and returned to the castle before the sun rose.

Doctors and healers surrounded the queen's bed. Heavy incense smoke clouded the air. All faces turned toward him when he entered. Alerik tucked the flask away out of sight.

"Sire, the queen has drifted closer to the twilight realm. We searched the castle for you but had to proceed with her final preparations. The sages say she will pass into the shadowed veil this night."

Emotion choked him up. "Leave us. All of you."

"But Majesty. It is customary for..."

He gazed at his wise-man. "I said out."

All the servants and the queen's kin filed out of the room. The sage stopped and stared at the king with blind eyes. "Let her go in peace, Majesty. It'll be much easier than what you plan."

"I can't," he whispered.

"Then heed this warning. You will live with what you do and wish you could turn back time." The sage wandered out of the room, leaving Alerik completely alone.

He sat on his wife's bed.

They had washed her and dressed her in all her finery so she could meet the shadow god who would bring her into twilight. He pressed his lips to her forehead and felt the coldness of her flesh. Her breathing came in shallow gasps. Her energy lingered about her, so her soul hadn't yet left her body and sought the other world.

Alerik took out the container of precious water and cradled her head. "I need you with me, my love. I'm not ready to give you up."

He tipped the flask up and let the water pass over her lips. Some of it made it into her mouth and some spilled out of the corners. She took a couple of swallows. When the water was half gone, her body twitched. Her eyelids fluttered. Her fingers raked the sheets and her mouth locked in a silent scream. After a moment the reaction stopped, and she lay limp.

Alerik waited for her to recover like the creature said. Nothing happened. She lay as still as if she were already dead. Alerik pressed his ear against her chest and listened.

Silence.

It lied. What did I do to her? What abomination did I bring into this world? He rested his head on her stomach and sobbed. After a time, he heard a small thud and felt her take in a breath.

"Why so sad, dearest?"

He looked up through blurred vision and saw his wife's beautiful smile. Her skin remained pale and cold. He pressed his lips to hers and laughed. The dark one had been true to his word. It worked.

"You're alive. I thought I'd lost you. The sages and the doctors couldn't do anything."

"I'm here with you. I'll always be here."

Alerik hugged her to him. His love had returned from the brink of death. Nothing else mattered except that.

———

K aya closed the book.

He's describing a bargain with the creature in the Bone Forest. The king loved Eloise so much he didn't think about the consequences of what might come after. All that mattered was that his queen was alive.

She sympathized with him. Alerik sounded much like Stavros in how much he treasured his wife and would do anything to bring her back. Kaya knew the only reason Stavros had treated her nicely at their last meeting was because she was the conduit for him to communicate with Serena. With the silver on her wrists, she couldn't channel Serena for him without hurting herself.

She shook her head and turned her thoughts back to the dark being mentioned in Alerik's book. Kaya had no doubt it was the same thing she sensed in the Bone Forest. It had found her in the castle as it had found her in the mountains of her home and drawn her to the ruins. She set the ring aside and went back downstairs.

"Where have you been?" Stavros sat in her sitting room going through some papers.

She couldn't hide that she had appeared from behind a hidden door. "I went to the garden hoping to find you there."

"I was there looking for you. I thought you might want

to take a walk with me. We could enjoy the night. You prefer it to the day, do you not?"

Kaya saw he was trying.

"I do prefer the night, Sire, though I can withstand the daylight. None of the others can unless they have magical help. The cloak you tore from me when you captured me was woven with magic to withstand the light. It is the same with Valik's coat."

"Where were you?" His tone darkened as he inquired again. The veins in his temples throbbed.

"I was in the tower looking out the window. Waiting to see if my mother and the court were coming. Or if Valik was back ahead of them. Forgive me for lying to you. I didn't think you'd understand."

Stavros sighed and relaxed. "I understand why you wouldn't trust me. You need the connection to your people. Serena used to gaze out that window when she first got here. She didn't trust me either. She was so homesick. Her father and I signed a treaty so we would have access to the ocean ports in their lands. Having access to the seas has made us profitable. We are still on good terms, but he is getting older and his son will take the throne soon. Luckily, the river flows straight through the heart of the land and we can use it to ship goods."

"Trade is good. We have our mines. The mountains are rich with silver, gold, other ores and gemstones. There are tunnels through all the ranges we rule. It's one reason we are such a profitable kingdom. I'm sure you'll be happy when you receive my dowry—or ransom. Whatever you wish to call it."

"I think we both need to stop thinking of you as a prisoner. That's why I came tonight. As I said, I thought you might want to go for a walk. The lords are whispering I must've killed you because no one has seen you of late. Rumors are rampant."

"I appreciate your desire to treat me better. Believe me, having the collar off is wonderful...but please understand. I can't just summon up your wife anytime you feel like it. She might be lingering, but it's up to her if she wants to show herself."

Stavros hung his head. "I realize that. I've thought a great deal about what she said. Petra's been harping at me, too. Kewskin wants to examine you. The generals are telling me to skin you. My logic says to marry you and do my duty as king. Make you give me an heir any way I can."

"Would your people be fine with a child who is part Vyrkola?"

"I hadn't thought of that. Would it have a thirst for blood?"

"Maybe. I don't know. You know I haven't killed anyone by taking blood. Many of my kind don't actually kill people. We don't need a lot of blood to survive unless we've been wounded. There are good and bad among both our peoples. Have you ever been bitten? It can be quite pleasurable."

He paled as she stepped toward him. "I don't think that's appropriate right now."

Kaya saw the fear in him. It made her feel as though the scales had tipped in her favor. She looked down. "Forgive me, Majesty. Sometimes I forget you've had only bad experiences with my kind."

"Would you like to go for that walk and get out of your room?"

She curtsied. "I'd appreciate that."

Stavros offered her his arm. Kaya took it and they walked out into the castle.

CHAPTER TEN

The castle was buzzing about Kaya being on his arm.

He had servants preparing rooms for the coming Vyrkola entourage. No one dared defy him, but he heard the rumors.

Stavros hated to admit, after spending more time with Kaya, they had similar interests. He found her likable. She knew history and music. Even battle strategies. When he asked her about magic, she hesitated, but answered his questions. Her inquiry about biting him made him wonder what it would be like. Of course, he went back and forth on that one and he wasn't ready to confess his curiosity even to himself.

"Sire, only one has returned from the scouting party you sent into the Bone Forest."

He looked up as Kewskin entered his private study.

"Take me to him."

He followed the chancellor to his quarters, where he found the man huddled in a corner.

He knew this man. He was one of his generals' sons.

The man babbled to himself. He was dirty and his eyes wild. His clothes were torn, and he smelled of old blood and death.

Stavros knelt before him. "Nicero, tell me why are you in such a state? What did you see? What happened to the others?"

Nicero's eyes wandered. He kept on muttering as though he had gone mad.

Stavros looked up at Kewskin.

"Something has gotten to his mind. I don't know if he'll ever be right again," the chancellor said.

"We need his information. Your magic can't penetrate the ruins. All I've learned until now is half history and half fable from the princess."

"Has Princess Kaya told you anything useful?" the chancellor asked.

"Princess," Nicero muttered.

"Yes, do you know something of her?" Stavros turned to the man again. "Go get Kaya and bring her here," he ordered Kewskin. "Maybe we can get some answers out of him if he sees her."

The chancellor flashed him an indignant look, but he bowed his head and left the room.

Stavros put a hand on the young man's arm. Nicero cried out and scrambled further away from him. He clawed at his face and left gouges in his flesh. The king grabbed the man's wrists to try and stop him from hurting himself.

"Go fetch me some water and a healer," Stavros told a servant hovering in the background.

Kewskin returned with Kaya. She looked bewildered by being summoned to the room. Stavros motioned for her to come over, and she knelt beside him.

"Nicero, the princess is here," murmured Stavros. "Did you want to talk to her?"

The other man's eyes flicked to her. His expression returned to something that resembled clarity.

"This man was part of a scouting party we sent into the Forest of Bones so we could see what the Thralls were up to," Stavros explained to her. "Six men went in. He's the only one who returned."

"Why send for me?" Kaya asked.

"When we mentioned your name, he calmed down. No one's been able to get anything sensible out of him," Kewskin replied.

"All right. I'll see what I can do."

Stavros stayed beside her in case the man tried to lash out.

Kaya spoke to Nicero. "The king said you asked about me. Can I help make you more comfortable? Maybe you want to tell me about what you saw in the forest?"

Nicero turned to her as his head fell to the side. It seemed he had trouble holding it up with the way it bobbed up and down. Something about the man didn't seem right. Granted, Stavros didn't know what to expect from a man who had been into the Forest of Bones and come out the other side. It would be understandable if he wasn't exactly sane. To be alive at all was a miracle.

"Forest." A string of drool ran from Nicero's mouth and landed on his tattered shirt.

"That's right. The king said you went into the woods to

see what the Thralls were up to. Did you make it to the ruins?"

"Ruins?" Nicero shook his head. Each time he did, the bones cricked and creaked with an unnatural sound. Stavros didn't think the younger man understood what Kaya was asking him.

"Keep trying. Something about you gave him a moment of clarity," Stavros encouraged her.

She nodded. Stavros laid a hand on her back.

Kaya jumped and shot him a questioning look.

He smiled at her.

Kewskin scowled at the small touch, but Stavros wasn't going to let his chancellor tell him what was good for him and what was not. They needed this information.

As he touched Kaya, he realized he liked how she felt. For a moment, an image of how she would feel against him flashed in his mind. He shook it off.

"Did you see anything in the woodland? A darkness or some other entity? Did you feel anything?"

"Darkness. Yes. Things in the woods, growing in the trees. Screaming. All the dead who linger there. Half alive. Half dead. Swinging from the branches. I saw them. They're still there." Nicero grabbed Kaya's hand.

"That's good. You don't have to worry about them. They can't hurt you anymore. What else happened?" Kaya laid a hand over his. He pulled away and cried out.

"Silver. It hates silver. Get it away from me. You're not the princess. Impostor! It'll eat you alive if you go into the woods. They're waiting for you. They want out. *He* wants out."

"Who is this 'he?'" Kewskin pushed him for more information.

Nicero withdrew from the wizard. "You'll never get what you want, *varaz*. Get me the real princess, or I'm not talking."

Stavros grumbled and pulled Kaya away. "Did any of that make any sense?"

Kaya ran her fingers over the silver cuffs. They seemed to trouble her, but she never complained about them.

"A little. The dead remain in the forest. I've seen the ghosts flickering in and out. They don't bother me though. The dark presence I've encountered...I think it's the same one Nicero is referring to. If he has more information, he's not going to give it to me because I'm wearing the silver bracelets. Will you remove them, at least for now? I don't expect you to leave the room while I have them off."

"Sire, if you remove those, you risk this creature running off or mesmerizing us. She could kill us all. Those are all that is keeping her under your control."

"I can assure you, Chancellor, my head is not going to spin around if the king takes these off. Nor am I going to hypnotize the whole court. It's not one of my talents. My best skill is with magic. As I've told the king, I've never killed anyone by draining them of blood—though I have in combat. I'm as skillfully trained as the rest of our warriors."

"You're a Vyrk," Kewskin scoffed. "Majesty, I've been telling you—"

Stavros glanced between the two of them. He pulled the key from around his neck.

Kaya bit her lip and her eyes lit up with hope.

"I'll take these off so you can talk to him, but you do

nothing. No magic. No signs of aggression toward us, or I'll make sure you're locked in your room until our wedding night. Understand?"

"Yes, sire." She cast her eyes down, but he sensed she wanted to say something else.

He undid the locks on the cuffs. Once the last one came off, Kaya seemed to grow before his eyes. Her presence filled the room. Her eyes brightened. Her hair seemed darker now that her power was no longer suppressed. She rolled her shoulders, wiggled her fingers, and cracked her neck.

A cold power came off her that prickled his skin.

It also aroused him.

Kewskin opened his mouth to say something, but Stavros shot him a look that warned if he did, he would lose his tongue. He was getting tired of the man telling him what he should and shouldn't do. His father had appreciated the sorcerer's advice. At times, his magic came in handy, but there were other *varaz* and sages he could call upon.

Kaya walked back over to Nicero.

"Nico," Kaya called softly.

The man blinked and rationality returned to his eyes. "H-how do you know that name?"

"It's what your father calls you, isn't it?"

"Yes. Who are you?"

"I'm Kaya. You said you'd talk to the real princess about what happened in the wood. I'm here like you asked. Can you tell me what you endured?"

A smile appeared on his face like that of a happy little

boy. "He said I could have a treat if I could get you to him. Can I have a treat?"

"After this is over. You can tell me what happened when you went into the Bone Forest with the other members of your scouting party first. You were going in after the Thralls to see what they were doing as the king ordered. Did you find them?"

Nicero pulled away. He tried to hold his head up, but it kept rolling around as though he had no control over it. "How do I know you're really her and not an impostor?"

Kaya held out her hands. "See. No silver."

He touched the place on her arms where the bracelets had been. A smile spread across his face. Something shook Stavros. His instincts told him to get Kaya out of there. He reached for her, but he wasn't fast enough.

Nicero grabbed her wrists and pulled her to him. She cried out in surprise and struggled to get out of his grasp.

Stavros rushed over. Before he got to her, Nicero stood up and had his hand around her throat. The king noticed several knives pressed into her skin. When he looked again, he saw that the blades were actually the young man's fingers.

"One move, king, and her head will come off."

"Kill her if you want. It won't be any skin off my back. She's nothing to me."

Kaya struggled as Nicero's other hand went around her waist to keep her close. She tried to speak, but he tightened his hold on her.

"King of the Humans knows nothing about how special this woman is. What a beauty she turned out to be. Everything I had hoped for." Nicero opened his mouth and a long black tongue flicked along the side of her throat. "She tastes so good."

Kaya struggled again to get away.

"Have you told him yet, Princess?"

"Leave her alone," Stavros barked.

His eyes opened wider, now flecked with gold. "You can't do anything to me, King of Nothing."

"Get behind me, Majesty. I'll protect you from this darkness and vanquish both of them." Kewskin readied himself to throw a ball of energy at Nicero.

"You might annihilate this body, sorcerer, but I'm still going to be here. If you hurt the princess, you might lose your head. Your king feels something for her, although he denies it. He's in for a big surprise. Don't you want to hear my demands?"

"Kewskin, lower your hand. You can't hurt the princess."

"You don't know what you're saying. She's bewitched you. It's obvious this man is possessed by something he brought back from the forest. We can't let it spread to any others in the castle."

"Do as I say or find yourself with your head on a platter," Stavros ordered.

The *varaz* squelched his energy ball and lowered his hand.

"Of course, Your Majesty."

"What do you want, demon?" Stavros asked the thing wearing Nicero's skin.

"I have what I want, King of Nothing." The candles and torches winked out and darkness descended in the room.

Stavros made out a form in the blackness.

Kaya screamed. The sound echoed as the shadowy figure dashed out of the room.

The guards scrambled to get the torches re-lit. When the light returned, Kaya was gone, and Nicero was nowhere to be found either.

"No."

Stavros dropped the silver cuffs and fell to his knees on the spot where Kaya had been. "It took her." He felt the pain of losing his wife all over again. "What was that creature?"

"A demon, as you said. It must have taken on Nicero's guise to get in the castle."

"It knew the princess was here. That's what she meant the other night. She said the darkness had found her, but she wasn't sure how when she was wearing the silver."

"What else did the princess tell you? Maybe this has been her plan all along. Maybe this was her way of escaping. She must have sided with the demon and with whatever the Thralls are doing."

"Kewskin, stop with your accusations. Couldn't you see she was terrified? She's not what you're making her out to be. You just can't stand that she's more powerful than you. You sensed it even with the cuffs. You want to know what she told me?"

"Enlighten me, Sire. Up until now, you've been dead set on killing any Vyrk you saw. You banned your subjects from consorting with them and even killed their lovers. Her kind killed your wife. Your demeanor toward her of late has changed. It goes beyond this trumped up betrothal they have yoked you into. You're falling in love with the

125

princess even if you can't see it yourself. The whole court is talking behind your back—saying that the king is under her spell. That he is *weak*. You've gone back on your word to eradicate their kind. You stopped the raiding parties and the killing of any Vyrk you could find. Your sister, the queen, is known to have a Vyrkola lover and you do nothing."

All the chancellor said was true. Stavros had promised his subjects he would kill all the Vyrks in his kingdom. He had eradicated any he could find. Those subjects who wouldn't give them up, he burned. His sister traveled outside the castle to meet with her lover, but he wasn't about to kill his twin sister.

Serena's words came back to him, and he believed what she said was true. "No, they didn't. Thralls killed the queen. I was made to believe it was the Vyrks so we would start a war with them. All of this happened so that I would hate them so much I would exterminate them until there was nothing left of their kind."

"What do you mean, 'it was the Thralls?' Who told you that?"

"Queen Serena did."

"She's dead."

"I know that, Kewskin." Stavros recounted what had happened to him in the garden when Kaya was with him.

"It was a trick to get you to remove her collar and trust her."

"I thought that at first, too. Kaya had no way of channeling her power while wearing the silver. She's stronger than you think. I'm learning that. I know what I said, but she's really a remarkable woman. I might have been forced into this marriage, called out in front of the court, but I can't stop my heart from warming to her. I've tried—and I won't stop it, or I won't see Serena again."

"Has her ghost come to you again since you've softened?"

Stavros ran his fingers over the silver cuffs. The energy he felt coming from them raised the hairs on the back of his hands. He could also feel Kaya's energy entwined somehow through the metal. He wondered if she had begun to shape the energy of them to bend to her will. If that was possible. When she stood before him in all her glory, it had aroused him, and he wanted to see more of her. He had seen some strange things from magic. It might be possible that Kaya had been manipulating him all along. Stavros wanted to believe in her, but if she was in league with the demon, then maybe Kewskin was right.

"No. Serena hasn't come to me again."

"Then let the demon have the princess. Queen Serena not appearing to you proves my point—that Kaya was manipulating you all along. You don't need to go into the forest after her. That's what it wants."

Stavros shoved the bracelets into his pocket. "We have to go into the forest and see what the Thralls are up to. This far into the kingdom, they could be planning something and using the forest as their base. If Kaya is in league with the demon, then I'll take her head. If this is all part of some game, then the Vyrks will know my wrath. Prepare for us to ride once the sun rises. Gather a handful of my best warriors and the strongest seer you can find."

"Yes, sire," Kewskin bowed.

Stavros felt the fire in his blood as he twisted all the

moments he and Kaya had spent together. The words of the demon calling him King of Nothing only enraged him further. Stavros left the chancellor's quarters and went into the garden to find a moment of clarity. His clouded mind went repeatedly over everything with Kaya and the night she brought his darling back to him. She drained herself by using her energy even with the silver cuffs on to bring his wife back to him. It had weakened her severely, but she did it anyway. Stavros raked his fingers down his face and sat by the fountain Serena loved so much.

"Please, beloved, if you're here, I need to know Kaya didn't just conjure you. You told me to open my heart. I'm trying. I think I could love her, but I need to trust her."

Stavros listened for some sign of his departed wife. The night remained silent save for the chirping of crickets. He slammed his fist into the stone of the fountain when he didn't get an answer. All of it was a Vyrk ruse. The princess was in league with the demon. They had made him look like a fool on purpose in front of his whole kingdom.

Nothing would stop him now from hunting her down and taking her head. He stood to leave when he heard a faint whisper next to his ear.

"You must save her."

He spun around, but saw nothing. "I need more than that. Show yourself to me. Show me you're not this dark monster from the wood."

A white flicker of light winked on and off before him as it gathered strength. The faint form of his wife floated over to him. She pulled his ear and smiled. Her gaze remained sad, but he knew it was her. She used to tug on his ear to tease him when he they were alone. Tears slid down his cheeks.

"It's really you."

She nodded before winking out. "She's the key. It's waited a very long time for her."

Her voice floated away, and he knew what he had to do.

II

SHADOW

CHAPTER ELEVEN

K aya opened her eyes and found herself in a stone room. No light penetrated the darkness, but she could see perfectly because of her night vision. With the bracelets off, her full senses had returned, along with her magic. The last thing she remembered was talking to Nicero—and then she was pulled away by something.

"No. No!" Kaya realized where she was.

"No need to panic, Princess." The voice came from a corner of the room.

The outline of a form leaned against the wall. It was taller and larger than any man, but it had a hunched shape and burning gold eyes. She recognized those eyes from the descriptions in the journal entries she read in the tower.

"You're one of them, aren't you? One of the ones who lured king Alerik into the woods."

It chuckled. "I'm not just *one* of them. I am the first one who escaped. I'm surprised that you know about that. How did you find out?"

"I read about it. Alerik wrote about what happened when you infected his wife. Although, I didn't get past the part where he gave her the water from the pond. I assume this place was built on that well."

"Actually, it's the castle where the king lived. The well where my brothers and sisters are being kept is in Thrall territory."

"Then why aren't you there?"

"Because Alerik imprisoned me here when he killed his wife, but not all of me was trapped. Look what has spawned from all these years. Just as I hoped it would. With my knowledge and the queen's, I was able to form a spell. I looked at the long term and you are perfect."

"You're the start of all of this?" Kaya breathed.

It stepped toward her. The stench of rot made her gag as she moved backward. It snapped its fingers and candles popped to life.

Her eyes took a moment to adjust to the brightness. When they did, she saw more details of the demon's face. Long pointed teeth hung over its lips. Its cheeks were sunken. Stubby horns jutted around its forehead like a crown. Gray scales flowed down its neck in various places and mixed in with skin and fur. Short, sharp claws tipped its fingers. It was extremely emaciated, ribs protruding from its barrel chest. Golden, over-sized eyes that shone in the light stared back at her.

"Does my appearance bother you?"

She nodded. It shrank and became a woman. She had long brown hair and wore a green dress. Even though it took on this human appearance, its eyes remained soulless.

"Who are you? What are you? Tell me the truth. What

wasn't in Alerik's journal?"

"I'm Eloise. Alerik's queen—or what's left of her."

"But you're more demon than human."

"You call me demon. I call myself something else."

Kaya glanced around for a way out. She didn't see any, but that didn't mean there wasn't one. It had gotten out somehow. At this moment, she wished she could turn to mist like other Vyrkolas. "What would you call yourself?"

"Kin."

"Impossible."

"Really? You asked me for the truth. Why don't you experience it for yourself? Let me show you..."

The demon clapped its hands. The rubble and stones moved backward until the ruins became a grand castle decorated in tapestries and paintings. Power passed over her and took her breath away with its raw strength. Images of people flickered around until they came into view and were no longer ghosts of themselves.

Kaya found herself immersed in a living memory. The creature came over, but didn't touch her.

"This is my favorite part. Let me give you the words to go with the visual." It touched her face and then she could hear, as well as see, the memory.

———

"Eloise, my love, why are you acting this way? You've been cured of your fits for months now. Your power has been growing stronger. But you've been writing spells that make no sense. One of the servants said you tried to attack her."

The queen stretched. "Alerik, I'm fine. I'm just tired. I stood on the edge of the twilight realm and I came back with so many ideas I want to share. Sometimes I can't write them down fast enough. The servant is lying."

Alerik went over to the window and drew back to the curtain.

Sunlight poured in and hit Eloise. She threw up her hands and rushed into the shadows. "Close it, please!"

The king stepped between her and the window, blocking out the light.

"Tell me there isn't something wrong with you. The woman I know loves the sunlight. You used to tell me stories of how the sun gods banished the darkness from this world. You used to head into the forest and worship the gods of light. Now you hide from the sun. This isn't you."

Eloise's laugh turned into a sinister snicker. "This is the new me. There were consequences for what you did. Did you really think that making a deal with a fallen immortal would let you come out of it without having to pay anything?"

"You don't know what you're saying."

Eloise turned toward the light. Her skin began to smolder. Her grin widened as her eye teeth grew. Her skin paled and her fingers sharpened into claws.

"I know exactly what I'm saying. Now I'm going to collect."

She rushed him, landing on top of him. The queen wrenched his head to the side, exposing his neck. Alerik threw up his hands to protect himself. She grabbed his wrist and bit down. He grunted in pain and shoved her from him.

She came at him again, but he swung his sword and took off her head.

Alerik sunk down beside his wife and screamed.

———

The memory faded away and the room returned to the present. The candles flickered as Kaya turned back to the demon. All the pieces fell into place.

"You bit Alerik and turned him. Although, he didn't realize it until he was well into the turn. But you never gave him any blood."

"Very good. Smarter than I thought. When Eloise bit her husband, I was so ingrained in her that one bite was all it took. I'd been biding my time, eating away a bit of her at a time. Playing along until I could take him for my first. He thought he killed me—but when he entombed me in the crypt, he reattached her head to her body. Poor thing couldn't bear to see her defiled. It took a little time, but I awoke again. By that time, the transformation had taken hold. I could feel it in him."

"You confronted him again. He used all his power to kill you and seal you away in here."

"Something like that."

"Fine. What do you want from me?" Kaya asked.

"You're the ultimate outcome of what I wished to accomplish. I saw it all those years ago. A union of human and immortal. You're the key. You can open the gateway between worlds and let out our kin."

"I would never willingly free the rest of your kind. The

land would be plagued by evil. You would destroy everything."

"We could share the land. There's enough humans out there for all of us. Humans are merely meat, but you would be my queen."

Kaya laughed. "I don't think so. Nothing you do will ever make me rule beside you. As it is...if you're trapped here, how did you pull me from Stavros's castle?"

"As the Vyrkolas have grown in number, my range beyond these walls has grown. The more of you there are, the stronger I become. I've been imprisoned here for such a long time—and then I felt you come to my calling. I've seen you outside of these ruins, too afraid to enter. Now that you are here, I'm not letting you go. I don't care if the king is coming for you...or even Valik."

"What do you know about Valik?"

"I know all of you—all of those who are connected to me through blood. However, I also know something Stavros doesn't." The thing walked around and touched her throat.

She cringed away from the demon. "What is that?"

"You've claimed Valik for your mate. Your husband."

"I know what I did. Stavros wouldn't understand."

"Wait until I tell him how you lay with Valik. He'll enjoy all the gory details."

"That didn't happen," Kaya countered.

"You want it to. You want to feel him inside of you. You've even thought about what it would be like to carry his child, but you already know his seed is dead."

She looked at the ground. The demon was reading her desires. She *had* thought about it, though she knew what the demon said was true. Valik, like all Vyrks, was unable to have children. The spell her father had cast on her mother to conceive her was a miracle. The enchantment no longer existed and even if it did, she wouldn't risk his life for a child. Kaya knew she would never be able to have Valik's offspring, but that didn't mean she hadn't imagined it.

"I'm going to marry Stavros and bear his children."

"You are meant for more than just being a brood mare. You're powerful. Beautiful. Just the thing I've been waiting for."

"You're not going to get me to do anything for you."

The demon grabbed her chin and held her in place. "That's what you think."

Kaya struggled to get out of its grasp, but it was too strong. She summoned her power and called an energy blade to her hand. The energy felt good, and brought a quick memory of her and Adran sparring together with energy weapons since they were the preferred form of combat weapon for a *varaz*. She slashed the blade across the demon's middle.

It screamed and released her. Black blood dripped from the wound as it held its insides in place.

"You won't take me. I might be the culmination of some plan, but you can't possess me. I have a soul. Eloise stood in twilight and it gave you enough leverage to fuse yourself to her until you twisted around her spirit. I see her still in you."

The thing growled and retreated into the shadows.

Kaya slumped against the wall and let the blade dissolve. Having her magic at her disposal again left her energized and gave her hope she could find a way out of the ruins. She closed her eyes, spread out her mind, and searched every inch of the room. Grating magic stifled her senses. The power that laced through the rocks was old and more powerful than anything she had encountered before.

It threw her back into her body.

She sighed. *I can't give up. I will get out of this.*

Kaya grounded herself again, but this time followed the link she shared with Valik. It flared to life like a beacon in her mind.

"Valik," she whispered mentally.

"Kaya, what's the matter?"

"I need your help. The demon came into the castle, possessed some human, and snatched me away. I'm in the old ruins in the Bone Forest. I can't get out. You have to help me."

She shared with him the memory of what had happened with Nicero and how she had been whisked away.

"I'll be there before nightfall. We're on our way to the castle now. Don't let it get to you, my love," Valik replied. A surge of love followed the words and made her shiver. Then all went quiet.

"Even if he comes here, he can't enter. The ancient magic binding me here also keeps out any other Vyrkolas. You're not getting out unless you're rescued by that human king of yours. You could have the whole Vyrk army on their way and they couldn't free you," the demon told her.

"But I've been to the ruins before and I've never been stuck."

"You've only been to the outskirts of the old castle. Underneath us is the very spot where Alerik buried Eloise and trapped me here using all of his magic. It killed everything around him, and made sure that no other Vyrks can wield magic," the darkness said to her.

Kaya wrapped her arms around herself. She pushed its words away and plunged her mind downward, to the source of the power she felt in the ruins. The further down she went, the stronger the magic became and the more painful. The energy pushed upon her like nails being driven into her skull. Kaya went still further, searching for a way out, or to pinpoint something she could use as a weapon.

In her mind's eye, she saw the effigies of the queen and the king in the tomb. *Alerik killed himself in the process of trapping the evil here. How does that make him the father our race?*

The pain from the magic beat against her skull like a drum. It was designed to work against Vyrks, and she was only half. *What would it do to one of the others?*

Kaya examined the stone likenesses in the tomb and noticed something. On the side of Alerik's crypt was a faint oval impression.

Not able to take the onslaught anymore, she returned to her body. She sniffled and tasted blood on the back of her tongue. When she opened her eyes, the demon stood in front of her. Its tongue flicked out and licked up a drop of her blood from the nosebleed. It grinned and dashed away.

"Leave me alone," she spat after it.

Kaya wiped the blood onto her dress and felt the ring in her pocket. She had forgotten about it when Kewskin summoned her. She had been going to read more of Alerik's journal when he knocked on her door and told her Stavros wanted her. Kaya paced the room. The ancient magic might hold up the tower she was in and the crypt beneath, but she was determined to find a way down to the tomb.

She trailed her fingers along the wall, slipping the ring onto her finger. The demon's presence retreated. When she ran her fingers over the bricks, the ring glowed purple. As she searched her prison, the glow from the ring brightened until it lit up the room. She stopped and placed her palm over the stone. The ring's violet hue fanned out along the wall.

Gears ground together, and a doorway swung open wide enough for her to squeeze through. Inside the passageway, she found a stairway that led downward.

Kaya summoned an orb into her palm. She tossed it into the air, and it broke into half a dozen tiny balls. The lights hovered around her as she descended, and the wall closed behind her. When she got to the bottom, she looked up and saw the core of the tower. The room she had left remained dark, but the demon hadn't followed her.

The globes doubled in size to penetrate the shadows. Three of them merged together and flattened against the opposite wall. The ring glowed again. When she touched the stones, they melted away. Kaya slipped through the wall and stood in the crypt she had seen earlier. The blanket of magic made her gasp as it wrapped around her and tried to beat her back. She steeled herself and examined the stone image of Eloise. She appeared peaceful, showing nothing of the darkness her husband had infected her with. Time had changed nothing on the coffin.

Kaya studied Alerik's effigy. His stone face been scratched and gouged until nothing remained of it. She trailed her fingers over his hands and saw the same ring she now wore.

The ring glowed purple again as she circled the sarcophagus until she reached the opposite side. She studied the carvings until she found a small depression buried within a stone wreath and some filigree. She pressed the ring into it. A quick bolt of energy surged across the stone coffin and the top slid open. She peered inside, expecting to see bones, but there were only more stairs.

Kaya cast the lights below until they illuminated the disturbed dust particles on the floor beneath. She didn't sense the demon, but she wasn't going to wait around for it to come upon her. Kaya climbed in and started down the stairs as the coffin lid closed above, leaving her with no way back.

The lower she went, the harder it was to breathe. Her head felt like someone had it in a vise. The orbs brightened into flames. Kaya no longer fed them energy because the place was steeped in it. The flames fanned out around the cave she emerged into. The flares illuminated jewels embedded in the walls. It looked like the night sky, shot through with silver. On closer inspection, wide ribbons of the metal glowed in the walls. She had seen the same veins in the tunnels of the mines below her home castle.

That's why it's trapped here. It needs someone to let it out. Someone alive, but not someone who's already been turned. It can't get me because I haven't given it permission to enter me.

Kaya searched the entire room but found no way out. No decoration adorned the cave walls, but an intricately carved raised capstone rested in the center of the cave floor. Carved on the seal was the same image tattooed on her back. Her royal crest.

Ripples of power pushed tiny bits of stone away from the capstone like waves pushing up sand. All the concentrated energy surged against her head and made it hard for her to breathe.

This has to be what Alerik tapped into when he sealed the demon here. So much raw power flowing through a human body—even one that had started to turn—would burn out the magical circuits in anyone.

As she passed her hand over the capstone, the ring glowed again as did the seal upon it. Kaya was drawn to the stone.

She shook her head and tried to ignore the urge to examine it more closely.

However, the energy had a voice. The words weren't something she could understand, but they translated into a knowing that if she went closer to the seal, the power would unlock something inside of her. She stepped to the edge, about to break the threshold of the pattern.

"Kaya, no."

Valik's sharp command within her mind broke her from the trance. She found herself about to cross into the energy waves.

"Why not?" she answered.

"All that power would destroy you. I can't lose you. I

can feel you below. *Listen to me and I'll help you get free."*
His love for her poured through their bond. *"Move toward
the south of the cave."*

"How do you know where I am?" He had to be close if
she could hear him this clearly. All the magic in the place
made it impossible for her to feel him. Then again it could
be a trap.

*"Dearest, I can see through your eyes. We're bound
together."*

"How do I know you're Valik and not the demon?"

*"Would I know that your mother calls you Anna or that
you mourn for Adran? You wish to feel his bond with you
again. How his blood is the only human's that truly satisfied
your desires because you're bound together in ways that
even I don't understand?"*

She teared up at the mention of Adran's name. It was
true. Some part of her didn't feel whole without him in her
life. The darkness wouldn't know that.

"Okay."

She pulled herself completely out of the hold of the
magic and went to the south side of the cavern.

"What now?"

*"Halfway down the wall will be a small indentation.
Press the ring into it."*

"How do you know I'm wearing a ring?"

*"I see it on you, but only barely because it's made of
silver."*

"Right."

Kaya felt along the jagged rock face and found another
depression. The ring fit easily, and the wall melted away. A
line of silver ran across the door. She hesitated for a

moment. A tingle of power irritated her flesh. It was different than the energy coming from the node of magic. Another spelled barrier so the demon couldn't get out, she guessed. Kaya stepped over it and didn't feel anything holding her back. Once she entered the passageway beyond, the wall behind her became solid again.

Tree roots scraped her head as she walked through the passage, which sloped upward. When she touched them, they were hard as bone. The pitch blackness of the small space made her feel a little claustrophobic. This tunnel didn't feel as secure as the ones in the mountains of her home. The darkness seemed all encompassing. The hot air made it hard to breathe. She shared the space with unseen creatures that scurried across her feet and brushed along her arms. Kaya tried to ignore them as she walked a long way in the tunnel until she saw a pinpoint of light at the end of the passageway.

Rocks and dirt from a partial cave in blocked the exit. She summoned up an energy ball and blasted the rocks out of the way. The cave shook, but nothing else came down around her. Kaya winced at the incoming sunlight and passed her hand between the cavern and the outside world, testing to see if any magical impediment remained.

Nothing barred her way, so she stepped out of the ruins. A blast of cold air rushed by her. Kaya turned quickly to see a dark shadow wind out of the tunnel and undulate before her, sucking in all the light around it. The burning golden eyes confirmed what she already knew.

"You said you were trapped."

"I was, but—thanks to you—I'm free. I needed someone to get me out. You were the only one. All the others died or went insane. You're special. I told you that before. Now the real work can begin."

"You tricked me. You made me believe you were Valik."

"Yes. It was so easy. You forgot that I'm attached to all of you. My blood is inside you. I know all of your deep, dark secrets."

"What are you going to do now?"

Its grin widened.

"So much to catch up on. So many plans. We'll see one another again, Princess. I'm not done with you yet."

It lifted its nose to the air and sniffed. A black tongue caressed its thin lips.

"First off, dinner. I'm famished and you'll be a good appetizer."

The demon rushed at her before she could defend herself. It wrapped her in darkness. She swatted at the thick shadow, but her hands passed right through it. Tiny needles of pain jabbed her body. Kaya fell to her knees, suffocating. Each place it touched it drained the energy out of her. Her pulse raced as she fought to stay conscious. Her vision blurred. The demon sucked the vitality out of her until she was sure it would kill her.

"I'm not going to kill you, Princess. I need your heart beating for you to wield the magic that opens the seal to release the rest of my kind. I just required a little something to get me going. There's other fresh meat not far from here. Your beloved king has come to rescue you."

The demon pressed its lips to hers in a kiss, sucking the last bit of air from her lungs until she blacked out.

CHAPTER TWELVE

Stavros opened his eyes. His body ached.

It was night now and the utter silence in the Bone Forest shattered his nerves. The last thing he remembered was riding into the depths of the wood looking for the ruins where the demon had taken Kaya.

All around him, his men and horses were dead; their bodies shrunken husks of what they used to be. Someone moaned beside him. Stavros looked over and saw Valik lying on his stomach, but slowly moving. He rolled over, his pale skin gray—but he was alive.

Valik staggered to his feet and offered his hand to Stavros.

The king ignored it.

"What happened here? What did you do?" Stavros demanded.

"I saved your life," Valik responded. "If it wasn't for me throwing myself on you, you'd be as dead as your men—a mere pile of ashes."

Stavros glanced at the remains of his trusted men and the generals who had ridden with him. He couldn't tell any of them apart. As the air stirred, their dried forms blew away.

Even Kewskin was gone.

Stavros looked back at the Vyrk. "What happened?"

"I came here looking for Kaya. She said she was in danger. A dark figure, almost a cloud, was attacking your people. It almost had you until I threw myself on top of you. Apparently, I wasn't appetizing, so it passed over me. You struggled for a moment and flung me off before you went unconscious."

He hated to admit the Vyrk had saved him. "Thank you."

"You're welcome. Why did you come here? Humans hate this place. Even our kind stays away." Valik adjusted the sword and dagger on his belt.

Stavros's body felt like lead, but he had come to rescue his fiancée.

"A demon took Kaya. It came in the form of one of my men. It fooled all of us. At first, it was answering questions about the Thralls. When she tried to entice him to answer more, it snatched her away and disappeared into the shadows. I couldn't get to her."

"Suddenly you want to save her after all the humiliating things you did to her?" Valik snarled. "If you were another man, I'd rip off your cock, make you eat it, and torture you the same way you did to her. Then, I would turn you and do it all over again—but you wouldn't grow your cock back. You'd be a eunuch for the rest of eternity, as well as my whipping boy."

Bile rose in his throat as he thought about being turned into one of Valik's kind.

"Things have changed regarding how I feel about the princess. I admit I treated her horribly. I did those things because each time it felt like I was getting a small piece of revenge for what happened to my wife and son. I've apologized to Kaya for it. I've gotten to know her some since you've been gone. My coming after her should prove to you that things have changed."

"I'll believe it when I see it." Valik looked up at the darkened sky and grimaced.

"What is it?"

"Kaya. She's in pain. Something's happened to her. I couldn't feel it before because of the shadow around us."

"How do you know that?"

"We're connected."

"Right. The way you're connected to the queen. She can see through your eyes and speak to you." Stavros wasn't sure what other abilities the Vyrk had, but Valik frightened him.

"Not exactly."

Stavros had to look up at the Vyrk which, he hated to admit, unnerved him.

"If you harm another hair on her head, I'll make sure you pay," Valik told him. "She's precious to me. Don't expect me to leave once you say your vows, if it even comes to that."

Stavros didn't look away. "I expect that when the queen leaves you will, too. I'll make sure of it. Kaya won't need you to protect her anymore."

Valik drew his dagger. The blade rested against

Stavros's neck before he could blink. "The only reason I left her this time was because I had to report back to the queen and make her aware of what you were doing to her daughter. She isn't happy about it. Queen Mila will have a few choice words with you. You have no idea how special Kaya is."

"It sounds like you're in love with her." Stavros was determined not to show his fear to the other man.

"Who wouldn't love her?" Valik replied.

"Are you going to use that knife, or are we going to go look for Kaya? Even if you don't believe me, I care for her, too. Let me prove it to you by helping you bring her out of this accursed place." He stepped into the blade until the pain of it sliced into his flesh.

Valik's nose twitched and his mouth stretched into a sneer. The Vyrkola holstered the weapon.

"This way."

Stavros followed him through dense forest. The thick branches scraped at his clothes. He touched one of the branches and found it hard as yellowed bone. All the trees had been petrified by some dark magic. He didn't need to be a sorcerer to feel the darkness and evil that lingered in these trees. Glints of things caught his eye among the bone underbrush. With the night growing darker, those flickers became lights that drew his attention. The further he got into the woods, the more it felt as though he were being watched.

An unholy presence blanketed the woodland. Something giggled in the distance. The wind kicked up until the branches creaked. A hollow sound, like crying, filled his head. Drawn by the wailing, Stavros found himself in a clearing.

A perfect ring of trees held their latest victims. Every branch had bodies hanging from them. Some were fresh—he recognized one of them as Nicero, the man who had supposedly came back to him—the others were either skeletal or rotting corpses. The longer he listened to the music the swinging bodies made, the more he wanted to join in the tune. Stavros wandered toward the middle of the circle and gazed around the trees, deciding which one he could become a part of.

The tall one would be perfect, and there's a fresh rope waiting for me.

He moved to the trunk of the tree, grabbed the rope, and slipped the noose around his neck.

"Stavros!"

A sudden shake broke him from the trance he was under. He blinked and saw that he wasn't standing at the base of the tree. He had fallen, and his backside hurt where he had landed.

Valik had his sword in one hand and the broken rope in the other.

Stavros grabbed his throat, only to find the noose still around it. His neck hurt where it had pulled tight.

"What the hell just happened?"

"I looked back, and you weren't there. It's this place. The evil, restless specters want people to join them. Nothing can prosper here. It used to be beautiful, or so I've heard. You must have been seduced by one of the spirits and not even realized it. Come on. Kaya isn't that far. Something's scaring her." Valik hacked at a small branch and looped the rope around it. He waved his hand over the hemp and it lit up.

He handed the torch to Stavros. "The light will keep both the dead and the demons away. Come."

The Vyrk lit the torch using magic. I felt it. But that's not possible. None of them can use magic. Unless they've been keeping that secret to themselves. What other secrets are they hiding? If it's not the Vyrks, then what secrets is Valik hiding?

The Vyrk had saved him twice now. Stavros hated owing him a debt.

The light cut through the shadows, even as they tried to encroach upon the two of them. Darkness overwhelmed the rest of the forest, stretching over it like a cloth. Fear grew stronger in Stavros the longer they remained. The images he saw out of the corner of his eye grew more frequent as they got closer to a large tower that loomed above the trees.

As they approached the structure, half-pitched tents fluttered in the breeze. He stopped and grabbed a discarded cloak and examined it. It appeared to have belonged to a Thrall. A few feet from the campsite were pits surrounded by piles of dirt. He nearly tripped over a shovel thrown haphazardly onto the ground.

"What were they doing?" He bent down to examine one of the holes. It didn't look like anything was in it.

"They were looking for a way into the ruins."

"Why? What good would that do them?"

"Because something was reaching out to anyone who would listen."

"Kaya said something about a darkness. Is that the same thing that attacked us?"

"I think we'll both get more answers once we find Kaya. She's close."

"Kaya," Stavros called.

"Quiet," Valik growled. "You'll draw the attention of the dead who don't know we're here—or something else altogether. I can't protect you from all of them if they swarm us. They ignore me because I'm almost one of them, but you and Kaya. You're alive. She..."

A scream split the night.

Stavros recognized it as Kaya's. Something in him broke upon hearing it.

He had enjoyed hearing her scream by his own hand, but now the shrill sound made his stomach curdle. He raced ahead of Valik and found Kaya surrounded by the transparent figures of the dead.

She flung a purple flame burning in her palm at the apparitions. As each one retreated, two more rushed her.

Stavros swung his torch through the ghosts. As the light hit them, they howled and backed away.

He pushed Kaya behind him. "We're going to get you out of this," he said to her.

"Thank you. There are too many of them. After the demon attacked me, I was too weak to call upon much of my own magic," she replied.

The specters inched closer even with the torchlight.

Stavros couldn't see their faces, but he felt the hollow echo of their pain as their wails grated on his ears. He thought he would go mad if he had to listen to them for much longer. A great wave of blue energy appeared out of nowhere and rushed at them. Kaya held onto his waist as it advanced. The spirits cried out in agony as they were hit with it.

Cold encompassed him and stole his breath away, but it only lasted a moment.

Valik came up to them after the surge passed. "Come on. They won't be gone for long."

Stavros wrapped the Thrall cloak around Kaya and grabbed the torch.

She flashed him a small smile and stepped over to Valik. "What were those things?"

"The hungry dead. Ghosts of those who want a taste of life."

"They're like your kind?" Stavros asked.

Valik's fist clenched. Kaya put a hand on his shoulder, and he calmed.

Stavros saw the look that passed between them. He knew that look because he used to gaze upon Serena that way. *They're in love, even though she's set to marry me in a moon's time.*

A flash of anger burned through him, but he pushed it aside. After all he had inflicted upon Kaya, it was only reasonable something might bloom between her and Valik. She would have sought him for solace after the humiliation Stavros put her through.

I'm not going to give up. She gave me Serena back. I can't let him win.

"Are you coming, Sire? We have to get out of the forest."

Kaya wrapped the cloak more tightly around her as Stavros kept in step with them both. It took all his energy to keep their pace. The adrenaline from finding Kaya had worn off.

He wanted to find a good place and sleep. They were a couple of hours ride from the castle. It would take them a good part of the day if they kept on walking without stopping. He didn't know how badly Kaya was hurt or how much sun the Vyrk could handle. Unless they came upon a farm where he could commandeer some horses, he didn't see them getting back to the castle until at least the following nightfall.

By then his remaining generals would be out looking for them. He prayed they weren't captured by the Thralls.

They walked in silence until Valik stopped at an abandoned farmhouse. Part of it had been burned, but the damage didn't look recent. The structure was falling down, but it would do for a roof over their heads. Valik gathered materials to make a fire in the hearth. Stavros found a rickety chair under some fallen wood and brought it over to Kaya.

"It's not much, but it's better than the ground."

"Thank you, but I'm just as comfortable being on the ground." She sat next to him before the fire. Kaya took off the cloak and handed it to him. "You should wrap up with this and get some sleep, Your Majesty."

Stavros took it, sliding his fingers along hers. "Stavros. You should call me by my name, and no other titles, since we're to be married."

"Stavros, then. You should get some sleep. You need it more than I."

He gestured to Valik. "What about him?"

"I don't need to sleep, Majesty. There are still hours

yet before dawn. You both should rest. I'll see if I can find food and water for you. We're on the edge of the forest; there should be something. I won't be long. You're safe here. I've already warded the perimeter so nothing will cross it."

He disappeared into the shadows.

"Didn't you tell me that Vyrks couldn't do any magic?" Stavros asked Kaya, hoping to figure out more of the mystery surrounding Valik.

Kaya stared into the fire. Her dark eyes were troubled.

"They can't. *We* can't."

"You can."

She glanced at him. "I was born with magic because I'm half-human. My father died so I could be born. I don't know all the details. Every human with magic who is turned loses the ability. The energy wave Valik performed isn't something he should have been able to do. I don't know how he did it. Maybe it's because he's so old. His magical wards are stronger than mine even. I can't explain it. How he can do it is something he hasn't revealed to me. He's older than he lets on. I don't know much about him except he's always sworn to protect to the sitting queen. No one knows much about him. He stays to himself mostly."

"How do you know that his wards are stronger than yours?"

Stavros never understood how some people could wield magic and others couldn't.

"I can feel it. Here, I'll show you. Give me your hand." Kaya extended her hand to him.

Stavros hesitated. A sudden mistrust of her reared its

head, along with a resurgence of his hatred for all her kind. Serena's face flashed in his mind. He had to get past these emotions in hopes of seeing her again. *Kaya's not going to hurt me.*

He placed his hand into hers. She extended both to the fire. The heat flared against his skin. He nearly pulled away, but she held tight. He gritted his teeth against the burning. "I don't see the point of trying to scorch me unless you're getting back at me for all the hurt I gave you."

"What? No. You feel the heat?"

"Yes."

"Okay." She pulled their hands away from the fire. "Now what do you feel away from the fire?"

"The air is cold." His breath came out in a cloud of mist.

"Yes. Hold up your hands. Now feel my energy." Her eyes lit up purple. She held up her hands before her and he mirrored her.

A zap of violet energy raced between their two hands, warm and cold. In his right palm he felt a warm pulse of energy and on his left he felt a stinging cold. It tickled his flesh and made the hair stand up on his arms. A metallic taste gathered on his tongue. The flash of energy washed over him and then settled above his heart.

Stavros could feel a second heartbeat within his chest. It was slow, and—for some reason—stirred his passion. He moaned. The scent of vanilla rising from Kaya's skin caught him off guard. He gazed into her eyes and leaned toward her. In that moment, she was the most beautiful thing he had ever seen.

She didn't back away from him. Their mouths touched.

A zap shot along his spine. An energy passed between them as Kaya returned the kiss.

It felt as though he had swallowed some of the energy. It burnt his tongue and sliced his throat, but it only made him kiss her harder, until she broke contact.

"What was that?" Stavros gasped.

"I-I'm not sure. I was showing you how to discern the different types of magic the way I was shown. Fire and cold, so you understand how they burn, and then the magic. It scorches, but in a different way. Once you get a sense for someone's magic, you can tell whose it is. Each *varaz's* magic has a signature."

"What just happened between us hasn't happened to you before?"

"No."

She pulled away from him. "Forget about it. You don't want me doing magic. You deny what I am. I'm surprised you haven't slapped those damn silver cuffs back on me."

"I don't intend to do that. I admit I was a bastard for making you...pleasure me. For all the things I did to you. For having you whipped. I hope one day you can forgive me for all that. You let me see Serena. I owe you a debt that can't be repaid. This past month we've spent talking has shown me how much more there is to you than I first thought. I can't say I understand what you are, but I respect and care for you. My feelings toward Vyrks aren't something I can easily cast aside, but I'm trying. Since we are to be wed, we should have some modicum of trust between us. I understand that some *provisions* must be made." Stavros took her hand in his.

"What do you mean?"

He trailed his fingers over the ring she wore. "I know you're in love with Valik. I can tell by the way you look at him. How you touch him lightly on the arm for reassurance when he's near you. How protective he is of you."

"I didn't think it was that obvious." She stared into the heart of the fire. "Are you going to have him exiled or killed?"

He turned her head back to look into her beautiful eyes. The light from the flames accentuated the beauty of her pale skin. Even with all the smudges on her face and clothes, and the tears in her dress, Stavros saw the magnificent creature underneath all of it. The one he should have seen when she first saved his life. "A month ago, maybe. Two months ago, most definitely. But no—it would hurt you too much. In the past, rulers have had lovers on the side as long as they fulfilled their duty to their country and were discreet."

"As long as the kingdom gets an heir, you would cast a blind eye if I have a relationship with Valik?"

"I didn't say that. No man likes to share a woman. I don't know how it is with your kind."

"We choose our mates carefully because we are long-lived. Sometimes...it just happens, as it did with Valik." She turned away from him again.

It was clear she wasn't ready to talk about this type of arrangement. He didn't want to discuss it much either, but if all this went ahead, then they would have to clear the air eventually.

"We can discuss it later. I'm going to get some sleep. The demon's attack has left me drained. Valik saved me."

He stretched out along the floor and closed his eyes. He tried to clear his mind and concentrate on relaxing. All he could focus on was the tingling on his lips and his hand where Kaya shared her magic. Something had awakened in him that tied him to her in a way he couldn't explain. He didn't know how he knew it, but he did.

———

"You need to feed," Valik whispered to Kaya.

Stavros opened his eyes.

The Vyrk leaned against the stone foundation of the farmhouse with Kaya nestled in his arms. She snuggled against his chest as he wrapped a cloak around her to keep her warm. Valik lifted her chin and brushed his lips across hers.

Stavros watched as Kaya molded her body to Valik's. He stroked his hands down her back until she moaned.

Stavros wanted it to be him that she was kissing.

The Vyrk warrior closed his eyes and stretched his neck out. Kaya broke from his lips and worked her mouth down his throat. Valik groaned.

The sound grated along Stavros's nerves.

This was a private moment he was witnessing. His breath quickened as Kaya opened her mouth. Her fangs flashed in the firelight. A moment of disgust gripped him at what he was watching, but then she bit into Valik's throat. The warrior's expression was one of ecstasy as she drank in his blood. Valik's eyes were clouded with emotion.

Stavros sucked in a breath. The Vyrk looked over at him and growled. Stavros took a step back, but Valik had crossed the room by the time Stavros blinked. Valik's hands wrapped around Stavros's throat. Stavros gripped Valik's fingers to pry them off but was unable to.

Kaya rushed over. "Valik, let him go."

"I should've ended him long before this."

"You can't. It would bring on a war. Release him," Kaya urged.

Valik tossed Stavros to the ground. The king rubbed his neck until he could breathe again.

Kaya knelt beside him. "Are you okay?"

"Fine," he managed to get out.

The Vyrk kicked a piece of the foundation of the cottage, sending debris raining down around them. Valik turned back around and drew his dagger. "You've been at his mercy all this time. It's time he knew what it felt like."

"Valik, this isn't the time. Stavros apologized to me for all that."

"He got off watching us. I can smell his desire. He's said he's accepted you. I want to see you feed from him. You need the blood."

Kaya turned to him. "Not like this. It should be done when he trusts me and we're alone."

Valik threw the dagger. It sliced the air and slashed Stavros's cheek.

"He made you service him night after night while he reveled in it and debased you. He made you stand naked in front of the court and whipped you so badly the flesh was peeling from your spine. I want to see the great king squirm."

"It's fine. Here." Stavros undid his collar and pushed the fabric away. He arched his neck the way he'd seen Valik do.

"Valik, I—" Kaya looked between the two of them.

The Vyrk's gaze was filled with hatred for being interrupted.

Stavros knew this was all about putting him in his place.

He took Kaya's hand. "It's fine. I said there had to be trust between us. You warned me that you bite. Take what you need."

A shiver of revulsion raced through him. The image of Serena and his son being slaughtered by the Vyrks flashed in his head. He nearly pulled away, but he forced himself to stay where he was. If he moved, Valik would kill him. He'd told Kaya he wanted to trust her, and that was the truth, but all he could think of was that she was about to rip out his throat.

Sweat trickled down his forehead. His body shook, and he went cold. Kaya came toward him, but he stepped back.

Valik growled and shoved the blade of his dagger against his throat. "You will let her drink from you."

"Valik, give us a minute." Kaya touched his arm. "Please, love. If you wanted him to feel some of what I felt, then you just did. Give us a little space."

"If he does anything...."

"You'll kill me. I know," Stavros answered. His stomach dropped as he glanced at Kaya. He hadn't felt this afraid since he watched his wife die. He took in a few breaths and realized he was breathing fast and his head was spinning at the thought of her draining him.

Valik stepped into the shadows, but Stavros knew he was still there.

Kaya touched his face. "Hey, look at me."

Kaya's voice helped to calm his nerves.

Stavros gazed into her eyes and tried to wrangle his raging emotions. Her smile was calm, but behind those sumptuous lips were fangs that could tear out his throat. "I can't," he whispered.

"Kiss me." She placed a small kiss on his mouth.

Stavros returned the kiss, but his heart hammered against his ribs.

Kaya placed her hand over his heart.

The burn of her magic entered his body. His nerves quieted, but he still felt the terror. Stavros kissed her a little harder as he wrapped his arm around her. Valik growled in the darkness, but it didn't stop him. Kaya's power wrapped around him until the same burn played against his lips.

She broke the kiss and moved her mouth slowly down his cheek.

His terror morphed into desire. Maybe it was the magic she used to make it easier coursing through him. Kaya planted a few kisses along his throat.

"Do you want me to stop?" Kaya whispered against his ear. She nipped his earlobe.

"No," he admitted. The intensity building in him with the scorch of her magic had to be let out.

Kaya bit at his throat. The graze of her fangs made him jerk away. She smiled and kissed him where she had nipped. He slipped his arm around her and balled his fist into her dress. Stavros jumped when she bit him with regular teeth. And then, her fangs broke his flesh. He groaned and leaned against her as her lips worked on his neck. The blood rushed from his heart to her waiting lips. Stavros held his breath as the flush of energy brought him a bliss he'd experienced only when he had an orgasm. The burn of her magic singed his veins. She wound her fingers into his hair, positioning his neck a little better so she could drink.

"Oh God," he muttered. He unclenched his fist and laid his palm on the small of her back. Part of him didn't want her to ever stop, but she did, lifting her head.

"Was that so bad?"

"No."

Once she parted from him, the burn of her magic left him. He felt strangely empty.

"Good."

Valik stepped out of the shadows and sat before the fire. "There's food and water over there. You've had your fill of her tonight. For the rest of it, she's mine. Problem with that?"

"Not at all."

Stavros went to the provisions the creature pointed to. He took some of the water and watched as Kaya and Valik slid down before the fire. Kaya closed her eyes and settled against Valik.

Stavros felt emptiness and caught the smirk the Vyrk directed at him.

CHAPTER THIRTEEN

The next day they walked until the sun was too much for Valik to bear. Kaya gave him her cloak, but it did little to block the light from his face. He endured, but her concern for him grew.

She also worried about where the demon was, and what it was going to do next. They hadn't discussed what had happened while it had her in its clutches.

Stavros was another issue. She hadn't wanted to feed from him the way she did, but she couldn't let Valik kill him either. Her other lingering question concerned what had happened between them when she shared her magic. He had no magic ability she could sense, but something had awoken in him when she tried to make him understand what magic felt like. Now she felt tied to him as well. Kaya couldn't comprehend it.

"Maybe we should seek shelter and stop for a while," she suggested.

"No. We have to get back to the castle. With the

demon loose, we have to find a way to seal it back in the ruins or destroy it," Valik forced out.

Horses galloped toward them before she could answer. Men surrounded them. "State your business," ordered their leader.

Stavros stepped forward. She glanced up at the soldier and saw he wore Stavros's colors. He was young, with barely any hair on his lip. "Sergeant, do you not recognize your king?"

The other men looked at one another. One of them smirked. "Our king wouldn't be traveling with a Vyrk and its whore."

Valik growled. Kaya barely stopped him from rushing forward.

"You sure about that?" Stavros showed the scoffer his hand with his Crest ring.

A look of fear passed between the horsemen. The soldiers dismounted their horses and bowed before him. "Sire, forgive us," the soldier begged.

"Get up. I don't need your begging. We need your horses. The princess and her guardian have been injured. We have to get back to the palace at once."

"Anything. Take them."

"What's your name?" Stavros asked.

"Jona."

"Well, Jona, when I get back to the castle, I'll speak to the sergeant-at-arms about you." Stavros mounted a horse and motioned for Kaya and Valik to do the same.

She helped Valik onto another of the horses. "Can you ride?"

"I'll endure. I'll feed when we get to the palace, then

sleep. Getting you to safety is the first priority. The demon could emerge at any time. It wants you."

"I know. We'll talk about it later."

Kaya rode behind him as Valik slumped over the neck of the horse. She urged their horse into a gallop. Stavros passed them and stayed ahead of her, though she kept pace with him until they reached the castle. Once they got to the stables, Kaya helped Valik off the horse. He was barely conscious.

"Is he going to be okay?" Stavros asked.

"I think so."

Valik stood, but he wobbled.

"I'll come up to your chambers to check on you after I have informed what remains of my command about the demon. We need to discuss what happened." Stavros hesitated for a moment before brushing a kiss along her lips. He turned away and left the stables.

She slung Valik's arm over her shoulder and helped him back up to her room. Once there, she locked the door and peeled the cloak from his body. Bits of flesh came along with the fabric. His skin was blistered and raw from the long exposure to the sun. That he had survived at all raised questions she needed to ask him, but now wasn't the time.

Kaya offered him her wrist. "Drink. To regain some of your strength."

"No. You need your strength, too."

"Rest and food will do that for me. You need the blood so you can sleep and let it heal you. No argument."

Valik nodded and bit into her wrist. She shivered at the rush it brought. He drank a few swallows and then lay back against the pillows. She didn't know what he had seen of her memories or if he had gathered any feelings from the sharing. He closed his eyes and slept.

Kaya filled a bath and slipped into the water. At least it was heated, and she was able to relax after what had happened. She re-played everything that had happened in the ruins in her memory—focusing on how the demon had tricked her. She hadn't even suspected it wasn't Valik who spoke to her.

She had learned how King Alerik had become infected and killed his queen, but she still didn't know how her kind evolved, or how Alerik had sealed the demon in the ruins. Kaya studied the ring she still wore.

Was it all a trick? Was the demon powerful enough to make me think Serena led me to the ring?

"What did I do?" she whispered.

There had to be some kind of answer in Alerik's journal.

Kaya finished washing and dressed. She checked on Valik. He lay sleeping as though he were dead, but his burns had healed some.

Assured he was asleep, she snuck up to the tower to read more of the journal. Once she entered the room, a whoosh of cold surrounded her. She recognized it as Serena—the queen's energy didn't feel anything like the demon's.

"Are you really the queen?" Kaya asked the thin air.

The spirit tugged on her energy to form as it had before, but it didn't make her sick. She could barely feel the drain now the bracelets were off.

The light radiating from the phantasm lit the room.

"Yes, I am the queen. I know what you must be thinking, but I didn't bring you here to release the demon. I brought you here, so you'd know what you're up against. The answer to imprisoning it forever is in those pages. You're the one so many have been waiting for."

Kaya didn't like the sound of the ghost's reply. "You make it sound like I'm part of some great prophecy."

"Sometimes prophecy isn't spoken until it's too late or it doesn't become recognized as one until certain things fall into place. I needed you to turn Stavros's heart. You did that."

"Why show me all this? You're dead. What cares do you have for the mortal world?"

"I was murdered at the behest of someone in this castle. Thrall mercenaries were hired to slaughter me, and my son, and they framed the Vyrks for it. Whoever ordered me dead wanted Stavros to start a war with the Vyrkola. Killing you would have started it. If you find my killer, then you find the one the demon is working with.

"Think about it, the creature must have had help over the years to gain such knowledge and know you were here. With you wearing the silver it couldn't sense you, that much I know."

What the queen said made sense. In the guise of Nicero, the creature wasn't sure she was really the princess. The silver had blocked her magic and her presence from it. "How do you know the demon is working with someone in the castle?"

Serena sighed. "Because I found out something I wasn't supposed to."

"Then you should know who killed you."

"I wish it were that easy. All of these events are intertwined. I heard the demon talking to someone, but that someone didn't answer. All I am sure of is that it was making plans to get free. It mentioned the Vyrk princess, and you being the key to letting it out. When I heard that, I knew it was evil. I tried to get away, but it heard me. A shadow darted out of the room, grabbed, and marked me." She held out her wrist and showed Kaya the black zigzagging line it had left even on her soul.

"I tried to tell Stavros, but he thought I was telling stories to scare him. By that time, I had discovered Alerik's journal. It wasn't hard to put the pieces together. It's been planning this for a very long time."

Kaya sank down on the rickety chair and absorbed what Serena had said. Someone had been working with the demon trying to let it out. It had shown that it could possess or take on the guise of someone for a short period of time. It had enough power to whisk her from the castle and transport her to the ruins.

I played right into its hands. It's all my fault.

She put her head in her hands and sobbed.

"It's not your fault, Kaya. You're its destruction. I know it. You are life and death wrapped up in one package. Look at the life you brought back to Stavros. You ignited his heart and bound him to you with your magic. The same way I did."

"How do you know that?"

"I can see the thread connecting you. Dark purple and bright blue light over his heart."

"I don't know *what* I did. Stavros asked me how I knew the difference between my magic and Valik's. I tried to show him—the way I was taught—but it did something to him...to us. I can feel him like I do Valik." Kaya had never had anyone she could talk to this way about magic. Adran never would've understood, and her mother certainly didn't.

She thought about Stavros. She had tasted his blood. When she reached out her senses, she could feel his mind and sense his emotions. It was more than the usual temporary bond formed from ingesting blood.

"My people believe magic is a part of the air we breathe," said Serena. "Even those born with no proclivity to magic can weave spells because connections are forged within them as infants. You know how to sense the signature of a magic worker. We feel it with people as well. Stavros had no such ability to work magic. When we married, as is my people's custom, I forged a bond with my spouse. I did this with Stavros so I could always have a piece of him. He always has a piece of me. You've done the same with him in your own way. You asked me what keeps me here. He does—because of my link to him."

"Will you always be here because he's alive?"

"No. You should look in the diary. See who Alerik was to find answers or...perhaps...more questions." The queen faded out as her words echoed in the tower.

Kaya pressed the ring into the side of the diary. The pages flipped themselves to a chapter near the back of the tome. She jumped back until the pages settled and then read on hoping to find some answers.

———

Alerik itched at the wound where Eloise had bitten him. Each day dark streaks spread further along his skin, inching up his veins. Each day he tried to hide them—even from himself. Each day a hunger grew within him that he couldn't shake and his grip on his magic lessened. Overwhelmed with the sadness of losing the queen, he moved the court from their winter castle to the summer one. He needed a fresh start away from where the demon was. Away from where his beloved Eloise lay interred. At night he locked himself away in his tower trying to find a way to entrap the demon.

A knock sounded on his bedroom door. A servant entered. "Sire, there's an emissary in the throne room to see you. He says it's urgent."

He glanced at the woman. She smelled wonderful. Alerik got up and sniffed her. She stiffened when he trailed his finger along her throat.

"What should I tell him?" Her whisper came out as a pant. The fear in her eyes snapped him out of his daze.

"Bring him into my study and draw the drapes."

She curtsied and left the room. Alerik licked his lips, attempting to ease his parched throat. He took a deep breath and tried to push the gut-gnawing feeling away. Each day it grew stronger and harder to resist.

He grabbed a glass of wine and downed it, but it did little to quench the thirst.

Instead, he focused on this strange emissary waiting in his study. As soon as he entered the room, he sensed the strong blast of energy coming from the stranger. This man was another powerful magician.

"My servant says you wanted to see me?" Alerik stayed in the shadows.

The other man turned from the book he was perusing. "Forgive me. I don't want to bother you, but I—and a few other practitioners—felt a change in the magical energy of the environment. A darkness, a magical sickness if you will, is spreading out from the old castle. The magical node there has been corrupted."

Alerik felt as though he had been punched in the gut. The demon had infected the magic at his winter castle. This spreading darkness wasn't going to stop unless it was capped off and the demon truly destroyed and not merely trapped in the crypt by the silver that ran naturally in the caves underneath the castle. The veins ran strong in the land and wound into the mountains.

"Thank you for informing me."

The magician nodded. "If I may, there has been some talk about the queen...and yourself."

"There is always talk. The queen died of her sickness. It looked like she might survive for a time, but she had another bout and it took her into the twilight realm."

"Yes, I've heard that—but I've formed my own theory. I've also heard the voices which whisper in the darkness in the bowels of the forest. Those who wish to rejoin our world. Those who were driven into the dark by the sun gods. Sometimes what they offer isn't worth the sacrifice. I know the queen was deathly ill. Maybe you heard the voices and listened to them. The entity said he could heal her. Maybe for a time she seemed better, but in the end, she wasn't your wife any longer."

"H-how do you know that?" Alerik asked.

"Because your wife wasn't the first to fall victim to these demons. The society I belong to keeps records from before the demons were locked away—detailing how they were banished. Their plague spread in this world once before, when the gods first locked them away. It took all the members of my order to subdue it. Many of them perished in the fight against the monsters, but a few remained to chronicle the ordeal. Those who were left were told to guard the pit in case the demons possessed another, and it let loose the plague once more."

"Why have I never heard of this plague?"

The wizard shrugged. "Many tales have turned into bedtime stories to frighten children or been lost altogether. I'm here to make sure the pestilence doesn't occur again. You've trapped the demon in your wife's sepulcher with the silver. We too discovered it hated the element. My lord, forgive me, but why don't you come into the light?"

He hesitated, but Alerik wanted to know more about this order and how they had handled the demons before. He had pored through his books and found nothing about how to eradicate an entity such as the thing that had infected his wife. If this man knew a way, he had to chance it. Alerik stepped into the light.

The wizard gasped, fighting to keep his composure, but the king caught the sour scent of fear. The man's heart thumped like a drum. Alerik licked his lips and tasted the terror. His gums tingled at the thought of that taste.

He already knows something is off.

"Sire, you've become tainted with the demon's blood. It's changing you."

"Eloise attacked me before I took her head. By then it wasn't her anymore. It was that thing."

"It was both. It was the queen and it was the demon. When the demon possessed her, it wrapped around her soul and ate her from the inside until it had all her memories. Your wife died."

"Tell me, sorcerer, what am I then? Will I become this demon the same as my wife? I already feel this insatiable thirst. I fight it with all my being. Each night it gets worse and I feel less like myself. I'm losing my ability to wield magic. Do you have any lore in all of your society about that?" Alerik snapped.

"Calm yourself. Strong emotion will only increase the thirst." The wizard reached into a bag at his side and withdrew a small leather-bound journal. The edges were lined with silver. "This is a chronicle of one of those who was tainted by the demonic plague. The thirst nearly drove him insane. He called upon the gods to kill him. He was in our order. It talks about taking on some of the demon's powers and the weaknesses it had. Each day the infection spread within him until he could no longer stand in the light. He found he could shift his shape, but he didn't hear the demon's voice within his mind. He was his own man even in the end. He did not want to pass along the plague. He sacrificed himself so we could devise a spell and hunt down all those who were infected using his blood. They were all wiped out in the end."

"Are you here to take my head?"

The sorcerer slid the journal across the table. "Not yet. I'm here to cap off the magical node below the castle and make sure the demon doesn't escape. I need your help.

You're a powerful wizard. I need your knowledge of the castle and your power—while you still have it. I need to make sure the demon isn't going to get out. Look in these pages and tell me what you want to do, Majesty. I think—"

———

"**K**aya?"

She jumped when she heard Valik's voice behind her.

"Valik, why aren't you resting?" she scolded.

"I woke up when the sun went down, and you weren't there. I felt you up here. What is this place?" Valik glanced around.

Kaya met his gaze. He did look better. His burns were healed.

His eyes swept the tower and then settled on the book. His gaze went from there to the ring on her hand. He crossed the room in a bound and clutched her wrist, holding it in a bone-crushing grip. "Where did you get that?"

Pain shot up her arm. "You're hurting me."

He released her wrist and grabbed for the ring. "Answer me. Where did you get this? How did you find this journal?" He slipped the ring from her finger and held it in his fist.

"How do you know about it?" Kaya asked. "How did you even get in here?"

Valik sunk down on a trunk and hung his head.

She tried to read his emotions through their bond, but

he blocked her out. Something about all of this didn't sit right. Too many questions bloomed inside of her mind.

He took a deep breath and played with the ring. It was a few minutes before he answered her. He rose to his feet. Each time he turned the ring over in his hands, Valik paced the small space of the tower room. He picked up the book and hissed as the silver touched his hands, but he endured the pain. He trailed his fingers over the pages before setting the book down. Tears gleamed in his eyes.

She had never thought he could be this distressed. It felt as though some dark hole had opened inside of him. All she could feel was the abyss.

"Valik, what is it?" Kaya took his hands and knelt before him.

He slipped the ring back onto her finger. "It belongs with you. If you've found it, then that means you're the one who it spoke about all those years ago as Alerik died. The demon came into him at the last moment and said it would one day get free. The one who found his ring would be the key to the darkness spreading across the world. By that time his spawn would cover the earth. He would be there to lead them, and the owner of the ring would stand beside him to free his brothers locked away in the pit. That's why I did what I did."

"What are you talking about?" His words confused her.

"I'm talking about what led to all of this and why I'm going to have to kill you."

CHAPTER FOURTEEN

Stavros felt refreshed after he had taken a bath and eaten. He thought about what had happened between him and Kaya. The echo of her presence lingered in his thoughts. It was as though he could feel her in the castle. As he thought about her, he could see the purple energy in his mind that connected them together. He wanted more of her, but he knew she was looking after Valik and probably resting herself. He touched his lips where they had kissed.

"Sire, Chancellor Kewskin has returned and wishes to see you."

"Show him in."

The sorcerer came into the room looking as though he had aged ten years. His skin hung off his bones. His robes were torn. He shook as he helped himself to a goblet of wine. He drank it all down and poured another one before he sunk into the chair by the hearth.

Stavros poured his own goblet and sat across from him.

"What happened to you? I thought you were lost like the others in the forest."

"I-I saw...I saw...it. Them. I felt the darkness. I know what it is."

"Calm down and tell me what happened. I led a group of men into the woods with you at my side and then this darkness descended. I didn't know what had happened until I awoke. Valik saved me. All the other men and their horses were dead and shrunken to ashes as though they had the life sucked out of them. I looked for you, but there was nothing left." Stavros sipped the wine and thought of those haunted woods and the total eerie silence of that desiccated place.

"I saw something in the trees and heard the dead calling to me. I wanted a branch from one of the trees deeper in the forest. They make bone wands that hold a lot of power. I was enthralled by the thought of them and wanted to see if I could get one.

"Once I started hacking away at one of the smaller branches, I heard a shrill cry and was overcome by one of the spirits. I tried to fight if it off, but I wasn't strong enough to keep the wraith from me. I blacked out. When I came to, I heard your own screams. I tried to get to you, but this looming darkness rushed me. It tore at my clothes." He opened his robe and showed Stavros the silver breastplate he wore underneath. "Once it latched onto this, it let me go. I saw its true face. Teeth in a mouth too big for its head. Horns jutting out all over its skull and seven talons on each hand. Long yellowed fangs and the hunger...that never-ending hunger." He took another drink of his wine and finished it.

Stavros had never seen the man so shaken.

"It's okay. You made it back alive."

"The princess? Did you find her?"

"Yes."

The chancellor grabbed Stavros's tunic and shook him. "She let it out. You must kill her. She's the key to all of it. If you don't, I will."

Stavros ripped Kewskin's hands from his tunic. "No one is killing my future wife."

"You're still going to marry the bitch even though she released it into the world? She's going to be the ruin of us all. It wants her for *its* bride. It wants to fill her with its spawn—and it's going to keep doing it forever. You won't be able to save her. Killing her is the only option."

"Guards," Stavros called.

They rushed in.

"Take the chancellor to his room. Make sure he is cared for and keep him under guard."

The guards took Kewskin away as he struggled to get out of their grip.

Stavros thought about what his chancellor had said. On some level he knew the man wasn't crazed. He remained sane. They hadn't talked about what happened in the forest or how Kaya had gotten out of the ruins. They were too focused on getting out of the forest alive and keeping Valik conscious. Now that they were out, they had to face up to Kaya having had a hand in them being attacked.

Where did the demon go?

He glanced at the silver cuffs, tossed forgotten onto the table, and wondered if he ever should have taken them off her in the first place. If he hadn't, none of this would be happening. And yet, he never would have felt the things he felt for her.

"Serena, I need your guidance. You always were my conscience."

He raked his fingers over his face to clear away the fog. Everything had been so easy since she died. Black or white. Kill or not kill. Now he didn't know what to do because the lines were blurred.

He felt something for Kaya. He didn't know if it was love, but he didn't want to see her hurt.

"What do I do?" he whispered.

A small light, like a candle flame, appeared in the center of the room and grew into the shape of a woman. It floated over to him. Stavros didn't have to fear this being like he had the shades in the forest. He would have known her if he was blind. Her beauty lingered even in death. He fell to his knees before her.

"You're here."

"I've always been here. Since the moment I died."

"Why haven't you come sooner? I needed you."

Serena laid a hand on his shoulder. The cold touch calmed his nerves, but it wasn't like he remembered. "I've been here, but you weren't able to hear or see me. I'm here now because your heart has changed, and the connection forged between us is open once more."

"What do I do? The demon's been freed. It will stop at nothing now to feed and destroy the kingdom. It was my fault it got out. I didn't see that it wasn't Nicero. It wanted Kaya and I gave her to him."

"It wasn't your fault or her fault. Sometimes events

happen. You could say it was fate...or not. Within this chaos you found that you love Kaya. She fashioned a bond with you she wouldn't have been able to do if you didn't love her."

He chuckled ruefully. "She doesn't love me. She has the Vyrk. I saw how they were together."

"She has feelings for you, or she wouldn't have shared her magic with you the way I did. It's the reason I'm here now. I'll tell you what I told her. I was killed by someone in this castle. They set the Thralls on me and made you believe it was the Vyrks. I don't know who it is, but they were consorting with the demon. I was killed because I heard too much. I heard it say Kaya was the key to letting it and the others of its kind out. It wanted you to go to war with the Vyrkola. It wanted to draw Kaya out."

"It got what it wanted."

"Maybe. If you find the demon in the castle, then you find the one who killed me. Don't blame yourself or Kaya. Don't shut down. She's going to need you."

"Right. I'm *sure* she will." Stavros didn't believe that. When he turned to ask Serena more questions, her spirt had vanished. The ache of her leaving him welled up in him once more. It reopened the wound in his heart of loosing her all over again. And yet, Serena's words lingered about Kaya needing him. She had Valik. How was she going to need him? He felt the wetness in his eyes. He wiped his unshed tears away as his vision blurred. He heard footsteps behind him. When he turned, he found Kaya and Valik—with a very nervous servant boy.

Kaya had a book in her hand and a knife at her throat.

"Valik, what are you doing?" he asked, moving toward

them slowly. Stavros gestured for the boy to leave. The terror in his eyes worried Stavros. At this rate he would alert the guards, and Stavros didn't want to make the situation worse.

"I have to kill her," the Vyrk muttered. "It's the only way the others don't go free. Without Kaya, it never would've gotten out."

"Valik, you said you'd explain all this," whispered Kaya. "What's happening?"

Stavros pulled out a chair and gestured for Valik to sit. "Yes, let's talk about this. I can't let you hurt her. I care about her. I know you do, too."

Why doesn't she use her magic on him? Why doesn't she try and get away? Stavros didn't understand what had happened in the short time since they got back.

Valik led Kaya to the chair and made her sit down. This was not the same man who had saved him. Something else lived in his eyes. Stavros could see the stone around the Vyrk's heart. He recognized it because he had been the same way for years. Looking at his reflection, Stavros didn't like what he saw.

"Tell him about the book," Valik ordered.

Kaya proceeded to tell Stavros how Serena had led her to the ring and the chronicle.

"Serena showed you where the ring was so you could open the book?" Stavros asked.

"Yes, she wanted me to know the truth of where we came from. How you're a descendant of Alerik. This castle used to be his. The ruins were his winter castle, and she wanted me to know there was a way to fight the demon in these pages. I was getting to that part when Valik found me."

Kaya glanced at the Vyrk.

A rush of guilt and heartache hit Stavros. He gripped the chair and realized it came from Kaya through the bond they shared. He squeezed her shoulder. A current ran along his arm that made him gasp.

Kaya slid her hand over his and flashed him a sad smile.

"Valik, tell us so we can make sense of it," urged the king. He heard the rushing of footsteps coming toward the room. The servant boy must have alerted the guards. "If you truly wanted Kaya dead, you would've done it upstairs. Something in you cares about her. You wanted to kill me for how I treated her before, and I intend on spending a lifetime making up for it to Kaya. You're treating her like I did. Do you really want that?"

The Vyrk thrust his blade into the table by Kaya's hand.

Stavros pulled his own short dagger and held it close to his chest in case the Vyrk came at him. The guards rushed into the room ready to swarm Valik.

"Tell your guards to stand down. Summon servants to bring you food and drink. This will take a while." Valik moved across the room to sit in the shadows as far away from them as he could get.

Stavros calmly sent them away. He requested food and wine for him and Kaya. Once they were delivered, he told the servants he didn't want to be disturbed.

Valik got up and locked all the doors.

"I will tell you all I know. No one interrupts us. When I'm done, Kaya dies."

Valik trailed his fingers over the journal, but he didn't open it. Instead, he slipped back into the shadows. Stavros kept his eye on him, but the Vyrk's gaze became unfocused and he began to weave an impossible tale.

———

Alerik watched the magician flip through his books. Three weeks had passed since the stranger arrived. Each day the infection spread, and his hunger grew. He hadn't succumbed to the temptation but ate an increasing amount of raw meat. Each time he thought about the warm blood in a living being, he thought about Eloise.

It gave him the cold realization of what he was turning into. He avoided speaking to anyone in daylight unless he stood in shadow. His magic sputtered during the day but grew stronger at night. Silver grew hard to touch and writing in his journal was painful, but he endured because he had to chronicle the events so it would never happen again.

Each night he told the sorcerer how he felt and what was happening to him. The other did not judge him, but only tried harder to stop the demon.

"Do you have the spell yet?" Alerik paced the room.

"Almost. The language is ancient and the power to do this even older. We must tap into the magical node. The magic will be erratic. I can't predict what it's going to do, but it'll close off the well of power. I have the symbols to carve into the cap so it can't be opened again."

"What is my part in this? What will happen to me once I help you with this spell? Are you going to take my head?"

The sorcerer sized him up and Alerik saw the truth in the other man's eyes.

"You read the journal, my Lord. When the member of our order who wrote it finally succumbed to the beast, there was enough of him left to beg us to kill him. Every day I see part of you is less human. I know you feel it, too. It will kill you if you don't feed. If you do, you become the thing your wife did. A darkness. A demon."

Alerik stared out the window. The energy of the night called to him. He closed his eyes and listened. The heartbeats of all his subjects erupted in his ears. He pushed past all that and heard the animals in the stables and the voices of the people. Smells were enhanced. He had started to detect what was human, what was animal, and the scent of magic that lingered around the sorcerer. The changes evolving within him that went into creating the hunger made him wonder if it would be worth it to see what he became—but, as the mage said, he had read the journal. He didn't want to evolve into a demon.

"I can't become one of those things."

"Then I suggest you write your will and choose an heir. You have no children who will reign after you."

"I've already done that. My nephew will rule after me." Alerik ran his fingers over his crest ring. It contained a bit of his magic. He used it as the key to open his journal. It was also the key to opening the chamber in the vault to get to the magical node in the old castle. That was the reason his ancestors had constructed the palace—so they could draw upon the magic below. Being so far away from it, he had taken it for granted.

"Good. Get the rest of your affairs in order because I have finished it." The wizard held out a parchment.

Alerik took it from his hand before he even realized he had moved across the room. It clearly shook the sorcerer. It shook him too, because he had never done anything like that.

He read over the spell. A simple binding spell which he could have written, but the blood ritual was not something he expected. It involved him and the sorcerer shedding their blood to seal the node once the symbols were carved into the cap. As he read more of the incantation, he understood it was also sealing in the demon and making sure there was some kind of barrier in the crypt so the foul creature couldn't escape.

He laid the parchment onto the table. "When can we do it?"

"The dark of the moon is in two days. We do it then. Can you abstain from hurting anyone until then? Can you stay true to yourself?"

"I can only try. I'll get the rest of my affairs in order." He left the library and went into the tower to record all of what had happened.

. . .

Two nights later, dressed in a dark cloak, he sat atop a horse. He had left an envelope on his desk so his advisors would find it along with his will, naming his nephew as his successor. The sorcerer was beside him with a bag of supplies they needed for the ritual.

The wizard kicked his horse, and off they went toward the old castle. It had been months since Alerik had traveled into the forest. All was silent. He could feel the evil in the air and the prickle of energy from the magical node.

He moved up next to the sorcerer.

"The magic is darker." Alerik shivered.

"Yes. The demon is feeding off the power. It's grown stronger, but the power has also grown. It's a never-ending cycle. Be glad it hasn't gotten strong enough yet to cross the silver. Then again, the silver is threaded through the land. The strongest vein runs down from the mountains. Magic travels along the metal. There are smaller nodes along these veins, but they are mostly all connected. Although where they start or come from, I can't say. Our order has tracked some of them. There is another magical well far to the north past the mountains. Another to the east in a great pine forest. I've heard the trees there grow so tall they blot out the sun."

"The magic lesson is interesting, but we're not here for that."

"No, we're not. I was trying to make the point that if this doesn't work then all the nodes could potentially be infected. Silver might purify, but I'm not sure how much it can handle."

"Then we can't fail." Alerik urged his horse forward at a faster pace.

As they got to the castle, the feeling of malice grew stronger, as did the sensation of the magic rubbing on his flesh. Even in the darkness of the night, he could see clearly. All of his senses were enhanced.

The sorcerer lit a few mage balls, but Alerik didn't need to. The magic within him jumped and sparked—wanting out. The stronger the darkness within him grew, the more his magic expanded in the dark of night. Tonight it writhed under his skin, almost like it had a life of its own. They reached the palace and secured the horses.

Alerik could feel the evil in the ground and the heat of the silver deep within the earth. It made him uncomfortable, but he could stand it. He ran his fingers over his silver ring. The burning against his flesh made him aware of his hunger and it kept him focused on not giving in to his growing appetite for blood.

"Which way?"

Alerik was pulled from his thoughts. "Follow me. Do you have a plan on how you're going to distract the demon?"

"I have an idea how to contain it long enough for us to complete the ceremony, but I'm not sure you're going to like it. That's why I haven't brought it up until now."

"What is it?"

"We have to burn your wife's body. Without flesh for the demon to cling to, it will be free—an incorporeal being. It won't have the strength to take on form to stop us. At least I hope it won't. I need you to distract it for me."

He didn't want to think about burning Eloise's body.

Even though he had beheaded the creature, it had risen and tormented those in the castle. "If it has to be done. She's gone. It's nothing more than her shell."

"Thank you."

He brushed past the sorcerer and headed toward the side entrance of the castle that would lead down into the caves beneath the tomb directly where the node was. "Follow me."

The deeper they went, the more he could feel the heat of the energy beating against his flesh, even underneath the ground. Mage orbs flew ahead of them so he could see in the dark. Roots grew down from above and he could feel the life around him in the earth.

"What is this place?"

"It's an escape tunnel built underneath the tomb that leads to the node. I found the cave years ago and had the tomb built over it. Come on," he told the wizard.

They reached the end of the tunnel. Alerik pressed his ring into a block of stone and the wall opened. The sorcerer wanted to enter first, but the king stopped him. The rush of magic overwhelmed him. He could feel the darkness in the magic as the sorcerer had said, but it was far worse than he had imagined. He and Eloise had once pulled from the magic here, but now the gritty feeling disgusted him. However, there was more to his unease than that.

"Wait. It's here." Alerik slipped his ring off and handed it to the sorcerer. "Straight across the cave to the left of the fifth brick, press the ring into the indentation. It will lead you to the stairs and up to the tomb. Do what you need to do. I'll distract it the best I can."

———

"What happened after Alerik went into the tomb?" Stavros asked.

Valik blinked at them both, as though coming out of a daze.

Stavros glanced at Kaya. Her eyes were filled with tears. He could sense her emotions but felt the echo of something else. His gaze turned to Valik, and he understood the feelings were coming from him. For some strange reason, he could sense Valik's emotions through Kaya.

A profound sadness overwhelmed him, along with the sense of a single purpose that burned within the Vyrk's mind. Years upon endless years, of that solitary goal. Stavros felt for the Vyrk and understood how such a dedication could drive a person mad. Once Valik realized something passed between them, the flow ceased.

"He faced off with the demon while I went up into the tomb and burned Eloise's body."

"But how?" Stavros gasped. He was not sure he understood what Valik was telling him. If he did, then it defied all logic. Could the Vyrk be that old?

"Let me finish," Valik answered. "By the time the demon got wind of it, she was already on fire. It was weakened enough by the fire and the silver to be dealt with. When I got back down into the crypt, Alerik was dying. The demon had slashed him across the chest. The creature was weak now and tried to stop the fire, but the flames were fueled by the magic in the node.

"Alerik begged me not to let him die a monster without a soul. He didn't want to turn into one of those beasts. He helped me cast the spell with the last bit of his power. I carved the sigils into the stone using magic and placed the capstone over the center of the well. I used to have a good affiliation with earth magic.

"Alerik died a hero. He saved us all from the demon getting out and becoming the scourge of the world. If the darkness had infected the magical node it would have spread to the rest of the land."

Kaya opened up Alerik's diary to the last entry and read aloud. The bindings of the spell that originally drew her into the ancient king's tale had fallen away allowing her to simply read from the journal and not witness the story as it happened. "I pray to all the gods we are success-ful, and that the demon is contained. I never thought I would be saying this, but the sorcerer is correct. It gets more difficult every day to hold onto the man I was. I can't become the thing that my beloved turned into. This marks the end of my journey. I know I will not come back from this. I pray future generations will understand my sacrifice and not make the same mistake I did. Don't give in to the darkness. Don't listen to the whispers in the night. They will only bring you heartache." She closed the book. "How did you become...?"

"How did I become this? How did our people start?" Valik asked the questions she had started to voice.

She nodded.

Valik returned from the crypt. He wanted nothing more than to get away from the evil place and return to his home. To Betha, his beloved wife, and Bem, their sweet daughter, who was only six summers old. Bem loved to be with him at night and stare at the stars. Before the order sent him out for this task. Meeting with Alerik was not something he had wanted to do, but it had been needed. Rumors of the darkness were spreading.

He sensed the evil lurking in the shadows, but he could not see the demon. The king lay on the floor. His stomach looked like ground meat and his blood was leaking onto the seal.

Valik whispered a spell. The earth rumbled, and a mound of stone formed over the mouth of the node. With a few quick strokes of his fingers, he carved the sigils into the stone. Seven symbols. As he formed each one, he could feel the power collecting in the node. The symbols drew the demon to it. The silver in the cavern hummed with power as the energy traveled along the veins of metal.

He reached out with his senses and drew the power from the node into the sigils so it would cap the magic in the well. The last thing he needed was Alerik's help and his blood to bind the magic for good. He prayed there was enough of the man left to assist him.

Valik knelt by the king. "Sire, I need your help with this. I've set up the enchantment, but we need to seal it. Can you help me?"

Alerik's sallow skin was streaked with the lines of darkness from the infestation in the bite. He barely looked human now. His eyes had gone dark and his skin gray. His nails were sharp—nearly talons. His gums had receded around his teeth, showing off his fangs. The king was very nearly the thing he didn't want to become.

But a spark of humanity remained in his eyes. "Help me up. Let's finish what I started. I'm losing myself as the darkness takes hold," he whispered.

Valik slipped his arm around the king's shoulders and lifted him. The king's blood smeared on his flesh, but he needed blood to complete this. He walked Alerik over to the seal. "All I need is your blood and your magic. You don't have to say the words. I can do the work as long as you can funnel your magic into me."

"You don't know what will happen," Alerik managed to get out.

The king was correct. He didn't know what was going to happen, but it was his job to make sure the node was sealed off. He had built into the binding spell the ability to make sure the demon never got out.

Playing with wild magic such as this meant anything could happen. "It doesn't matter what happens to me. Give me your hand."

Alerik's nails sliced Valik's palm as they joined hands. He ignored the pain and felt the king filling him with the warmth of energy. Valik gathered his own energy and spread out his power until he rubbed against the raw magic of the wellspring. Within it he sensed the evil influence of the demon and how far it had seeped into the land. It was heading further north into the mountains along the veins of silver.

He prayed the enchantment would do its job. Valik

pooled his energy with the king's. Their blood mingled and dropped onto the sigil. A shadow darted in the corner.

The ancient words of the binding incantation flowed from his lips. The sounds and the spell came from a time when all magic was untamed; when the old gods still walked among them. As each syllable came forth, the symbols on the seal brightened. The magic from the node flared in the cavern and rode the silver veins.

Alerik screamed as the energy blasted between them, but Valik proceeded with the chant. The magic surged upward like a large geyser, but the flow had lessened.

The spell was working. The node was closing.

Alerik's magic began to slip away. Valik uttered the last syllable to seal off the magic. As he did, a shadow dashed into the center of the geyser.

The demon.

As it impacted the node it created a vacuum, sucking the remaining power from him and Alerik. It drew the magic from the crypt along the silver veins, pulling back the toxic energy it had left behind. The silver glowed around Valik as the energy backtracked into the well. The power flashed back into the ground and brought him to his knees. Valik breathed a sigh of relief, but then a flair of magic shot out from under the cap before his spell took complete hold and hit him square in the chest.

Valik screamed as the demon laughed. The sigils brightened and then the illumination faded. The well was sealed.

Alerik reached out to him. "You did it."

"Maybe. The demon jumped in at the last moment. It altered the enchantment somehow. I felt its influence."

"Do one last thing for me. Take this ring and my journal. Hide them away so they will be preserved in my tower. Will you do that?"

"Of course."

"Tell them I died well and I'm sorry."

The light dwindled from Alerik's eyes. As he passed on into twilight, his face returned to its human appearance —as did the rest of him. The evil taint in him had been cleansed.

Valik gathered his tools and took a last look at the newly-created capstone. It glowed. He could feel the magic below, but it had been contained. He prayed it would hold. Before he could leave the cave, a dark laugh stopped him.

He turned and stared into the shadows. A pair of golden eyes gazed back.

"You can't leave this place, demon."

"Maybe not now, but one day I will. I've lingered a long time in the darkness with the others plotting. When I took over Eloise, I learned a lot about this time and her magic. Plans were made and hidden away. It might not be today or in a thousand years, but one day, one of my blood will free me. When that happens, I'll bring the world to its knees."

"I won't let that happen."

"You won't have a choice. One born of night and magic will free me."

"Those who come after me will know about this and be warned. It will be preserved in my order."

The demon snickered. "About your order...you'll be surprised when you find them. I felt them when the magic went out and they felt *me* in a big way. Although, it might take them longer to realize it."

Dread shot through Valik. He needed to get back home. He needed to see what damage the demon had done when it interfered with the spell. The dark entity didn't stop him as he slipped out through the tunnel.

When he finally reached the outside, the sight before him was baffling.

The sun crested over the horizon. The lush forest he entered had vanished. Everything remained standing, but it had all turned bright white, with no life. When he touched a tree, he found the branch hard as bone. He searched for their horses and found them stripped of all flesh and turned to bone. The shock of what happened hit him.

When they tapped into the node—and the demon jumped into the mix—it pulled all the evil taint of magic from the forest. It blasted back out through the veins of silver and this was the result. Valik didn't like the feeling of the place. The air now thrummed against his skin with a life of its own he couldn't understand. All he knew was that he needed to get out of there.

He trekked back to Alerik's palace. As the sun rose higher, he found it irritating his skin more and more. It started off like an itch. When the sun reached directly overhead, it felt as though he were burning up from a bad fever.

He took refuge in an abandoned barn and fell asleep. When he awoke, it was night, and he felt much better. Valik continued his travels to the castle.

By the time he arrived, they had discovered the king's

letter naming his nephew as heir. The resulting chaos made it easy for him to slip into Alerik's rooms and find the journal. He took it and the ring into the tower. Even as he stepped into the structure, he could feel the magic around it. More warding had to be done so it would remain hidden from prying eyes.

Valik hid the ring in the room at the top and then left the journal out in the open, locked. As he ran his fingers over the silver, he found it burned his fingertips. Dread flowed through him as he realized what had happened. He and Alerik had mingled blood, and the infection was passed. All he had was lost.

It was now too dangerous for him to return to his beloved Betha and their child.

The demon's words echoed in his mind about the order. They were deep within the mountains. The demon's meddling in the spell must have affected the other members. Valik had to get back there. As much as he wanted to stay away, he had to tell the others what had happened. He saddled a horse from the stables and raced back into the mountains to his order's headquarters.

———

"And when I got back to the order, I found the others were changed by the demon as well. We weren't like Alerik or Eloise. We had become something different. We bound ourselves to certain rules. How many in the bloodline would be made. The head of our order, Thesia, was the leader then. We kept the leadership under a female rule. As the years passed, our magic dried up. We could shift into an animal. Each of us had a specific form we could take.

"We needed blood to survive, but we were never invaded by the demon. Its words lived within me for eons about one day being freed. I couldn't let that happen. I slipped into the background of our people and waited while the world changed. We survived deep within the mountains, gaining trust from the people around us and our servants whose families always lived with us. We mined the silver and that made us wealthy."

"If the silver burns you, how could you mine it or even be around it?" Stavros asked.

Valik glanced up at him. "Members of our order used to mine it for our spells. Those who chose to stay with us enchanted the tools so we could work the mines. It's uncomfortable to be around, but something you get used to while in the mountain. The workers wear masks and guard their flesh. It's a deterrent, though it burns if we have long exposure to it. Some are more sensitive than others.

"We adapted because we controlled the mines and needed the safety of the darkness to live. Humans came to fear us over the years, but they couldn't stop trading with us. There is more than silver in the mountains. Tunnels have been built throughout the range and we have found gems, minerals, and artifacts older than even me—and we haven't even scratched the surface.

"I alone could still perform certain spells although why remained a mystery to me because in the end no other Vyrk possessed the ability to do magic. I kept this a secret and devoted myself to learning the art of the sword and other weaponry until I mastered several fighting skills. The man I was died. I tried to find and destroy to the demon. I returned to the Bone Forest several times, but I couldn't enter the ruins. It couldn't get out either. It needed a key. A thing born of magic and darkness. I swore as part of my duty to see it returned to the hell it came from.

"When you were born, Kaya, I knew you were the key foretold. Your mother conceived by magic and your birthright is part of the darkness. I've kept watch over you all these years waiting to see if you would turn to this evil. I never saw its taint in you. I thought I might be wrong as one century passed into another. Now the demon is out and it's going to come back for you. I won't let it have you so that you can release the others in the pit."

CHAPTER FIFTEEN

B efore Kaya could ask Valik any questions, the blade
was once more against her throat.

He looked deep into her eyes. She saw her death in his
gaze, but his hand trembled. The edge of the dagger cut
into her flesh.

Stavros was behind Valik tugging at his arm. The Vyrk
shoved the king away and returned his focus to her.

She understood his dilemma, but there had to be
another way. Stavros lay on the floor, out cold. Valik
pressed the blade into her throat harder. Kaya didn't flinch
from the pain. She stared her death in the face. As a
warrior she understood what he was doing—showing her
the one who would kill her—and she didn't show any fear.

Kaya placed her hands on his face. The edge of the
blade went deeper into her flesh.

"Don't try and stop me."

"I'm not. I just want one thing before you take my
head."

"What?"

"A kiss. We're bound together. You can shut me out all you want, but before I die, I want a kiss from the man I love."

Valik didn't lower the dagger as she pressed her lips to his. He stiffened, but his mental armor opened a small chink. She didn't bombard him. Instead, she let him feel her love for him. She pressed her lips harder against his and showed him what she imagined being with him would feel like. How it cut her heart that she would leave him without ever knowing the sweetness of him. She slid her tongue along his lower lip, seeking entrance. She wound her fingers through his hair and dared another image of them together with a child in her arms.

The knife slipped from her throat. He raked his fingers down her cheeks and pulled her close to him. His lips mashed against hers. The wall around his resolve crumbled completely. Valik held her closer and broke their kiss as he breathed hard.

"Can that be true?"

"It can."

"How do you know that? I'm dead. Everything about me is dead."

Kaya placed her hand on his chest. "Not all of you is dead. The magic in you is still there because you have a spark of life. That's why our kind can't weave spells—because they are dead. Magic has always been said to be a gift from the gods. Whatever happened to make you into the first of our kind, it didn't kill you."

He shook his head and stepped away.

"I took an oath. It doesn't matter what I want, or who I

love. I swore to stop the demon along with the one who was the key to getting the others out. I won't let that happen. I can't."

"So you're going to kill me for something I haven't done yet and don't plan on doing? The last thing I want to do is let out this evil. I want to put it back. There has to be another way. There must be something.... What about asking Eloise?"

"She's long dead." He grabbed the dagger and held it against her throat once more. His eyes glistened. "I never thought I could love another, but I love you. I've tried to fight it. I don't want to do this."

Kaya slipped her hand around his wrist. "Give me a chance to fix this. The demon said it learned a lot from being with Eloise and her magic. Together they wrote spells. Those enchantments have to be hidden somewhere. Let me try to find them."

He lowered the dagger.

Stavros rose to his feet, swaying slightly. He drew his sword and stood behind Valik with the sword at his throat. "You make her bleed again, and I *will* take your head."

"Stavros, put it down," Kaya whispered.

She couldn't lose them. It dawned on her how much she cared for both. It had started badly between her and Stavros, but he had come to save her, and they were also connected. She stood, looking between the two of them, when trumpets sounded. Stavros stiffened.

"Your mother is here. Perfect timing." Valik straightened.

Stavros took his sword away from Valik's neck.

Dread dropped like cold stones into her belly knowing her mother had come.

"Looks like you can't kill me now," Kaya told Valik.

"What are you going to tell your mother?" Stavros asked.

"About what?"

"About how you two are mated, if that's the correct term."

"The same thing I'm going to tell her about how I'm bonded to you. She won't like it."

"What won't I like?"

Kaya turned. Her mother stood in the doorway. A large black cloak covered her head. She lifted the hood from her face. Her silver hair flowed over her shoulders.

The power that radiated from her always made Kaya take a step backward. Along with her pale skin and ice blue eyes, it was difficult to believe her slender mother had given birth to her. They looked more like sisters. The queen was shorter than she and wore heels to give her more height.

Valik dropped to his knee before her.

"Your Majesty. Forgive me for not being there to greet you. I—we were discussing..."

"Get up, Valik," Queen Mila ordered him.

A servant burst into the room behind the queen trying to catch his breath. "Sire, the queen is here along with her entourage. What do we do?"

Stavros shot Kaya a look and then glanced at Valik.

"I can see that. Make sure Queen Mila and her entourage are shown to their quarters and afforded all the courtesies of my kingdom." Stavros bowed before the queen and moved to stand beside Kaya. He slipped his fingers through hers and squeezed them.

She felt his slight tremor.

"I am Stavros, King of the Pressions. It is a pleasure to meet you."

"I can't say the pleasure is mine. You nearly killed my daughter. I should rip out your throat and drain you dry," she growled, showing off her fangs.

"I can assure you that I now realize that was a horrible way for me to treat Kaya. I have begged her forgiveness." Stavros knelt before the queen and bared his throat. "I don't yet know all of your ways, but I know I can offer my life to you."

Queen Mila slipped her hand around his throat. Her nails trailed over his flesh. She stuck her thumbnail into his skin until a bead of blood welled onto the tip.

Stavros grunted.

She flicked her tongue over it. Her expression darkened. Her gaze flicked to Kaya. She snarled and wiped at the blood on Kaya's throat. "Who bled you?"

"I did, Majesty." Valik didn't look at her.

Before Kaya could comment, her mother had a short sword against Valik's throat. "You dared to touch my daughter? I will take your head."

"No. Mother. Kill him and you kill me."

"You would take *him* for a mate? A lowly warrior of a defunct bloodline? When you know you are to be married?" She let him go.

"Do you know what this means?" Mila asked Stavros.

"I understand that in your culture it means she's married to Valik," Stavros replied.

"You are going to allow this?" Her mother's stunned expression wasn't lost on Kaya.

"Mother, there's more to it than that. Valik saved my life after the last incident with Stavros. He's not some defunct bloodline. He's always been loyal."

"I don't care if he's been loyal or not. He laid his hands upon you. He mixed his blood with yours. It's against our laws even to touch you," Queen Mila railed.

"Kaya has told me all about what happened between her and Valik," Stavros reassured the queen. "In many ways, it's my fault. I accept her for who and what she is—even with Valik. We can work it out."

"You say that now, but what happens when your court finds out she has a Vyrk lover and her king condones it?"

"Then I'll deal with it. You were the one who sold your daughter to me," Stavros replied.

Her mother slapped Stavros across the face hard enough that he rubbed his cheek.

"I didn't *sell* my daughter. I made sure she would live. I'm quite aware of your decree to kill my people if they are in your kingdom. She is my most precious commodity. I'd do anything to make sure she lived. Her dowry awaits inspection in front of your court. I know our presence here will make your people uncomfortable. My entourage is well aware that they are not to feed on anyone in the castle unless it is a consensual relationship."

"The kingdom will see how much I love your daughter when I lift the edict to have all Vyrkola killed on sight," Stavros told Mila.

"That remains to be seen. Kayanna, come with me to your rooms. Make sure my things are brought there. I will be staying close to my daughter." Queen Mila walked past her out of the room.

Kaya looked back at the two men who held her heart. She couldn't say no to her mother, but she knew that what was between her and Valik wasn't over. What Stavros said about loving her made her heart beat a little faster because he wasn't bluffing. If he had been, her mother would have killed him.

She showed her mother to her rooms.

The woman closed the door and removed her cloak.

"I admit it's much nicer than I thought it would be." She surveyed the quarters.

"You assumed I'd be in the dungeons?"

"That was my first thought when I felt your pain that day. Why didn't you just listen to Adran and come back home?"

"Something about Stavros drew my attention when I saw him sneaking into the Thrall encampments. Thralls are raiding our borders and you weren't doing anything about it. I learned that they were going into the Bone Forest."

"For your information, I knew all about the Thralls going into the Bone Forest and trying to get into the old ruins. There's nothing of value in them. The only Thralls that made it back out went insane. I'm doing more than you think to keep the Thralls from our borders. I've been negotiating with some of the clan leaders."

"That's good to know. You should have told me sooner. And there *is* something in the ruins, because I let it out."

"What do you mean, 'you let it out'? What did you let out?"

Kaya told her mother the short version of the story about the demon and how it had kidnapped her. How Valik and Stavros had come to her rescue.

Her mother took a step away from her and slumped onto the bed. The shocked look on her face was more emotion Kaya had ever seen from her mother.

"You don't know what you've done. I should have told you all about our past. About where we came from and the prophecy about the darkness taking over the land once more."

"Wait. You knew this could happen? You knew about the demon and how our race came to be?"

Her mother patted the bed next to her.

Kaya sat down. She barely remembered a time when her mother showed her so much attention. Once she was old enough to take care of herself, her mother had left her to her nannies until Adran came along.

"Kaya, I know I've been harsh with you...and distant. Not what a mother should be. You were my miracle your father gave his life for. When I was pregnant with you, it didn't even dawn on me to wonder about the prophecy. It had been so long since my coronation and my talk with the Old One. I'd completely forgotten all about it until I had a dream when your magic awoke in you. I dreamed you were older, and the forest was burning. All were dead around you. You were something darker. The Old One has remained from the original people who started our race— our first queen. She awoke from her long slumber and I told her my dream. She told *me* you were either our salvation or our damnation."

"Why haven't you told me any of this before?"

"Sometimes prophecies only come to pass if we know about them. I didn't want to worry you. I prayed it wasn't true. We only speak with the Old One when it's time for a new queen. She picks the next successor. In the catacombs deep within the mountain, is the truth about us and the order we originated from. The others have gone into a deeper sleep or are dead. Their texts are preserved by magic and the environment."

"Then I have to see what's in the archives. I have to talk to her."

"You're not allowed until you're anointed as queen. The magic will keep you out even if you bear royal blood."

Kaya had to tell Valik about this. "Then I have to go back to the source, just like I was telling Valik."

"I forbid it."

"Mother, it seems your view of who we are and where we came from is a little skewed. All of it," she told the queen.

"What do you know?"

"More than you think." Kaya got up and unlocked the door.

"Where do you think you're going?"

"You've forced me into this marriage, but I made the best of what was dealt and found two men who I love. They're different from one another, but they accept me for who I am. The demon got out and I'm going to find a way to put it back in. And somehow avenge Adran."

"Avenge him?"

"He died when I was captured."

"Princess." The door opened a crack, and a serving girl peeped in. "The king has requested you and your mother come down before the court. He asks you wear this." The servant handed her a package wrapped in fabric. She curtsied and left the chamber.

Inside the package was a shimmering gray dress. Kaya ran her fingers over it.

Her mother touched it and jerked her hand away. "Damn it. It's made of spun silver."

"It's beautiful. Not many can take silver and spin it into a garment. It must have cost a fortune."

"He gave it to you on purpose."

Kaya put the dress on. It was lightweight, and a little big for her, but after she adjusted it, the scooped neckline showed off her breasts. Her mother swept part of her hair off her neck and left the rest down, fixing it with a bit of ribbon. When the queen set her hands lightly on Kaya's shoulders, and Kaya smelled the burning of skin.

"You do look beautiful," her mother said softly. "I've never really told you that. I'm sorry about all of this. I should've told you so much more. Now it's too late and you've been brought into the middle of it. You're leaving me...I thought we had more time."

"I'll outlive Stavros, so we'll have more time in the end."

"Not if you turn him."

Kaya glanced at her mother. "I don't know if I can do that. I don't think he'll want to become one of us. I hadn't planned that far."

"We'll just have to see what the future holds. Come, we can't leave your future husband waiting." She offered Kaya her hand and led her out of the room.

CHAPTER SIXTEEN

The throne room was bursting, with Vyrkolas on one side and his court on the other. The animosity was so thick he could taste it. Stavros hoped Kaya would like the gift he had sent up to her.

His father-in-law had once commissioned it for his wife, but Serena had worn it after her mother. Stavros thought it would look beautiful on Kaya. He felt the weight of his office crushing down on him, with his crown and the emblems he wore around his neck to mark his station.

The doors opened. The queen walked in with Kaya behind her. He waited as she approached. Her mother moved aside and held out Kaya's hand. "Your Majesty, I present to you my daughter, Kayanna EbonWing, Princess of the Vyrkola."

Valik stood with the queen's people.

Stavros glanced over at the Vyrk and saw awe in his eyes. He half expected Valik to say or do something, but as he read the man's expression, Stavros knew he would never hurt Kaya.

The king directed his eyes to his betrothed and his heart nearly stopped when he realized how beautiful she was. It had been right in front of his face for so long. He saw her now the way he should have from the beginning. He should never have put her through the torture he had inflicted.

All he had seen was rage—but now it was gone. He rose from the throne and took her hand. He turned her around and presented her to the court.

"Lords and ladies, may I present to you your next queen."

Petra stood up from her own throne and moved to the smaller one next to it that was her birthright. Stavros led Kaya to sit in the queen's throne next to him. Once she was seated, the room erupted into applause. He was surprised at the reaction.

They adjourned to the dining hall and ate. The Vyrks sipped on blood they had brought with them.

Stavros didn't know how long the visitors would be at court. He didn't think it would be long, since now they had arrived the wedding would be expected to take place; but with the demon out and plotting, he wondered if he should postpone the ceremony. That would look bad, so he dismissed the idea. All he knew was that he wasn't going to get the time he wanted alone with Kaya.

He glanced at Valik. The Vyrk kept his attention focused on the princess.

The feast went on, and then there was a break for dancing. Stavros offered his hand to Kaya. She took it and he led her onto the dance floor before the rest of the court.

"You look ravishing," he commented.

A splash of color filled her cheeks. "Your gift is quite beautiful."

"It belonged to Serena. Her father gave it to her as part of her dowry. I hope you don't mind. I thought it would suit you. It brings out the silver in your eyes."

"I don't mind. Although, my mother thought it was a slight against her because she can't touch it. The silver."

Kaya spun out of his arms and into Valik's as Queen Mila came to join Stavros.

"Do you still plan on killing my daughter?" she asked.

"No. I couldn't mistreat her even if I wanted. If I harm her, then I harm myself."

The queen's mouth remained in a stern line as her eyes narrowed. She didn't appear to be any older than he was, but something in her eyes told him she was ancient. That otherworldly energy made him a little afraid of her. He sensed her cold power as it pushed along his skin and recognized she was definitely not of his world.

Valik gave him the same feeling, but his power wasn't as strong.

"You sound as though you're connected to my daughter."

"I am—more than you realize. I don't know how much she's told you about what's been going on, but I don't intend on letting anything happen to her."

"She's told me enough. I know the dangers the kingdom faces because of the evil that's escaped. That's partly my fault. I should have told Kayanna certain things about our history long before this. It doesn't bother you that my daughter will outlive you and she's apparently mated to one of her own kind?"

"I'm aware of it."

The music shifted again, and he found himself partnering his sister. Petra gave him a gracious smile. "Your new bride-to-be is lovely. Although, her mother doesn't look very happy to be here."

Stavros chuckled. "I'm sure she's not. Are you sure you're okay with stepping down as queen?"

"I never really liked being in charge anyway. You never liked it either. I prefer being in the background and pulling the strings."

He pulled his sister closer while they twirled. "What strings did you pull, Petra?"

Her expression darkened. "Are you accusing me of anything, Stavros?"

"Things are happening we have to be aware of."

"I guess we should have a meeting then. There are whispers going on about the dead coming back."

Before he could ask her another question, Kaya was back in his arms.

Having her there felt right. He didn't want to let her go again. Her bright smile lit up his heart for the first time in a long time. The more he looked into her eyes, the more he saw in her the same light he'd seen in Serena—but, in Kaya, it was brighter. It made him want her more.

The music stopped and the rest of the court clapped. He was breathing hard and Kaya laughed. Stavros claimed her lips in front of everyone. He wanted to make it clear how he felt about her. Gasps erupted in the gallery, but he didn't care. Kaya returned the kiss. His tongue swiped across her bottom lip and he felt the tips of her fangs. She pulled away, her cheeks reddened.

"Let them talk about that," he whispered in her ear. Stavros led her back to their thrones. Once they were seated, the rest of the court sat.

The next course was served. He noticed Kaya ate a little, but she also drank from the chalice Valik offered her. Stavros guessed it was filled with blood. He wasn't sure he was ever going to get used to that, but he would have to make do. He was about to signal the next of the festivities when the door opened.

Kewskin walked in, dressed in all his finery.

The music silenced.

The chancellor bowed before the king and the rest of the court.

"Majesty, esteemed guests, I have come to pay my respects."

"Chancellor, you are looking well. What is your gift?"

Energy crackled around Kewskin's hands. "Just a reminder that she's mine. That you're *all* mine. I giveth and I taketh away!"

A ball of energy shot from his hand directly at Kaya. It hit an invisible wall around her and flamed out.

Stavros glanced over and saw Valik muttering and waving his hand.

Kaya responded with an energy ball of her own. It flew from her hand and hit the chancellor's chest. His robes caught fire. Kewskin screamed and went up like a quick candle. What was left behind was black sludge.

Screams erupted in the hall. One of the Vyrks had grabbed a servant and sunk its fangs into her throat.

"Let her go," the queen commanded. "Stephen, this isn't you."

Stephen looked up from the girl's throat. "It is me, Majesty. It's always been me. Can't you see that?"

"It's the demon," Valik whispered. "It can manipulate those who are descended from its blood and are weak." He drew his sword and started forward.

Stephen threw the woman at Valik and raced toward the door for escape. Stavros signaled his guards to go after the Vyrk. Kaya stood up. He felt a blast of power go out from her. It passed over him. A rope of energy wound around the Vyrk's throat and took off his head.

"Sire, I would suggest we cease the festivities for the night," Mila said to him.

Stavros nodded. "I would agree. We need to discuss this to see how we can stop it."

"I think you're right. Any ideas, Valik, on how we keep this demon from infecting the rest of our people?" the queen asked.

"Silver. Everyone needs to wear something silver," Valik said immediately.

"Which will hurt us," Queen Mila replied.

"It's better than the alternative. Some have a stronger tolerance than others," Valik responded. "It's the only defense."

Mila nodded.

Kaya stood by Valik's side.

Stavros smiled and went over to her. "Let us convene in my war room in an hour. Your Majesty, bring your top advisors and I'll have mine. We can discuss how we are going to fight this creature."

The queen scowled but didn't say anything as she left to gather her council.

Stavros pulled Kaya aside with Valik. He looked at the hardened warrior. "I know you love her—but I also know you took an oath to stop the person who let the demon out. I need your word you won't hurt her."

"Stavros, what is this all about?" Kaya asked.

"I can deal with this on my end, but you two need to find a way to put the demon back and trap it again. I think we can distract it. With so many other Vyrks here, it's not going to realize you're gone. Call it a feeling. I don't think you have much time. Valik, you can protect her. You know the demon better than anyone. Swear to me you won't hurt her?"

"I-I swear it."

Stavros held out his hand to the other man. Valik hesitated a moment and then grasped it, clasping him at the elbow with his other hand.

"Thank you, Valik. Now, go. Do what you need to."

"Stavros, I—"

He trailed his finger down her cheek. "Kaya, this is partly my fault. This is the only way I know how to defend my people. I love you. I know you might not believe that, but I do. Valik can help you in this. Go."

Kaya kissed him quickly and then left. Valik nodded as he went after her. Stavros turned back, and out of the corner of his eye he saw a dark shape chase after Kaya and Valik.

CHAPTER SEVENTEEN

K aya changed into traveling clothes her mother had brought for her. She rummaged through the things and found another black cloak like the one she had worn before she and Adran had been caught by Stavros and his men. The familiar stirring of magic slid over her as she let it settle over her shoulders. She slid on Alerik's ring in case she needed it again, along with the smaller crest ring her mother had brought her.

Valik came into her room and handed her a long dagger.

"What's this for?"

"In case you need to use it on me."

"I don't think that's going to happen."

Valik shot her a dark look. "You saw how easy it was for the demon to influence Stephen."

"You said yourself it could only get into the minds of the weak." She threw it down on the bed. "You might need to use that on *me*, if you're so worried about it taking over you."

"It can't. You were born the way you are. You still have a soul."

"And you don't think you or the others do?"

"After what I did? No. Come on. Take the dagger just in case. You never know, I might renege on my promise and try to kill you." His voice was cold. The gulf between them had returned.

Kaya tried not to focus on it. Instead a brush of energy across her side caught her attention. She felt the breeze and knew it was Serena trying to get her attention. She followed the dead queen into the tower. Serena's light was brighter than she had ever seen it before.

"You're heading back to the ruins," the spirit murmured.

"Yes. I'm about to head out. I hope the demon doesn't realize I'm gone. Why did you bring me up here?"

Serena pointed to Alerik's diary. "I brought it back here so it would be protected from the demon. It can't come up here." She passed her hand over the journal. It flipped over to an entry near the end.

Kaya hadn't read that far.

Serena pointed to the passage. "I don't know what it says, but I get the sense it's a summoning spell. If it's hidden in the journal, then it has to be something. Take it in case you need it."

Kaya tore the page from the diary and tucked it into her pocket. "Thank you, Serena."

"I can do one last thing to aid you. I'll buy you as much time as I can."

"Thank you."

"Just get him back to the hell he belongs in."

Kaya left the tower and rejoined Valik in her room.

"Find something interesting?" he asked.

"Just try and keep up." Kaya let her magic slip into her limbs and let go of her human self.

It felt good to feel her bones realign and become wings. This was the natural shape granted to her from being a Vyrk. It allowed her to soar out of the window, letting her be free. Flying was one of the only times she could let go of all her responsibilities. Kaya flew with purpose and homed in on the old ruins. High in the sky, the mountains were small hills in the distance. The Bone Forest was to the west and to the northeast were the Thrall lands. To the south, beyond Stavros's kingdom, was the sea Serena had come from, but Kaya had never seen the ocean. Just the vast lakes in the mountains where her people ruled.

From the air, the Bone Forest was even larger than she had imagined it to be. The times she had been to the ruins she could never remember getting there. Now she had a clear head, and she could see how immense the place was —how much the magic running from the node underneath the ruins had really affected the forest so many years ago.

She couldn't imagine what Valik and Alerik had given up to cap the node and trap the demon. Valik had survived all these years and never let on that *he* was truly the first of their kind, and yet—like her—he was different than the rest of them.

Part of him remained alive.

She had sensed it when all his barriers crashed down and she could see into his soul through their connection. It was the reason he could do the magic he did. The others of his order had been infected by the demon and their magic had died off over time.

Magic had created the bloodlines she was descended from, and magic was the thing that had created her. Without it, she wouldn't be alive. She shook her head as she moved downward toward the ruins and transformed back to human form.

Once her feet touched the ground, a jolt of power surged along her backbone. Something had changed since the last time she was there. The air had thickened. It left a metallic tang on the back of her tongue.

Valik shifted to human form from a large black eagle. His hardened exterior showed him to be the warrior she had grown up with, but she had seen another side of him and wished he would open up to her.

"What is this wonderful idea you have?" Valik lowered the hood of his cloak.

"Can't you feel it?" Kaya asked. "There's something different about the forest since the demon left."

"The magic has been released from its binding spell. The node is active again," an unexpected voice answered. A cloaked figure stepped out from behind one of the larger bone trees.

Valik drew his sword and had it at the stranger's throat in a blur of motion Kaya couldn't even follow. A green arc blasted Valik across the clearing, where he crashed against a tree trunk, but didn't even make an indentation in the bone bark.

The coolness of the magic washed over her. She would know that feeling anywhere.

"Adran." Kaya rushed over and threw her arms around him.

He returned the hug lightly then pushed her away. "Hello, Kaya."

"I thought you were dead. Stavros's men ran you until you dropped behind their horses. Why didn't you come to the castle and try to get me out?"

"I was at the castle, but you never knew I was there. I wanted to reveal myself to you. I almost did a couple of times when Stavros was torturing you, but I was told to watch and wait. I spun a concealment spell around me so I wouldn't be seen."

"Let me guess. The order sent you." Valik got up and dusted himself off.

"Yes. They sent me."

"Wait? The same order of *varaz* you were a part of?" Kaya asked Valik, trying to understand.

Adran replied instead. "The very same. Kaya, I've wanted to tell you all these years, but they made me stay quiet."

Her mind whirled. "It was all a lie. All my life I thought you were my only friend. You taught me how to do magic."

Her rage exploded as her fangs ripped through her gums. She landed on top of him with her hand wrapped around his throat. He didn't fight her as tears of betrayal burned her eyes.

"I won't stop you, but if you kill me then you won't be able to send the demon back to hell. I'm not talking about trapping it. I mean killing it altogether," Adran rasped.

"We need to hear him out. Let him go, Kaya," Valik urged.

She reined in her anger and forced it into an energy ball she lobbed at the tree trunk. The energy didn't even leave a scorch mark except for the one on her pride.

Adran put a hand on her shoulder. She whipped around and slapped him. He grunted and worked his jaw. Kaya was furious—and hurt, as well. All the years they had spent together. He had been her confidant. The one and only person she truly thought understood her. He might have reported her whereabouts to the queen, but he kept her other secrets. They had played together as children. He was her first in everything...and now the betrayal she felt only made the wound worse.

"Feel better?"

"A little bit. Why couldn't you have told me?" Kaya asked him.

"I did my best. I resurrected Serena so she could help you."

"I thought she was hanging around the castle until someone found her killer and she was trying to get Stavros to open his heart again."

"All of that is true. I just made it so she could communicate with you. She led you to the tower and to the journal. I didn't know about any of that. I'm sorry, Kaya. Valik —I wish I could've told you I knew about you."

"The order died out when the Vyrkola were created," Valik told them.

"It didn't. A few of the original members who turned brought together other members who remained human. They had not been monitoring the node in the mountains when you preformed the spell, so they weren't affected when the demon interfered with the enchantment. They bid those members to gather information about the demons. A couple of the original members went deeper into the mountains, along with some of the others to find out more about the new race that was created. We've learned a few things over the eons. Our families were integrated into the current families so we could keep an eye on the race as it grew."

"The order knew all about this. Why haven't you done anything about it? Why didn't you come to consult with me?" Valik growled.

"Everyone believed you were like the rest and had lost your magic, but from what I saw tonight, that isn't the case. Part of you is still alive if you can wield that much power. It's the same reason Kaya can channel energy—because she's alive."

"Told you," Kaya said to Valik.

He shot her a glance, but it was clear even he didn't know any of this. "I feast on blood the same as the others. I have all of their abilities and their weaknesses. My heart doesn't beat, and my seed is dead. How can I be alive?"

It hit her. "You have a soul."

"Are you saying the other Vyrks are damned?" Valik growled.

"I didn't say that. Think about it. The others were all infected with the demon's essence when it got into the stream of magic you and Alerik were using to bind the magical node. Alerik was bitten by his wife who was possessed by the demon, but he could still use his magic. His journal said he could feel that he was losing himself to the darkness. That he could hear the voices of the others. You mingled your blood with his to perform the ceremony. Something about it must have changed the parameters of the demon's blood within you and made you slightly different than the others. You were still alive while you had the blood in you working on your human body and then the blast hit you."

Valik rubbed his chin. "I've been trying to figure out what it was all these years."

"So has the order. They've always wanted to know about their origin. You never told them about Alerik or what happened. They have a theory it has something to do with the silver," Adran explained.

"Somehow, you retained the bit of yourself that could do magic. When the spell hit the others, the magic got sucked out of them. Look what the incantation did to the forest. It sucked the life out of the trees and turned them to bone. You said yourself dealing with magic as powerful as this could be erratic. It made you different than the others. You had no way of knowing the demon would put himself into the spell, or that it would rebound all the way up the lines of silver to where the order was headquartered, or that the members were monitoring you, or even that they were using the magic at that point in time. You are different than all of them—just as I am. Magic created both of us. Doesn't that mean anything?" Kaya tried to get him to see how unique he was. How he wasn't like the others.

Valik's cold glare met hers. "It only means magic is going to get us out of this and once it's done, then I'm going, too."

His words cut at her heart. She pushed back her tears

and focused on why they had come here. The past didn't matter nor did how the Vyrkola were created. They had to get the demon back into its realm.

"Adran, do you have any idea how to contain the demon again? You said the order has been working on it for years."

"That's why I followed you. I overheard your conversation with Stavros. If you had an idea, then you were my best bet. The order has sent many sorcerers to the ruins. Of the few who returned, they couldn't find a way in. No one could except you, Kaya, and you got out again."

"Then let's go back in. I'm going to need your help, Adran. I have a plan."

Kaya walked around the ruins until they came to the mouth of the tunnel she had come out of. She passed her hand over the entrance. "It's different as well."

She stepped inside and Valik followed.

"The barrier was broken when you left and let it out. Now anyone can get in. Another reason it needs to be sealed once more. I hope we can find what you're looking for. If Eloise is even still here. It's been a long time."

Valik walked down the tunnel, leaving her alone with Adran.

He touched her shoulder. "I really sorry. None of it was a farce. Your friendship was very dear to me. They put a binding spell on me so I couldn't talk about any of it. I tried, but the spell caused severe pain. I've always been your friend."

Kaya hung her head. "I'm still mad at you, but I'm glad you're alive."

"I can deal with that. You and Valik? How does Stavros feel about that?"

"Oddly enough, he's okay with it, but Valik's shut me out. It's been his lifelong mission to destroy the being who would be the key to letting the demon out. I'm hoping Eloise might still be here—or at least some part of her that can help me. The demon bragged about learning a few things while his essence was enmeshed with hers and accessing her magic."

They made it to the end of the tunnel and caught up to Valik.

Valik pressed his hand against the door, but it didn't open. "Kaya, use the ring. Place it here."

He showed her where the ring went, but he avoided touching her. They entered the cavern together, and Valik screamed.

CHAPTER EIGHTEEN

Stavros stood in the garden he had shared with Serena. The energy of the night felt off. The brush with the evil of the demon had contaminated everything. He sat on the bench and tried to find his footing once more.

"Mind if I join you?"

He glanced up and saw Kaya's mother. She wore a necklace of silver around her throat. Black marks from her singed flesh healed quickly as the silver necklace shifted on her skin. She didn't seem bothered by the pain.

"Not at all. I'm surprised you found this place. It's not known to many."

"It is, if you know how to listen for a specific heartbeat."

Stavros nodded, not sure how to answer.

"I wanted to apologize for how all of this happened. I sensed my daughter's distress and sent Valik after her. She's precious to me. I couldn't let anything happen to her. You were not the ideal husband I imagined."

He chuckled. "She wasn't the typical wife I hoped for either."

"It seems you do love her even after the hell you put her through."

"I did it out of spite. My—"

Mila waved off his statement. "I already know about your queen and the way she died. You killed quite a few of my kind. Many of my subjects call for your blood, but I don't want a war. The Thralls are enough to deal with. They feel they can invade our lands, steal from our mines, and kill the families who are loyal to us."

"You and I have a common enemy besides the Thralls."

"This demon?" she asked.

"I suppose so."

"Do you have any idea how to defeat it?"

"Not yet. But that's what I'm hoping we can find out."

"You mean what Kaya and Valik can find out?"

He shifted uncomfortably on the seat. "Yes. That's the idea. I hope they can figure something out. My chancellor was obviously possessed by something, or even already dead. I don't know."

"While they aren't here, we have a wedding to plan. Maybe it's time we talk about combining forces to keep the Thralls out of our lands and drive them back into theirs. I've been talking to some of their chieftains, but they don't want to budge. They feel they are entitled to the territory. It's very frustrating."

"We could use another perspective about where the Thralls are coming into our borders. Let me assemble the generals I have left."

He stood, gave the queen a bow, and moved to gather

his generals. At the gate to the garden, he paused. "One other thing, how are you going to keep the demon from possessing your people?"

"The silver hurts, but we can withstand the pain as long as it keeps the demon out. Some of us are better at handling it than others. We do live in the mountains where the halls and rooms are lined with it. If we all had Kaya's resistance to silver, we would be so lucky."

"Before you leave, can you tell me about Kaya's father?"

"Why do you ask?"

"Kaya said her father gave his life so you could give birth to her. Vyrks are creatures of twilight. You die and are reborn, so you cannot procreate the way you would have as a human." He moved back to the bench and sank down beside her once more. "If you have magic, then it dies with you, when you reawaken. How did Kaya come to be birthed?"

A flash of pain crossed the queen's face. "I loved Laris with all my being. I never thought I could love anyone more. I've been what I am for almost two thousand years. One day a traveling *varaz* came to court and asked if he could entertain us. I needed the amusement, so I allowed it. He was no ordinary magician.

"I might not be able to do magic any longer, but I know the feel of it. Laris was powerful. We fell in love. The more I was with him, the more I wanted to be human so I could bear his children. We spoke about the future and how I could turn him, make him like us. Laris didn't want the life of a Vyrkola. After a few years together, he told me there was a way I could bear him a child. It seemed impossible, but he told me it was true and showed me a spell he had happened upon in his travels. The enchantment was in an old tongue from before my time. It required the sacrifice of a life for a life to grow within me. I agreed to it thinking the sacrifice would be a prisoner.

"We went to a part of the mountains where there was a magical node. He had me stand over it while he recited the ritual. I had to drink from him. We made love at the height of it and he told me to drink all of him. I couldn't kill him. I loved him. Laris slit his own throat. I couldn't resist the blood. I lost myself a little. The energy of the incantation hit me like hammer. It kick-started my heart and I felt a spark of life ignite within me."

"How did you keep your heart beating?" Stavros asked.

The queen shook her head and looked up at the stars. "Something I'm ashamed to admit. I've never told anyone. The spell did something to me while I carried Kaya. It made me alive again and my hunger for all things doubled. I could eat food, but my blood hunger differed. I didn't just take in blood to keep my heart going, I drained my victim's souls. Seven months after the ritual Kaya was born—a healthy girl child with a heartbeat. I loved her because I saw Laris in her eyes."

"What about taking souls? Do you still do that?"

The queen shook her head. "Once Kaya was delivered, my heart died once more, and I returned to my former self. Please don't tell her. She wouldn't understand. I know I sound like a monster for doing it, but she was my link to Laris. Once my advisors discovered I was pregnant, they wanted me to terminate it. I couldn't. You understand why she's so dear to me. I can't lose her." Mila wiped away a bloody tear.

"I understand. Those who took my wife also murdered our son. I'm not sure what drove me over the edge. Losing her or losing him. They were my life, and then they were gone. I remember the day Serena told me she was pregnant. I couldn't have been happier. Not because I would have an heir, but because she bore a part of me. A symbol of our life together."

"Yes. Children are our most precious commodity. That's why I did what I did. Your reputation had grown so that they were calling you the Night King because you killed so many of us. Almost like you knew where to find my people."

"You don't need to worry about that now. I won't kill any more of them unless they break the laws here. They will be treated like anyone else."

"That's good to know. I'll gather my advisors."

She bowed and left the garden.

CHAPTER NINETEEN

Kaya rushed into the cavern and pulled Valik back. He groaned in pain as his hands covered his eyes. Her breath hitched in her throat at the sight before her. The left side of his face and both eyes were burned. Almost as though they had melted.

"It's going to be okay." She bit into her wrist and offered it to him.

Valik pushed it away. "No. You'll need all your strength to face it. I can't enter."

"You need to drink so you can heal. Even a couple of swallows. Please," she entreated him.

He growled, but he took her wrist and latched on. Kaya tried not to lose herself to the sharing and stay focused. Their link expanded, but it was gone too quickly for her to get any kind of a read off him except his pain. "Enough. Take Adran in with you. You'll understand."

He slid down the rock wall. Kaya didn't want to leave him behind, but they had to get this done.

"Come on. He'll be fine." Adran touched her shoulder and motioned for them to go into the adjoining room.

As they entered the cavern, Kaya was hit by a wave of pure energy. It tingled, but it didn't hurt like before. Silver light emanated from the center of the wellspring like a liquid sea. She walked closer to it.

"Kaya, don't." Adran yelled, as though he were caught in a great storm, but Kaya felt none of it. He shielded his eyes from the light, but it didn't bother her.

Kaya pointed to the seal. "The seal is cracked. The magic is loaded with silver now. It's been amplified from all these years of being sealed off. Can't you see it?"

"All I see is the silver energy. It's like a heat on my skin. I can't get near it. How can you even look into the well, let alone step into it?"

She shrugged. "It's using the silver from inside this place. I don't know what the binding spell did, but it's fused the silver with the magic."

"Whatever it's done, the node has grown stronger. You're the only one who can handle the power of it. You had better do whatever you're going to do, because I can't stay in here much longer."

Kaya nodded. If she was going to have any chance of contacting Eloise, then she had better use her time wisely. "I need you to use the same spell you used to bring Serena forth. If you can do that to help pull in Eloise then I can reach out with you, lend you my energy."

"I can do that. I think. Remember when you used to repeat the spells after me when we were little? I think that's our best chance. I don't think it's a good idea for me to mess with this kind of power. No one has touched it in so long.... It's become untamed."

"Fine. Say the spell and I'll repeat it."

Kaya relaxed and stepped into the magical storm. The power enhanced all of her senses, but it didn't hurt as the silver-infused magic passed over her.

She looked at Adran. He stood with his back against the cavern wall. From the way he cupped his hands around his mouth, he must be yelling, but she could hear him as if he were next to her. The power both warmed and chilled her at the same time. She could feel it moving into her soul. Adran's voice was clear. She kept her focus on summoning Eloise. She couldn't feel any of the darkness or evil that had tainted the chamber before within the magic. The magic in the ground that ran along the rest of the magical threads in the earth up into the mountains and beyond was untainted. Her own power stirred and, for the first time in a long time, she didn't hold back.

"From restful sleep I call thee. From twilight side, I summon you forth. Eloise, Ancient Queen, I need your wisdom. In this place where your bones lie, I beseech you to appear."

Energy left her in a great rush—a whoosh that forced her back a few steps. For a quick second, the silver light turned purple, and then the silver illumination of the magical storm died.

Eloise's transparent form floated in the center of the node. She looked lost. Her form wavered in and out. Kaya couldn't believe the spell had actually worked. She had never pulled a spirit back from the dead before.

"Why have you called me from the twilight realm?" The queen's low voice echoed in the chamber.

"I need your help," Kaya told her.

The queen turned her green gaze to Kaya. "Abomination," Eloise growled. Her mouth stretched and revealed fangs as her eyes darkened, but it passed in an instant.

"You know what I am."

"You are an unholy creation born from magic and the dead. You have no soul."

The words irritated Kaya, but she pushed the comment aside. "The demon has been set free. He confessed that while you shared a body he wrote the spell that enabled me to exist. There must be more to your shared magic. You must know how to send it back to the realm it came from."

"Why would you want to send the one who created you back to its hell?"

"I have no love for the demon. It wants to cause havoc in this world. I can't have that. I accidentally let it out and I have to put it back or destroy it. Please, you must know something."

Eloise floated closer and grabbed her chin.

Kaya grunted at the frigid touch.

"I will never help you. He tricked my husband into using me as a vessel. Alerik did it out of love. Send me back to my grave so I can be with my husband. He would warn you that the evil will destroy you. He would never help you, either."

"Alerik would want the demon gone from this world. He fought the infection to the end, and died human," said an unexpected voice. "He never took a life. Alerik wanted you well, but he also wanted to be sure you knew he loved you. He stayed with you until the demon consumed you. You were the one who bit him, Eloise. Kaya has no love for this foul creature."

Eloise turned toward Valik. Part of his face had healed, but his eyes were white.

Kaya's heart went out to him. She wanted to be sure he was well, but he wouldn't let her get close. She wondered if they would ever be close again.

Eloise floated toward him and laid her hand on his cheek. "You're the one who sealed the magical node. When the demon jumped into the silver it separated my soul from its essence. You made it possible for me to move on. You're with her?"

"I swore when the demon told me it had future plans to let the rest of them out that I wouldn't let that happen. I've lived all of these years to see it return to hell. You can help."

"You face has changed some since the last time I saw it. You, I'll help, but not her."

"Fine. Do you know how we can send him back? Where is the book of spells the demon wrote while he was twisted up in you?"

Eloise whispered in Valik's ear. He nodded and the ghost of the old queen drifted back toward the center of the seal.

She glared at Kaya. "Release me now. Pray Valik does the right thing. You don't deserve to live," Eloise spat.

Kaya waved her hand. "Be still the ghosts of the past. Return to twilight and wake no more." The power left her, and the node flashed purple.

Valik cried out as Eloise faded away. The full power of the well rushed back over Kaya. Something about it was different. It hit with more strength than she could handle, shoving her backward into the wall.

Adran ran to her side.

"Are you okay?"

"I'll be fine, but something's going on with the node."

"It's starting to overload. It's going to blow up and it will destroy everything around here," Valik told them.

"Did Eloise tell you how to send the demon back to hell?" Kaya asked.

"Yes, and where the book is hidden. I'll retrieve it. You and Adran contain the node before it consumes everything. I need Alerik's ring."

Kaya slid the ring from her finger and handed it over to Valik. He dashed out of the room. It didn't seem as though he felt any pain from the silver now.

The node threw another burst of energy at her that struck her in the chest.

Adran grabbed her hands.

"We need to close this."

"Do you know how?"

He nodded. "I've been studying the old texts. We have to mend the seal and divert the energy back into the land. By you tapping into it, the crack in the seal widened. At least we know there's no taint of evil in it. The silver veins must have cleansed it. The others in the order are going to be on the lookout for this."

"What happens if it rebounds like it did with Valik?" Kaya asked.

"It's a chance we have to take. Kaya, I can't do this by

myself. I don't have the power. You have more magic in you than a handful of the collective working together," Adran told her.

"What do we have to do?"

"The spell to seal the rift is about visualizing and using our power to heal the wound in the capstone. Close your eyes and feel the energy building between us. Resist the temptation to pull from the well."

She closed her eyes and mentally envisioned the space between their joined hands. Adran's energy played against her palms and burned yellow as hers was dark blue. Their energy swirled together and formed a green light in her mind. The silver energy from the magical node blinded her with its intensity, but she forced herself to stare into it. The power prickled across her skin. Small flares of it shot out and hit the walls of the cavern. The earth rumbled beneath her feet. Debris fell on her shoulders. If they didn't get this done soon, the ruins were going to come down on top of them. "I see it."

"Good. Focus our combined energy into the crack in the stone cap. We've done this before, remember? When we were children learning about the elements."

"I remember, but this is a lot bigger...and there wasn't any magic involved on the other end of those games."

"We just have to seal it on this end. Once we do, the magic should shoot along the silver veins. The order has people at key points along the lines to make sure the magic stays contained. They're waiting on us. I need you to do this. Concentrate on the crack in the seal. Weave the two edges back together again."

Kaya took in a deep breath, trying to ignore the explosions of rock around her. She prayed Valik had retrieved the Eloise's spellbook. The magic bubbled up within her. She opened the tap inside of her which she hardly ever accessed and let the power flow. Once the energy between their hands grew to a good amount, she directed it downward. The magic of the energy node forced their combined power back up.

Kaya gritted her teeth and kept on pushing her magic against the flow. Adran cried out, but she sensed him with her.

His magic faltered.

They continued until their power touched the seal. Pain shot up Kaya's arm. She whimpered but kept on going. In her mind, she knit the broken seal back together. Adran's magic weakened until it left her completely. She fell to her knees and tried to weave a net of energy to catch the wild magic flowing from the node. The earth rumbled again underneath her.

She kept her hands outstretched. The power of the magic burned her flesh, but she kept on. She put all she had into stopping the magic. The flow didn't decrease. Something heavy hit her shoulder. Kaya didn't need to open her eyes to know the ruins were crumbling. Her power weakened until she felt another energy join hers. It steadied her and helped her regain her focus.

"Together again. Sealed to remain unbroken."

The node's energy rose up against her one last time. This time she was ready for it.

One final push, and she felt the magic rush back into the ground. The stone cap slammed back together, and she was thrown backward to land on top of someone.

She opened her eyes. The cavern had caved in completely. The tower above it collapsed around them. The area immediately surrounding them remained, unscathed by the destruction. When she looked behind her, Valik was there. His eyes had healed further, but he seemed different.

"Thank you for the help."

His eyes were now rimmed with silver. The pull to him overwhelmed her. She touched the side of his face. He frowned at her in confusion. His skin wasn't as cool as it had been before.

"You're welcome." He slipped her hand from his cheek and pointed at her friend. "Adran."

Kaya snapped out of it. When she tried to move, all of her bones ached. The world spun. She tried to go over to Adran, but she stumbled.

Valik grabbed her elbow and helped her over to her fallen friend. He lay motionless.

Kaya shook him.

"Adran, this isn't funny. Get up." She shook him again. Kaya touched his throat and listened. She didn't feel or hear a pulse. "No. You can't do this to me again!"

His unblinking eyes, and the absence of a heartbeat, told her he was really dead this time.

"We can't stay here," Valik urged her. "The demon's going to know by now that we've left Stavros's castle. Everyone along the lines of the node will know something big happened. You don't have the energy to shift, and I'm not one hundred percent either. Adran knew the risks of doing this. He gave his life to seal the rift. Come on."

She wiped her tears away. "Where do we go?"

"We go home." Valik helped her up. She noticed a satchel hung at his side, and it bulged with the outline of a book.

"You got the book."

"I did—and she told me how to send the demon back to hell and close the portal so he and his kind can't come back. I need some things back in the mountains that only the order has. I have to speak to Thesia. She's the only one I know of left from my time. She's the one your mother spoke about who picks the next queen. Come on." Valik offered her his hand.

"Are you still going to kill me?" she asked quietly.

III

SHATTERED

CHAPTER TWENTY

Valik's oath to kill the being that would unleash the demon had driven him since he turned into a Vyrkola. When he discovered it was Kaya, it tore him up inside, because he could see into her heart. She had her faults, like everyone else, but no evil lingered in her soul. Still, he had to stick to the plan. He shut himself off from her.

He knew it had hurt her, but he constantly reminded himself *she* had released the demon. That guilt had weighed on him as he searched for Eloise's book, but he had to keep his mind focused. Valik retrieved the spellbook encased in the wall of her crypt. He didn't have time to read it. The whole place shook from the enchantment Kaya and Adran wove. He rushed back to see their progress.

When he returned to check on Kaya, she was on her knees and Adran already dead. She was using all of her energy to seal the rift—and it was working—but she was losing the battle. He could let her use up her energy and die, but as he watched her struggle, Valik knew he loved her too much.

He raced to stand behind her. As he did, a bolt of the wild magic hit him in the chest. It didn't burn him the way it had when he first looked at it and it damaged his eyes. Instead, it stole the breath from him, and he felt something ignite within him. Valik placed his hands on Kaya's shoulders and funneled his energy into her. Once she finished the words of the spell and knitted the capstone back together, a great explosion rushed over them. The veins of silver in the cave burned white. The cavern collapsed round them, leaving them safe in a bubble of energy. The power reverberated along the lines of silver that ran under the ground.

Valik and Kaya climbed out of the ruins. Nothing remained of the castle or of the crypts. The great surge of energy had leveled the closest trees as well.

The energy of the node surged around him. Kaya had done it. Her magic was greater than Valik had realized. As they walked through the Bone Forest, he could feel it flowing stronger than he ever had before.

The day grew warmer, and the sunlight singed his skin, but he didn't find it as bad as he had in the past. With the protection his cloak afforded him, he could keep going.

Kaya stumbled along. She needed to feed and get out of the light in this weakened state, but they had to be clear of the forest first. The ruins might have been toppled, but the phantoms who haunted the trees remained and called to the living, trying to add to their ghostly numbers. They had a long way to go before they would get to the mountains.

He would shift his shape, but he wasn't about to leave Kaya behind. She was too grief-stricken to think straight.

They walked until the middle of the afternoon and found shelter in a cave. Kaya sat beside him in the darkest part of the cavern. Her pale skin and thready pulse concerned him.

"Kaya, stay here. I'm going to find you some food. You need to have something in your system to get your energy back up."

"I'll be fine as long as you stay with me. I can't lose you, too."

"Kaya, the magic required to perform that spell nearly killed you. It drained your life-force. That was no small feat. Adran gave his life for the endeavor. You can't so the same."

She scoffed, "If I die, it makes your mission easier, doesn't it? You won't have to worry about me releasing the other demons."

"Kaya, I don't want you to die. I-I can't have you die. If I wanted that, I wouldn't have shared my magic with you back there."

Valik took her face in his hands and kissed her. Once their mouths touched, he couldn't deny the bond between them. He had shut his emotions down, trying to see her as a thing he needed to kill. It was simpler when she was just the queen's daughter and nothing else.

When she came so close to gliding into twilight after shutting down the node, he knew he couldn't live without her. It hit him so hard that he nearly released her, but instead he pulled her into his arms. Valik let her feel the love he had for her. Having her nearby healed a long-covered wound that had never quite mended. The loss of his family was something he had never quite gotten over.

It had been easier for him to shut down his emotions and become a warrior. To defend the royal bloodline until the one person who was his sole purpose for living came along. Kaya was the sunshine he'd been denied. She filled him with a warmth he'd long forgotten. He tried to make her understand that, for so long, he had been a Vyrkola and nothing more, but she made him feel human again.

He kissed her lips and worked down her throat. They both needed one another in ways he had never fathomed before—even in her weakened state. His fangs grew and he pierced her flesh. Valik didn't need to give her any encouragement. Kaya found his throat and they shared their blood, renewing the bond between them. The joy in the sharing lasted for several moments, until he pulled away. She continued to draw life from him until he had to ease her away.

Her color had returned, and her heartbeat sounded faster. She wouldn't die on him. Tears stood in her eyes as she looked up at him. He'd forgotten how young she truly was. He had seen thousands of years, and she only a couple of hundred.

"Valik—"

He placed his finger on her lips. "You don't have to say anything, Kaya. I can't hurt you. If I could, it would've been that first night I saw you reading Alerik's journal. Some part of me snapped. I needed to believe there was another way to send them all back to hell...and then, you found it. That's why we need to return home. I need to know if you're strong enough to shift and fly with me until we get there. It's a push, but we can't waste any more time."

Kaya stood, wobbling on her feet. He moved to catch her, but she shook her head.

"I'll be okay. I've been like this before. Your blood helped, but you're right. I need to truly feed or have food. Probably both. I don't normally perform strong magic like that. I didn't think I had it in me."

"I knew you did. Can you shift?"

"Yes, I'll manage. Are you going to be okay in the light?"

"I'll manage," he returned with a smile.

He looked outside into the direct sun. The light brought him dread, but not as much as it had before. As he'd grown older, the sun did less damage. He adjusted the bag on his shoulder and secured his sword. The world dissolved around him and the eagle emerged.

Valik flapped in the cave, but it limited his wingspan. He hopped forward until he came to the cave mouth and gained space to spread his wings. A few moments later, Kaya joined him in her grackle form.

They rose into the air and headed toward the mountains. From overhead, the trees in the Bone Forest had a shimmer to them. They had hundreds of miles to cover and he pushed it as hard as he could while the sun was out. They would feed when night fell. He could already taste the blood on his lips.

Kaya kept up with him through the day. After a while, he felt the strain of the sun and the need for blood. He descended outside of a farmhouse and Kaya followed him to the ground. Her shift back to human form was clumsy. It took her longer to take her natural shape than it should have. Her cheeks were hollow.

He caught her as she nearly fainted.

"You need human blood. We both know you're running on empty. Wait here." Valik stepped up to the house and knocked on the door. They were in no man's lands—a territory that didn't belong to the Vyrks or the Thralls.

He didn't know if the inhabitants were going to be friendly or if they would try and kill him. Either way, he was ready to entrance them with his eyes.

A young woman opened the door. She didn't look much older than Kaya. Her startled expression told him she knew what he was. "What do you want?"

"My mate and I were caught in the sun. She needs blood. We will gladly compensate you for the trouble."

She looked at him and at Kaya, who slumped in the shadows. "What do I get out of it?"

"Whatever she wants," Kaya whispered.

"My mate says whatever you desire."

"How do I know you're good for your word?"

Valik growled, but Kaya staggered up and joined him. She slipped the ring with her family crest off her finger and handed it to the young woman. "You can come to the Vyrkola castle and give them my crest ring. Tell them you want to see the princess. "

The young woman's eyes grew wide and a spark of recognition returned. "I've heard about you."

"Will you help us?" Valik asked.

"Yes—but in return, I want to be one of you. That is my payment."

"I don't know if that is such a good desire...." he began.

"If that is what you wish, but it will be at a later time. If I take your blood, I can find you at any time. If you don't come to the castle, I can come to you so I can eventually get my ring back," Kaya told her.

The young woman thought about it. "All right."

Kaya descended on the woman with a hunger he'd never seen in her before, but he could feel her dire need. She had hidden how weak she truly was from him.

The woman swooned, but Kaya still fed.

Valik touched Kaya's shoulder.

"You have to stop. You could kill her. You don't want that on your soul. Besides, I've never known you to break your word."

It took a moment, but she released the woman. Valik checked the farmer's heartbeat. It remained strong enough he took a few sips from her himself. The blood helped revive him. He left the woman in her own bed and then went out into the barn and fed on one of the horses. It wasn't his first choice, but it would do. He found Kaya looking down at the sleeping woman.

"What is it?"

"Her family was killed by our kind and yet she has no hatred for us. She still wants to be one of us. The horrible things that band of rogues did...I've heard about it, but it's like what Stavros did to me. I wanted to loathe him. I did—but he's so broken...like you are."

"Like her, you've learned to forgive him for what he did to you. And you've come to love him."

She touched his face. "I love you, too. It's different. I can't explain it. You're both a part of me and I want you both."

He took her wrist and kissed the inside of it, ignoring the urge to bed her. The warmth of her flesh and her scent enticed him. If they didn't have things to do, then nothing would keep her from him. "We should get going, if you're up for it. "

Kaya slipped her arms around his waist. "We could stay here a while. There's a little time."

"Yes, but each moment the demon is out, it schemes to free the rest of its kind and get you back helping it. As much as I long to taste your flesh, we have to go."

Kaya sighed. "I know. I just don't want to think about it all. I need something to keep my mind off Adran."

"I know, love. That is another reason you have to stay focused. Use your anger and sorrow to fuel your determination to put the demon back in its cage and seal its portal off once and for all."

"What did Eloise tell you about it and what's in the book? Why haven't you told me?"

"Because Eloise didn't give me a straight answer. It's a text of some sort that's even older than I am. That's why I need to talk to Thesia. She has studied ancient texts that were around when the old gods walked among us. She warned me dealing with the demon would be unpredictable. Eloise's answer has something to do with the spellbook. It's written in an ancient language I don't understand. Can you be patient a little longer?"

"Yes. You're right. Adran gave his life so we could stop this."

"He did. You know he's watching over you. He always did. Come on. Let's get home."

Valik took wing once more. This time Kaya led the way as their strength fully returned.

They flew to the spine of the mountains with the ever-present snow on their peaks. He prayed the demon didn't know what was happening. If not, they might have a chance. They might not, but whatever the outcome, he would stay until the end.

CHAPTER TWENTY-ONE

High in the mountains, Kaya landed next to Valik in a courtyard she had never been to before. Snow covered the ground and jagged icicles hung over openings carved in the rock.

She shivered and let out a breath that came out as a blast of cold air.

Valik ducked under the icicles into a dwelling that had seen better days.

Something about it seemed familiar. Laughter echoed in the rooms and they grew warm and cozy as she caught ghostly images of memory playing out before her. "This is where you lived with your wife and daughter."

The pain of the remembrance flitted across his face like ashes scattering in the breeze. "Yes. Betha and Bem used to stay here with me in the summer. They had rooms in the lower castle when it got too cold. I came up here to study the sky. Bem loved to look at the stars with me. After the demon was captured, I returned to the mountains to tell the order what had happened and found them and myself much changed. The hunger came upon me and Betha was the first to succumb to my thirst."

"I'm sorry for what happened to them."

She placed a hand on his shoulder. They might have shared their feelings a little bit more, and she knew he loved her in his own way—at least she had gotten him to admit that. But the gulf between them seemed so large she wasn't sure how to approach him.

He winced at whatever recollection went through his mind and she guessed what he was remembering.

"At least Bem got away from me. She wasn't here when it happened. Before I went to the node, Betha and I had been writing. She said Bem had some magical ability. She had been sent away to live with the other apprentices of the order. Betha...I didn't know what I was at the time. Once I realized what I'd done, I couldn't face myself. I didn't come back here for a long time.

"Later, I came looking for her ghost, but she isn't here. I come here on occasion to look at the stars. Sometimes I stay all night. We will rest here for a little while. Then I will lead you down into the tunnels to the deepest part of the mines where Thesia is."

"Okay." Weariness descended over her from the long flight. The woman's blood had helped her, but she was still weak.

Kaya slid down along the wall and stared up at the night sky. The energy of the mountains strengthened her because she was home—and because of the natural magic running through the stone. When she reached out, she could feel the convergence of all the different strands deep within the land, as well as the new one she had just unleashed.

"Have you ever wondered if your family kept on? I mean if your daughter had children of her own..."

"I've tried over the years to look for her. The order used to keep track of all the active *varaz*, but she was never recorded. After a while, she was lost to time. I don't know what happened to her. I can only hope she lived a full and happy life with no idea of what I became."

"I'm sorry. I never should've brought it up."

Valik patted her knee. "It's all right. You and I share memories now. I know how much you cared for Adran. You feel he betrayed you but are sad for losing him. The conflict between that and forgiving him plays within your heart. This place triggered that within you. I think about them."

"Did you ever try calling Betha back like we did with Eloise?"

"Her soul didn't linger as Eloise's did. Her soul crossed into the twilight so I let it remain. If there had been a glimmer, then...maybe. What Adran didn't tell you—or maybe he didn't know—was that Serena and Eloise could not have been called back if part of them was not still here. No one can truly control the dead."

"You're half-dead. I mean, you're not like the others and you're not like me. You kept your magic. The others in the order all died and were reborn. Maybe it happened to them so fast they didn't realize it at first. The demon can't control you or me."

"This seems to be the theory. You're forgetting about the silver. It affects us as it does him."

"Right." Her mind tried to work out a way to destroy the demon.

"What are you thinking?" Valik asked her.

"Let's talk to Thesia first and then we'll see."

"Fair. You're getting good at avoiding questions."

Kaya brushed her lips against his and felt him respond. "I'm learning from the best." She wrapped her arms around his neck and kissed him harder. She might have been wearied from flying, but right now she needed him.

He broke off the kiss. "Remember, the good of the many."

"I know, but sometimes we need a moment for ourselves." She undid her cloak and shed her clothes until she stood before him.

Kaya felt more exposed than she had been when standing in front of the whole court. The silence echoed between them, and she reached for her cloak. Valik snatched her wrist, removing his own cloak. He laid it atop hers on the ground. He didn't move his gaze from her while he undressed.

Her eyes swept over his lithe body and the pull between them overwhelmed her. Kaya slipped her fingers over his flesh, feeling coolness and warmth at the same time. Her mouth closed on his nipple while she slid her hand down and cupped his erect shaft. Valik groaned as she caressed him. He grabbed her ass and held her to him as his lips sought her throat.

She waited for the bite, but it didn't come. Instead, he sucked on her skin and moved along to her shoulder—nipping harder each time with regular teeth. His fingers swept along her belly until he found her buried bud. She jumped when he touched her.

Kaya moved to claim his lips. She wanted this to last between them, but something primal had taken hold of her. She didn't fight it. She gazed into Valik's eyes and saw the same force driving him. Kaya tugged on his lip as their tongues touched. His fangs lowered as she ran her tongue along them. He caught it with one of his teeth.

He worked her clit faster until she moaned.

She was ready for him.

He picked her up and lay her down on their cloaks. His eyes glowed silver in the darkness. He fondled her breasts until her nipples hardened. He kissed her chest and then the hollow of her throat. Kaya moaned as she wrapped her legs around his waist. Valik slung her arms around his neck once more. He plunged inside of her as he sunk his fangs into her throat. Kaya held him to her as they moved together.

She cried out as he drank from her. She'd never experienced being with another Vyrkola.

"*Drink.*" He offered his throat to her and spoke through their bond.

Kaya dug her nails into his back as she was cresting fast toward an orgasm.

He knew how to make sure they were both enjoying one another.

She bit him and his blood flowed over her tongue. She closed her eyes and got lost in the beating of his heart as it thundered in her ears. The taste and the feel of him inside her and against her enthralled her. She swallowed his blood and surrendered to the pleasure.

When it was over, he held her tighter as though he never wanted to part. It made her want more of him, but it was over too fast because he broke away and groaned.

"I love you, Kaya. Never forget that," he whispered in her ear.

"You make it sound like this is goodbye."

"We don't know what forces we're dealing with—invoking all this ancient magic. In case something happens to me, I want you to know."

"Nothing's going to happen."

He kissed her again and separated from her. As they dressed, his silence made her regret the statement. She wound her fingers through his.

"We should go," he said.

"I've never been intimate with another of our kind. I didn't expect it to get so heated."

He smirked. "It can get frenzied. Sometimes the animal comes out in us. Next time will be slower and more fulfilling for you."

She felt her cheeks sear. "It was. I just mean…"

He touched her cheek. "I know what you mean. I felt your enjoyment. I loved having you against me."

He kissed her again slowly and ran his tongue over her lips. She closed her eyes and sunk into the moment, losing herself to the subtle way his body molded against hers. Again, it was over too quickly, and she was left wanting more.

Kaya opened her eyes and smiled at him.

He settled her cloak back over her shoulders, but she could still smell him on it and that calmed her nerves.

He put up his hood when he entered the living room.

It took a moment for her eyes to adjust. The energy felt stale and dead. No one had lived there for so long. This was where Valik had killed his wife and thrown off his humanity.

She shivered as he moved down into the darkness without any light. She walked behind him into tunnels she had never known existed before, connecting his dwelling to the rest of the Vyrk kingdom. There were so many things that she didn't know.

The feeling of the silver in the ground pressed upon her stronger than she'd ever experienced. It made the air heavier to breathe. The heavy concentration was something she hadn't felt before. She tripped over a rock protruding from the floor and fell into Valik.

He stumbled but caught her.

"Sorry," she murmured.

"It's okay. You don't know these passageways like you do the ones in the lower mountains. Silver is extremely concentrated here. I need to get out of here as quickly as we can. I had forgotten how bad it is. Take my hand." He held it out to her.

Kaya took it.

Valik led her through the darkness into narrow corridors she had to squeeze through. A few of them were partially caved in. They finally got to the bottom of the mountain shaft and came to a large stone door carved with symbols. Valik touched it but jerked his hand away. She smelled the burnt flesh. The symbols flashed silver.

"Kaya, I need you to open the crypt. The spells on the door only let royalty in. Since you're the queen's blood, it should open for you."

She approached the door. The energy of the magic hit her like a cold wave. This magic was old. Not as old as the power from the energy node, but close to it. She placed her hand on the stone. The sigils flashed gold and then silver. Gears ground in the wall and the massive door swung open. Candles popped to life. Inside was a large library with a woman poring over books and parchments.

The woman glanced up. Kaya gasped. Thesia was nothing more than a withered skeleton with flesh stretched over her bones and hollow eye sockets.

"Valik, look at you. So much has changed since the last time I saw you. Princess Kayanna, it's an honor to finally meet you."

"We've come seeking your help. The demon—"

"I know why you're here. I sensed the magic from the node you sealed flash through the mountains. It gave me the strength to rise before my time and enabled me to let you in. I've felt his call. The one who made us."

"Can you help us?" Kaya asked.

"Tribute first, young one, and then I will help you. I thirst. All who visit must pay the toll." She gestured to the silver chalice by the door.

Valik grabbed it and bit into his wrist. He let his blood flow into the cup, and then passed it to Kaya. She did the same, filling it until it was close to the brim. Thesia snatched it up and guzzled it down. She traced the insides with her finger to get every last bit of blood she could. Her skin plumped and hair sprouted from her bald head until it reached her shoulders. She ran her fingers over her face and then smiled.

"You both taste different. I expected the uniqueness

from you, Kaya. But Valik, you've been holding out on us. Not like those who got hit with the backlash of the spell. You made first contact and the magic is changing you again. You never truly died like we did."

Kaya asked. "How did you become as you are?"

"Do you want me to answer that, or do you want me to answer the questions you came to ask? I can do both, but more tribute is required."

Valik fished Eloise's spellbook from the satchel and placed it on the table. "We need answers."

Thesia touched the book and howled as she pulled her fingers away from the cover. They were seared black. "This was written in our creator's own hand. The demon's dark power lingers about its pages. How did you come by it?"

"It doesn't matter. I need to know how we can send the demon back to its hell once and for all and close the portal." Valik told her. "The book's written in an ancient dialect I can't make out. We need your help."

"Help, I can give, by reading the pages—but I can't touch them. Princess, would you mind?" Thesia gestured to the tome.

Kaya touched the cover and expected to be burned like Thesia, but nothing happened. "Why can Valik and I touch it, but you can't?"

"Because both of you are still alive. The dead can't lay hands upon it."

"Thesia, I've had no heartbeat since the time I was changed. Like you all, it only beats when I feed, and then it stops once the blood has been absorbed," Valik responded with a sigh.

"You can still perform magic, can't you? I smell it on you."

"Yes, but so can you. You choose the next queen. You were the first to rule," Valik replied.

Thesia laughed. "I lost my magic the same as the others. My sight—my ability to see things—has always been there. It isn't magic in the same sense. It didn't die with me the way magic does when a human becomes like us."

"What about the spell on the door? It's ancient magic." Kaya asked.

"After I saw the next ruler, I had those who remained in the order copy our most ancient and sacred texts and gather them to place in here so only the next-in-line could open the door. I saw this coming. You see, Kayanna, I knew all about you long before you were born. The spell on the door was placed before all of our magic faded and our thirst grew."

"Then you know how to kill the demon?" Valik asked. "There was no point for us to even bring you the book?"

"But there was. You want answers that can only be found in here. My sight is good, but it hasn't given me the vision of our demise. There are answers in this tome written by the queen's own hand before she was overtaken." She pointed to the spellbook and read aloud, "I write this as a record for those to come. It starts with me, but I see to the end.

"My husband thought he was saving me from the disease that ravages my body. But I was ready to drift into twilight to return to my ancestors and be reborn with Alerik when the time came.

"Now, I'm damned. My soul will not pass on to the

hallowed halls, and each day this dark presence grows stronger and my magic to fight it weakens. I write this tome so others will know never to listen to the dark whispers in the wood. The shadowed gods were banished for a reason. They had darker appetites than any of us knew. The gods of light were right to lock them away. The shadowed ones still hunger. I feel that hunger grow stronger in my veins every day. I feel the presence of the god awakening inside of me as I lose myself.

"Sometimes I see its dreams. It wants to free the other old ones. It remembers a time when they roamed free and feasted on the blood of the living until the light gods expelled them to their shadow realm. Men willingly gave the gods their bodies as vessels for their hunger. It dreams of that time again."

"Didn't you tell Alerik you were sent because an outbreak or something had occurred before and it took all of your order to end it?" Kaya asked Valik.

He nodded. "It was long ago. Our order was formed to keep an eye on magic in general. Thesia, you foretold the coming of the Vyrks, but this wasn't what you expected, was it?"

"Not exactly. Turn the page, please."

She skimmed a few more and gestured for Kaya to keep going.

"She goes on about losing herself and how the demon awakened and how she can hear it. Ahh...here we are...'It thinks I'm too weak to resist. It vies for a place in my body. But I have power enough to keep it from taking over. It doesn't know I am witness to its dreams. It has gained knowledge from me and devised a way to free itself and to create a being perfect to do its bidding. So grotesque. This abomination would be born from death and magic with a sacrifice made. Blood and soul to give the evil life. He knows it will be the key to their freedom. When I look back over these pages, I find it's written in them as well. Spells and ramblings about the future. He can't use my sight, but he eats up my magic.'

"'I don't go into detail about what I see because I know he will read it. I've spun the strongest of my magic into my message so the dead won't be able to get to it and I've mixed the ink—and lined the pages that matter—with silver so it will be blinded to the things I write there. When it is free to walk among men, I pray my words find those who can defeat it.'"

Thesia looked up from the book. "That is all she wrote. The rest are incantations penned by the demon, and I don't dare read them for I don't want what it would unleash."

"There has to be something else." Kaya thumbed through the chronicle.

Thesia caught her hand. "There's nothing else written by the queen. What is left was put down by the dark one."

"Valik, you said Eloise told you the answer was in the book. But you needed Thesia to read it."

"That's what she said." Valik sank into a chair.

Someone banged on the door trying to get in.

Valik shot up and drew his sword.

"He knows you're here. He can't enter because of the silver." Thesia winced. "He's trying to take over my mind and find out what I know."

Kaya flipped to the back of the book and noticed a

loose corner on the end-paper. She tugged on it until it came free, revealing a small envelope with a wax seal.

She opened the letter.

Thesia moaned. "It's written with silver in the ink. This must have been what Eloise meant about keeping things from him. Valik, can you read it?"

He looked at it. Thesia guarded her eyes from the parchment. The banging on the door grew louder. Bits of stone fell from the ceiling. Valik looked away a few times and grunted.

"I can read it. It's written in the common tongue of the time, not what the journal was written in. It hurts to look at it. But I can read it."

Shouting erupted outside and the seals on the doors cracked. The magic that held them shut was waning.

"Quickly, take the book and get out of here. The demon's sided with the Thralls. They have invaded our mountain. He knows you're here. I can feel him pressing on my mind. The magic on the doors won't hold for much longer. The Thralls have their own *varaz*. The order is your only refuge. They can help you. You're what he wants, Kayanna, but he knows if he hurts Valik, he will hurt you." Thesia embraced her in quick, strong hug. "I can't see past the darkness that looms over the land, but a sacrifice will have to be made."

"Where is the order now?" Valik asked.

"On the other side of the mountains, where our kind can't walk."

"How do we get there?" Kaya asked.

Valik shoved the book back into his satchel. More pebbles rained down from above.

Thesia pressed a stone next to the large fireplace. "This leads to my sleeping chamber. You'll find a map from the old days with a few updates. Stick to the tunnels where the silver runs strongest. It will block his sight of you. Stay on the ground. Do not fly."

Valik embraced her. "Thank you, Thesia."

She brushed her lips across his cheek. Valik stiffened, then pulled away.

He nodded and grabbed Kaya's hand. "We have to go."

The door cracked as the magic that had held it shut faded away. Thesia gestured toward the door to her chamber. "I'll buy you what time I can, but you must hurry."

Valik nodded as they slipped into the darkness. Gears turned, and the door shut, locking them in the passageway.

"What did she say to you?" Kaya asked.

"There's a reason she couldn't see beyond the darkness. Come on." They reached the end of the hallway to the chamber.

Valik gave her a minute to rest.

A map lay on Thesia's bed. It looked old, but notes had been made around the edges. Valik tucked it into his breast pocket and motioned Kaya to slip behind the tapestries. As they entered another corridor, a piercing scream and a loud whoosh of dust raced along the tunnel behind them.

They ran until she grabbed Valik's arm, barely able to breathe, and gasped. "Stop. Have to stop." The air was hot and thin. She bent over to get more oxygen. "Where is the map leading us?"

Valik pulled it out. He waved his hand and a small flame appeared in the palm of his other hand so they could see. "We keep following this tunnel along a heavy vein of silver. The demon won't be able to track us. It'll bring us out to the other side of the mountain range. We have to keep moving. Are you going to be okay?"

"I don't have a choice. I'm stuck down here until we can get out. I'm good. Let's go."

Valik extinguished the light and they kept on walking through the darkness into parts unknown.

CHAPTER TWENTY-TWO

Valik lost track of all time in the dark. He stopped often because Kaya lagged behind. The longer it took them to get through the mountain, the more worried about her he was. They had no water or supplies. There was no blood to be had and neither of them could spare any, so drinking from one another was out of the question. The longer they were underground, the more he realized that something was happening to him from the blast of power from the node. He first noticed it as an itch in the back of his throat, and then it went dry.

He assumed it was a need for blood, but as they got closer to the rushing sound of an underground stream, he realized he thirsted for water. His lips were cracked, and his throat ached. His stomach felt uncomfortable as well. His night vision wasn't as strong as it had been. The little changes made him wonder exactly what the magic was doing to him. He felt a bit warmer, but he still didn't have a heartbeat he could discern. His magic increased. It swam under his skin, waiting for him to use it. It was an odd sensation. It made him feel more alive.

He studied the map as he listened to the water. It was getting closer with each step. The tunnels were narrower than he liked. They had to squeeze through some and crawl in others.

This was another slim passage. "How are you doing?" he called back over his shoulder.

"I'll be fine. I just need to get to that water."

"I know. We're almost there. A little bit further. When we get there, we'll rest."

"Okay."

They went on in silence except for the echoes of their footsteps and the rushing of the water that led them forward. Finally, the tunnel opened into a cavern large enough it could have fit Stavros's entire palace into it. A waterfall cascaded down at least a hundred feet into a pool below. Beams of moonlight coming from overhead reflected off gems and other minerals in the water, giving them some dim light.

All he could see, however, was the silver. It stung his eyes—but he could look upon it.

Kaya gasped. "What is this place?"

"The heart of the mountain, I think. I've never been this far myself, so I don't exactly know. These passageways are older than anything I've ever seen."

Kaya bent down and took in a few mouthfuls of water.

He knelt beside her and realized she was crying. He pulled her into his arms and held her. "It's going to be okay."

"All of this is because of me. We wouldn't be here if...."

He smoothed the hair from her face and kissed her forehead. "Hush, love. It's not your fault. It's a beguiling creature. You didn't know. Thesia was strong with her visions even when she was still human. She saw this was going to happen."

"She saw her own death. She told me a sacrifice had to happen. You can't read the letter and I don't understand it. We need to get to the order."

He held her to him and inhaled her scent. How could he tell her she had allowed him to love again after all this time? The anger that used to consume him no longer raged inside. She had tamed the monster. Valik would do anything to keep her safe.

"Sometimes things happen for a reason we cannot see. I don't understand that part of it, but you mean something to me. I love you, Kaya. I haven't said that to anyone in a very long time. I'd nearly forgotten what it felt like to be even remotely human and you've given me that gift." He kissed her lightly, savoring her sweetness.

"You mean that?"

"You know I do. How about you try and get some sleep? We've been going on little for days and I know you need it."

"What about you?"

"I'll be fine. Just close your eyes."

Kaya snuggled into his arms.

He hummed a tune he hadn't thought about in eons— one that he used to sing to his daughter.

Soon Kaya's breathing evened out, and she fell into a deep sleep.

The waterfall above them sprayed him with mist as he

lay her down on the stone floor and peered into the pool below. Fish swam toward the surface. It gave him an idea. He used a bit more of his magic and threw the flame from his hand onto a small pile of stones. Valik grabbed a fish and laid it out on one of the stones. He caught several more so they would have something to eat.

While Kaya slept, he pulled out the letter Eloise had written once more and trailed his fingers over the parchment. It still hurt to look at it, but at least he could read it better and understand it:

To the one reading this,

I don't know your name, but I know you are like him and yet you are different.
　　　You've set your life to killing the beast that would set our demonic father free
　　　along with the rest of his shadowed gods.

You seek to put him back where he came from and seal the portal for good. I
　　　write this in my last moments of control. Every day he takes more magic,
　　　and I feel myself grow thin. Blood must be shed to close the portal for good. It's
　　　not a normal blood sacrifice. The magic is older than anything you know. Once
　　　you know the words the rest will come to you.

. . .

There were more words recounting her thoughts about what might come, but he stuffed the letter back into his pocket.

The fish smelled too good and his mouth watered. He plucked it from the hot coals and dug into it. When he'd eaten the whole thing, he realized he wanted more. By the time Kaya woke up, he had consumed two more and prepared her a couple. He was cooking more so they could take some food with them.

"These are good."

"Yes, they were."

Her eyes widened as she licked her fingers. "You ate some? You don't eat."

"It appears I do now."

"Is this a result from being hit with the magic from the node?"

"Maybe. I don't know. I feel stronger. My night vision is not as sharp as it used to be, but I can feel the power inside of me and the energy around me. I don't know if it's from your blood or if it's a combination of everything working together. Now that you've rested, do you think you're ready to move on?"

"Yes, I think so."

"Good. Then we should get moving." Valik threw the rocks back into the water, along with the fish remains.

They crossed the pool and found a trail that led behind the waterfall. They walked uphill in water for hours until they came to a fork in the tunnel offering them the choice of one of three ways.

"Which way?" Kaya asked.

He took out the map again and studied it. As he did, he saw the silver vein veered off to the left. "This way. Thesia said to follow the silver."

They stayed with the silver line. Their climb upward got steeper and the passageway smaller until they were crawling. They were on their hands and knees for several more hours. The air was thick and hot. Finally, a pinpoint of light could be seen. He crept toward it until they emerged from the mountain. He squinted against the brightness of the sun, but it also didn't burn him. Valik held out his hand and let the sun warm his flesh.

Kaya laughed and slipped her fingers through his. The sun bounced off her hair and the smudges of dirt on her face. They both needed a bath, but they still had a way to go if they were going on foot. Looking down at the valley below, he saw they had to climb down and then cross the grasslands, as they had come to the other side of the mountain range.

"We're finally out," she said happily.

"Yes, but we still have a way to go. It looks like there's a path down—or what used to be one. It'll be slow going."

"Screw the path. I need to stretch my wings."

Before Valik could remind her of Thesia's warning, Kaya jumped up and let herself fall off the ledge. He shook his head and let his form shift as he fell too, and his own wings took hold. It felt good to be free of his human shape. Even as he flapped his wings to catch up to her, he heard the screeching.

Valik found a swarm of bats attacking Kaya. They were the largest bats he had ever seen.

He dove faster, stretched out his talons, and caught

one. He ripped the head off the bat and tasted the dark taint in its blood. These were no ordinary beasts. They were parts of the demon, which meant it was growing stronger. He fought his way through the cloud toward Kaya. They massed around him as the demonic influence pressed upon his mind. Valik fought the darkness. When he emerged from the cloud, three bats carrying a limp form hovered in the distance.

"Come after me and I drop her," it warned him mentally.

"You need her," he replied the same way. He flew toward her.

Two of the bats released her and the third sunk under Kaya's weight. They spiraled toward the valley floor. Valik couldn't see his love die.

If the demon could sacrifice her, then he was calling his bluff. Valik winged back upward, and the bats rushed down to grab her. As they did, they merged into one large dark creature. The demon laughed within his mind, but Valik swore he heard it echoing off the mountain walls.

"She's mine. Come after her and you die."

The dark entity completely enveloped Kaya and flew off.

His heart sank. If he went after her, then the demon would drop her. The only thing he could do now was continue on to the order and pray they would help him. He dove down to the valley floor and took refuge in the shadows. The coolness helped him think and gave him a chance to study the map further.

He understood Thesia's warning now about sticking to the path. In the air there was no silver to ward off the demon. He should have stopped Kaya. He kicked himself for that, but even though he knew the demon wanted Kaya alive, he couldn't risk it hurting her. His only hope of rescuing her was getting to the order and having them look at Eloise's spellbook to decipher the entries so they could send the demon back to its realm and close the portal it came through for good. According to the map, he had only a little way to go to the forest he could see in the distance. The map didn't show exactly where the order was, but they would find him. The need to get to the order and their help outweighed Thesia's warning. He needed to find the way to get Kaya back and overthrow the demon. Valik folded the parchment back into his pocket and became the eagle once more. It was the fastest way to get to the forest.

Valik flew to the edge of the forest just as the sun began setting. The coming darkness brought him renewed strength. He felt more like his old self as the shadows lengthened, without the gnawing hunger for human food or water—although, to some extent, that remained. His blood hunger had risen, but he shoved it down. Trees towered above him. This was an old forest that had seen many years and great magic. The power flowing under the ground nearly knocked him backward. The grass, and even the very air, seemed alive.

The very opposite of the Bone Forest.

He touched the bark of one of the large oak trees and pulled his hand back. His palm smoked from where he had touched the tree.

"You're not wanted here, Vyrkola. Go back into the mountain," a voice boomed from somewhere in the forest.

"I've come here looking for the Sacred Order. I need their help," Valik responded, gazing up into the trees.

"What do your kind need from the Sacred Order? The soulless do not enter this place," another voice, older, came from somewhere else.

Soulless. They think that because Vyrks can't wield magic we have no souls. I know now that's not true.

"If I were soulless, could I do this?" He summoned the same fire he had conjured in the cave. This time he drew on all his energy and threw a fireball at the nearest tree.

The tree didn't burn. The flame shot up into the sky like a column of air.

Someone landed next to the tree—a man with silver hair and piercing blue eyes with a silver tint to the irises. A half dozen others came out from behind the trees to look upon him. Most of them wore hooded robes, but he could see the glow of silver from their eyes. A few of the sun's remaining rays wove through the trees and bathed Valik in their light. Those who had come from the trees gasped.

"I need your help. The order I remember would never turn anyone away in a time of need. I know a lot has changed over the years, but this?"

"You're Valik."

"I am."

"Don't trust him, Ineth. He's one of them."

"And yet he wields magic and is walking directly in the light. No other Vyrks can use magic," Ineth said to the younger *varaz*. He turned back to Valik. "We know who you are. We've had our eye on you and the princess for many years."

"Kaya found out about Adran," Valik told them.

"Where is he?"

"Can we speak about this somewhere else? The demon could have spies everywhere." Valik gestured behind him and toward the forest.

The younger *varaz* laughed. "Nothing with the taint of evil or death can enter here. Why do you think your kind can't come in?"

"Enough," Ineth snapped. "Come this way, but understand you will not be alone while you're with us."

Valik sighed. "I understand, but I have one request. I must feed. Animal blood will suffice, but I will need more of it. Trying to save the princess has drained my strength."

"We will meet your needs, but you must be blindfolded." Ineth formed a strip of magic from thin air and wove it into a blindfold. He tied it around Valik's eyes, and he could see nothing. "Take my arm."

The others grumbled, but they said nothing else as they walked through the forest.

Valik could feel the life teeming around him, along with the magic. He didn't need his sight in order to see the outlines of the trees with the magic coursing through them, or to gauge how they spread deep into the earth. They all glowed silver from the magic racing within them. The air was saturated with it. The power sat on his tongue. In its own way, it strengthened him and eased the hunger within.

The heartbeats of those around him gave him an idea of how many surrounded him in the wood. Some were against bringing him back to wherever it was they were taking him.

Finally, they entered a building of some sort. The

doors echoed as they closed behind them. Stone made up the floor beneath him but that didn't stop him from being able to see the magic.

They led him through another door and into a room where they sat him down. The blindfold was removed. They were in a large hall with benches on all sides and five chairs on a platform. He sat in the middle of the room. Doors opened on all sides and more *varaz* filed in. They crammed together to fit in the seats, with others standing. If he said the wrong thing, he wasn't walking out of here.

This felt like he was being put on trial more than anything else. Still, the sight of all the *varaz* made him happy, because the order had grown considerably since the days when he was involved with it.

The council assembled on the platform and Ineth took the center seat. "I gathered you all together, brothers and sisters, because we have been asked for help by this creature who was once counted among our ranks."

"Why is the Vyrkola here?" someone asked.

"How is it he can walk within these woods? I thought we were protected from their kind," another shouted.

Murmurs spread through the crowd.

Valik didn't need to guess what an angry mob sounded like. He had seen many of them, but the questions posed made him wonder what the order had been dealing with when it came to others of his kind.

Ineth raised his hand to silence the assembly.

"We all have questions about why this creature is here. I'm sure he'll answer them all to the best of his ability. He came asking for our help. Rise, Valik, and address the order," Ineth said to him.

Valik looked around the room. The eyes on him were filled with both hatred and wonder. "You have me at a loss —you know my name, but I don't know many of you. Let me first say it's wonderful to see the order has so many members. In my day, we were stretched thin. It was difficult to fulfill the requests we had from other kingdoms."

"What do you know of the order, monster?" someone snapped.

"Enough. Let him speak," Ineth answered calmly.

"You're right. Many of the Vyrkola are monsters. On the other hand, many of them are the kindest souls I've ever known. I know from firsthand experience my kind are descended from darkness, because I was there when we were created. I was the *varaz* assigned by the order to seal the magical node because it had been tainted by the demon.

"King Alerik and I closed the node. However the demon interfered with the spell at the final second. As I said the last words, the wild magic from the node moved through the energy coming from the well. Its intrusion changed the magic of the spell. The magical energy backlashed. It hit me first and turned me into what you see before you. This tainted energy traveled back to those in the mountain along the silver lines and changed those who were monitoring the node into the first true Vyrkola. I went back there and discovered what had happened. The demon was trapped in the castle ruins and the forest was turned to bone. Now the creature has been released once more and needs the Vyrkola princess to free its brethren from their realm."

He reached into his satchel and pulled out the book

Eloise had given him. "This is the journal and spellbook written by Queen Eloise and the demon combined."

"Where did you get that?" Ineth asked.

"Princess Kayanna and I returned to the ruins to see if we could summon the queen from the twilight realm. Adran came with us and helped. We discovered the capstone cracked and the power from the magical well-spring swelling out of control. It took all three of us to close it."

"What happened to Adran?" A young woman who resembled him stepped forward.

"The spell proved to be too much for him. He died casting it. Kaya was almost taken too, but I helped stabilize her. The magic rebounded and did something to me. The node was sealed for good and the ruins destroyed."

The young woman burst into tears and swayed on her feet. A man next to her caught her and led her from the room. Valik looked at Ineth for some clarification.

"Adran's younger sister. What is it that you need from us?" Ineth asked.

"I need to know how to send the demon back to its realm and seal the portal. I pledged my life to stopping the entity. Now it has the princess."

It hit him in a rush. They were his last hope. He didn't know where else to turn and he only had a little time left. Valik felt his eyes burn with tears and fell to his knees before them.

"Please, no matter how much you hate my kind, I beg you, help me. If the demon releases his kin, it will spread his darkness everywhere it touches. The princess is innocent in this. I have nowhere else to go. The order was once my life and now I need its assistance." He felt the tears fall as he looked up at then.

Emotions flickered across Ineth's face.

Valik prayed the result was in his favor. The gallery talked among themselves. The silence that gradually spread through them made his heart drop. He had no idea where the demon had taken Kaya. He should be able to find her through their blood tie, but he couldn't feel her because the demon was too powerful.

One of the younger members of the order whispered something in the leader's ear. Ineth looked to Valik and then back at the man.

Something has happened.

"We will help you, Valik. Come with me."

Valik rose to follow the leader into a hallway behind the platform. He wiped his eyes. His fingers weren't stained red from blood tears; they were clear. He kept the amazement to himself and kept stride with Ineth. "Thank you."

"I'm not sure you're going to thank me when you find out what has happened to those in the mountain. The demon has destroyed all those who dwelled in the mountain kingdom."

Valik froze as the weight of the news hit him. All of those innocents slain because he had gone there for help. Half or more of his people had been wiped out.

Ineth gripped his shoulder. "It's not your fault."

The same words he had said to Kaya. "I'm not so sure of that."

He prayed that the Vyrkola now visiting Stavros's castle had been spared. He had to shut out all of that and focus on finding Kaya. "The good of the many," as he told her when she was mourning for Adran.

They stopped in a circular room open to the sky with a large well in the center of it. Carved into the stones were symbols he recognized. They had been on the seal he used back at the ruins ages ago, but there were also symbols to direct power and to keep the power contained within.

"I'm sorry to hear about the others in the mountain," Ineth offered. "Your family."

Valik glanced at him. "They were never my family. When I realized what happened all those long years ago, I took my vow I wouldn't let the demon get out. I stayed close to the queens and watched over them to insure it. I became a warrior and hid my magic because I was the only one among us who could do it. I've lived with the guilt of killing my wife by putting this life behind me. Luckily my daughter escaped my thirst and lived her life. Others in the mountain took over the leadership. I suggested the name of the new race that was created, and then I slipped into the background of history and let the years pass me by, learning all I could of fighting styles from the lands I traveled."

"How old are you?" Ineth inquired.

Valik sunk into the chair the leader offered. For the first time the weight of his long life came down on his shoulders.

Someone came in and set a goblet down in front of him. He smelled the blood. It was human. He nodded thanks at the servant. Ineth watched him. Valik took the large goblet in hand and sniffed it again, checking to see if there was any taint to it.

"It hasn't been poisoned. You and I are on the same side when it comes to ridding this world of the demon and sending it back to the hell it came from. We were alerted to its release and have been fortifying this place in case it came here. Everyone in the other room donated a little blood. It was...it was felt that it was the least we could do."

"My thanks to you all."

Valik sipped at the goblet and then drained it. He could taste the many lives put into the chalice. Each drop renewed his strength and satiated the beast within. With his hunger satisfied, he could feel the magic rush through him from ingesting the blood. But there was more to it. Even as he drank the blood, something in him felt odd.

"What is it?"

"I'm not sure. When I assisted Kaya with her spell, an errant magical bolt hit me. I'm not as I used to be. I can't fully explain it, but that's what happens with wild magic. I see you have the symbols here to seal and control the magic you pull from this node."

Ineth looked over to the well. "We had no choice. This enclave of the order goes back over ten thousand years. Were you ever here when you were human?"

"No. I didn't know there was a stronghold on the other side of the mountains."

"Thesia suggested we build something here in case of future need. It was a small settlement at first. She foresaw a great disaster in the south and a great miracle in the north. Not many understood what she meant." Ineth ran a hand through his beard. "You don't know how long I've wanted to talk to you, Valik. I've had so many questions. Thesia was my friend. I visited with her often before she became what she was. When we both became what we are."

"What you are?" Valik was confused by the man's speech.

Ineth flicked his hand. The sounds of the locks clicking on the doors echoed in the room. He unbuttoned his shirt and showed Valik a silver mark on his chest like a burned-out star.

"This is what happened to me when I was monitoring this well that day. You knew there was a magical node in the mountains which was why the order was headquartered there, but Thesia instructed me to follow the line of power. 'Follow the silver,' she said. It was a couple of years before the order sent you to Alerik. I followed that vein of silver through the mountains to this place."

"You built the tunnels."

"Yes. I came to the waterfall. It was more difficult to get through the rock after the cavern, but I kept on going. In some places you had to crawl, as you discovered. It took months to dig through using just my abilities, but I always had more of an affinity with earth magic. It was here, in this place, that I found the end of the silver line. The magic of the node goes a little further north, but it's only a trickle. It flows strongest in the mountains and at the ruins. A village had grown up around it here. They had no *varaz*, so I became their wizard. When I had my last visit with Thesia, she insisted I bring an apprentice back here with me. After you and Alerik did the spell, the energy rode the silver and hit those in the mountains, then it came here.

"It grew stronger as it spread along the silver. By the time it reached this place, the demonic taint had been cleansed. The order sent word for me and my apprentice to monitor the node here. They didn't give me any specific details, just to watch it during certain dark moon phases. I tried to contain the power from your spell with Alerik, but it hit us hard. We wrestled with it and got the magic to flare out along the silver lines in the ground."

"It went into the trees," Valik murmured as he listened to Ineth's tale. He'd had no idea the magic he'd done so long ago had rebounded this far north.

"Yes, it blew lines all along the forest until the whole place became a repository of magic. You felt it in the air. The magic was so hot it melted the silver and bonded with it. The trees have silver flowing through their veins. That's why no Vyrk can set foot here. It's been a haven for those who've been tortured by them over the years. When that magic hit me, I was imbued with the same longevity the trees possess. The same silver—and power—flows through my veins."

"This whole forest is living silver?" Valik asked.

"Yes. If you cut the trees, they bleed silver, and it hardens into metal. It's the strangest phenomenon I've ever seen. Or, it *was*, until I saw what Thesia had become. She warned me you would be the doom of the order."

"I didn't come here to bring doom to the order. I thought the order was all but dead until Adran said he was sent to keep an eye on Kaya and teach her how to handle her magic. I know I came here out of the blue. Kaya's in trouble and I'm sitting here getting a history lesson." He pounded his hand on the table and the chalice fell over. He took a deep breath. "I'm sorry."

"It's quite understandable. I wanted you to understand

the history of what happened to the order here and how your actions led to more than just the creation of the Vyrks. The children I had, and the ones down through the generations, carry the same powers within them as I do. Although, later generations are not as long lived as I am. They still age slower than even a normal *varaz*." Ineth flicked his wrist one more time and the doors unlocked. "Now it's time to take a look at your book."

"It's written in an ancient dialect. That's why I went back to Thesia. What Eloise said didn't make any sense."

"You spoke with Queen Eloise?" A female voice said behind him, as a new woman entered the room.

Ineth bowed his head in respect to the woman. It appeared Valik had been wrong, and this was the leader of the order, not the older man.

"Yes. Adran and Kaya summoned her back from twilight. Her spirit lingered in the crypt," Valik said, rising to his feet as the woman approached the table.

She was dressed in a dark green robe. Her black hair tumbled down her back in various lengths of braids. The power flowed from her in waves. She was strong when it came to magic. Her dark blue eyes were laced with silver.

There was something familiar about her. He couldn't place it.

She gazed at him, and her eyes seemed to hold questions. "What did she tell you?"

"Her spirit said twilight would come before the darkness was sealed away. For the darkness to be banished, twilight had to be cast upon the earth. Thesia couldn't find anything in the book, but...." He pulled the letter Kaya had found from his pocket and held it out to them. "This letter seems to be addressed to me. It was hidden away so the demon wouldn't find it. The ink is laced with silver so a normal Vyrk couldn't read it. I have trouble with the glare, but I can read it.

"Thesia couldn't touch it. She said no other Vyrk could. Only those that were somehow still partially alive. I suspect Eloise spun the spells to keep it out of the hands of the demon. I don't know. The letter said blood has to be spilled, but it's not a normal blood spell. Once I knew the words, then I would know what to do."

The woman took the book and the letter from him. She flipped through the spellbook until she stopped on a page about halfway through. "This passage is not written by the queen, but by the demon. The hand is different, and the energy is darker."

Valik looked over her shoulder. The words made no sense to him. The lines blurred on the page and rearranged. "I can't read it."

"I can," she said.

CHAPTER TWENTY-THREE

K aya opened her eyes and found herself laying on a bed. The stench of decay hung in the air. The room was dark, but the moonlight streaming into the room gave her enough light to see. The whole room had seen better centuries. Things scuttled around the room and remained in the shadows. She sat up and found her head spun a little. Something rustled in the corner like leaves skittering across the floor. She turned her attention to it. Her gaze settled on a man sitting in a chair.

Her blood turned to ice. She backed up as far as she could against the moldy headboard.

"There is no need to fear me. You are the one I've been waiting on for such a very long time. I have no intention of harming you."

The demon wore the face of Chancellor Kewskin, but its features were off—the smile too big; the eyes lit with an unearthly light.

"You used me to get free!" Kaya said. "You want to use

me again to open the gate and bring the others from your world here. I won't have any part of it."

The demon chuckled. "You're the key I've needed and dreamed about since I took form in Eloise. Alerik only took a part of me from that well. It took time for me to grow into her shell. I learned many things while snacking on her soul. The forming of an entire race was not brought about by accident. Nor was its destruction."

"What are you talking about?" Her heart sank as he said those words. *It can't be true. I would know if they were all dead.*

"Right. You don't know. The Thralls had a hell of a time plunging stakes through all those in the mountain. They were willing to allow me in for the ride. They've been very useful, even if their magicians aren't that powerful. They can perform a few tricks, but nothing like Kewskin and Eloise. I learned so much from her. It was a waste what happened. I only wish she had stayed with me till the end."

"How could you have gotten into the mountain with all that silver?" Kaya asked.

The demon gave her an abnormally large grin. "That's the beauty of possessing someone. I was deeply rooted within the wizard and, with a few enchantments from Kewskin, the silver didn't bother me as long as I didn't touch it. You, sweet princess, have a strong resistance to silver, a wonderful gift. One I plan to use to my advantage." The demon glided his fingers over her cheek. She pulled away and tried not to feel sick.

"I won't have anything to do with you. I'll kill myself first."

"If you take your life, then you'll rise again as a true Vyrkola. You'll be useful to me either way. Kill yourself. I won't stop you."

"What did you do to my mother? To the others at the palace?" Her thoughts moved to Stavros and how she didn't want to lose him either.

"Your mother lives—as do the others at Stavros's court...for now. I didn't want to take the queen's life just yet. I knew it would be too much of a blow for you to lose all of your kind at once. I promise if you do as I say, I won't kill them or your beloved Stavros."

Her heart fell. "What did you do to him?"

The demon waved his hand. A dark window appeared between the two of them. She could smell sulfur and feel the heat of flames through the window. Stavros dangled above the flames, with his feet barely touching a ledge projecting into them. He seemed unconscious which was a blessing. "He's my prisoner for now, in a place only I can get to—thanks to Kewskin. He was a good student of other worlds and realities. Of course, others have helped me more than he did."

"Who?"

The demon waved his hand and the window disappeared. He held up his finger and wagged it at her as though he was disciplining a naughty child. "I'm not going to put all of my cards on the table. Did you think I would tell you everything at our first meeting? Maybe after we get to know one another a little bit better. Once we've consummated our relationship, *then* I might let your little king go."

"What are you going to do to me?" she whispered. She

couldn't even think about being physical with the monster before her.

The demon grabbed her head. Kaya screamed, which only made his grin larger.

"Your fear tastes good. Better than all the others in your mountain put together. It's made me strong, but not strong enough to open the portal by myself. I want to know what makes you tick. Why only you can open the gateway." Black spikes that resembled fangs stretched from his maw.

"Stay away from me," she whimpered.

"No. No, dear. You're mine. You were made for me alone. Always remember that." He plunged his teeth into her throat.

Frigid pain entered her neck.

Kaya fought against him, but he was stronger than she was. The cold spread throughout her body. Something gritty rooted around in her mind. She pushed against the demon, but her fingers slid through the shadowy substance making up the creature.

"How can you hold onto something made up of shadow and nightmares?" taunted his voice inside of her head.

She could feel the gritty evil in her mind as he tried to get to the bottom of her soul.

Kaya struggled harder against him and found he was no longer in front of her. Something moved inside of her. It hurt like her insides were being scraped out and something else was being poured in. She felt crowded and knew the demon had somehow crammed itself into her body to share her flesh.

She glanced around for something that would get the

demon out of her body. The only thing she had was Alerik's silver ring.

Kaya grabbed the silver and felt it burn her palm from the demon's influence. She let her fangs grow and sunk them deep into her palm. When she tasted her blood, it was poisoned. She gripped the ring and tried to bring it to the open wound, but she couldn't move her hand. She pitted her will against the demon. She had a soul. It didn't.

"It won't happen, princess." The words came from her own throat in a guttural voice.

She could hear them, but she didn't have control over her body. Instead of moving her hand, she found herself looking through a small window in a thick door with the demon on the other side. It had trapped her in her own mind. Kaya pounded against the door in her mind and tried to throw herself out of a window in the imaginary mental room. A dark shadow appeared, and she bounced off of it onto the bed once more.

"Let me out!" Kaya screamed.

"I don't think so. You will do what I want you to do. You're staying in this room."

Kaya concentrated as she could feel the demon rooting around in her brain. He couldn't find certain memories. Trunks materialized in her room. She thought about other things. More chests appeared.

The demon screamed and pounded against the door.

"What are you keeping from me?"

"Nothing you need to know. You might be able to lock me up and take control of my body, but you're not going to know about the things in here."

"You bitch."

Kaya smiled. The demon rattled the doorknob. She didn't know how long she could keep him out. *Valik will come and save me. He has to. I have to hold out until then.*

That hope, along with the power of her anger, fueled her to keep the door shut. The demon banged until it nearly drove her mad, but it finally quieted. Kaya focused her strength and kept calm the best she could, hoping she could find a way of purging the demon from her body.

CHAPTER TWENTY-FOUR

Valik stared at the woman as she flipped through the spellbook. She sat at the end of the table and gestured for him to sit beside her.

"How is it you are able to read that?" he asked her, sinking into the offered seat.

She glanced up at him. "The demon's writing is meant for one of its own kind. It's not written in silver and the darkness coming off it is something I can understand."

"You don't feel like a demon."

The woman's eyes darkened until they were completely black. Black veins threaded through her pale skin. Her fingers sharpened into talons. "You think you know everything, Valik. You know nothing." Her voice grew deeper and gravelly. She balled her hands into fists and pulled the power back inside of her.

"Cyn, was that necessary?" Ineth asked.

She glanced at him. He laid a hand on her arm. Her eyes flashed sliver and she shook as though the silver within him had a calming effect on her. "He needed to know that there is more here."

"What are you talking about? Are you another product of the spell that went wrong who blames me?" Valik ground his teeth together. Kaya was in danger, and this delay infuriated him. When he reached out along their bond, he couldn't feel her and that twisted his guts into a fury he hadn't encountered in a long time.

"Peace, Valik," Ineth said. "There's no blame here. Cyn, why don't you please just translate what's in the book? I'm sure Valik would like to rest."

"You're right, Ineth." She took a deep breath and then turned to Valik. "The demon speaks about the magic he's learned from Eloise and how he wishes to be reunited with his kind. He yearns for the darkness to spread once more like back in the days when they roamed the land before their portal was closed. The people then called them the Shadowed Gods."

"How can I save Kaya?" Valik asked.

Cyn raised her hand. "Let me finish. The book is written by three different people. You might've been able to read what Eloise had written, but another hand, worked through her, you can't see because it's written in pure silver. Even the demon couldn't see it. This book is worth its weight in gold."

"Whose is the other hand?" Valik asked.

"It's written in response to Eloise's pleas to send her a way to rid herself of the demon. She called to the old gods she worshipped—those who were around when the shadowed ones also roamed the land. One of them answered. I have a feeling that was one of the reasons she was able to write this letter to you and weave some of her magic into the enchantments to keep the demon trapped for so long. That's just speculation. Sorry, I'm getting ahead of myself.

"The gods answered Eloise. This god writes that Eloise has always been a devoted servant, along with her entire family line. They go on to talk about the first time they drove the demons into the darkness. How one *varaz* had to channel the god into themselves so they could take on physical form. That sorcerer started the order, and when the god left the *varaz*, the knowledge remained, along with the pledge to drive the darkness back into the underworld if it arose again. That's why the order originally sent you to monitor Alerik. The god wrote a spell to summon one of his kind in case the need arose again. It was only to be used in dire circumstances—and it's a little odd."

"Why do you say that?" Valik asked.

"Because it calls for one of mixed blood," Cyn said. "It's a blood spell, as Eloise said in her letter to you. Ineth, pen and ink please."

Ineth got up to get her the things she asked for.

Valik looked over the pages, and all he saw were the writings from Eloise. "How are you seeing both writings?"

Cyn took his hand and ran it over the spaces between Eloise's words. "Do you feel the power in the words?"

He closed his eyes, and he could feel the heat coming off the pages.

"Yes, I feel it—but I can't see the words. It's a different feeling than either the darkness or Eloise's magic. I wasn't able to detect it before."

"That's because you didn't know what to look for. The

silver and the power behind it would probably burn your eyes."

Ineth returned with the pen and ink. Cyn wrote down the hidden spell written on the last pages. When she was done, she handed it to Valik.

He scanned the enchantment. He needed to call upon a deity of light. Most of the old gods were no longer worshipped at all, or they had become something else as the times changed. *Maybe that is what happened with this one.*

The wording called for a being of mixed origin to fight the demon.

"Thank you for this. I don't know what else to say. Forgive me if I jumped down your throat." Valik slipped the spell into his vest pocket. He reached for the book.

Cyn flipped to another page that looked blank. "This is a word of warning. Before you run off and do this spell."

"I can deal with the consequences. If I can get to Kaya and free her; reverse the damage I've done, then that's what I'm going to do."

"I understand that, but the god warns that when called upon, he will do all he can to wipe out the demon's influence completely. It could kill you and all the other Vyrks you created. I don't know what it would do to Kaya since she is only half Vyrk."

"Are you afraid it could come after you, too?" Valik asked Cyn.

"It could, and I can deal with it in my own way. That's all the book has to offer. I'm sorry there's nothing else."

"Valik, I can show you to your room to rest," Ineth said.

"It's all right, Ineth," interrupted Cyn. "I'll do it. There are some other things I want to talk to him about. Follow me."

Valik gathered up the book and slipped it back into his satchel.

Ineth gave her a look, but he didn't say anything.

Cyn rose and Valik followed her out of the room. They walked down a long corridor and up a flight of stairs. He could feel the magic that traveled in the walls, as the stone was also infused with the magic of the land. It was stronger when Cyn opened a door and stepped in.

A wave of energy washed over him. Cyn held the door open for him.

"Am I expected to sleep in here with you?"

"No. There's something I wanted to show you. This room is magically sealed so the things in here aren't affected by age. Ineth and I might be the longest-lived of the people here, but even with magical aid some things don't last forever."

He sighed. *This was all a wild goose chase.*

He wanted to get out of there as fast as he could. However, he still didn't know where the demon had taken Kaya.

"I understand. I have some things in my permanent quarters protected the same way. If they haven't been destroyed. The demon killed all the Vyrks in the mountain. I feel their absence like a hole in my soul."

She nodded and led him over to a small framed portrait.

Valik stared at the painting. It was old and faded, but the figures remained clear.

"How did you get this?" he whispered. He reached for it, but then pulled his hand back.

"I used to live on top of a mountain where my father would take me to study the stars with him before I was sent away to study. My mother was happy during those times. Other times, when it was colder, we'd go underground toward the heart of the mountain, where it was warmer, to be closer to the order. My father used to tell me stories about ancient magic and great beasts that lived in the forest. I adored him."

Valik sank down in a chair and looked between the picture and the woman standing before him. Her profile was very much like his deceased wife's. "It's impossible."

"No. Ineth and I were monitoring the spell together. The lines lit up and the power hit us. He stopped aging. I grew up—and then stopped aging too. When we realized what had happened, I went back to the mountain. I felt the darkness of the Vyrkola. They were hungry. I found the painting, and I looked for you. I sensed you had become one of them. I read the past and saw what you had done to Mother. You used to call me Bem, but I chose another name over the years. Cyn."

He recalled the day with clarity. Valik had found his wife—and his hunger overtook him. Tears filled his eyes and his heart expanded. "All these years, I never knew what happened to you."

He stared at the woman before him. The years spread between them and he didn't know if he could ever find the words to tell her what he felt. "How can you be my daughter?" He looked at her with disbelief. "Why hide away all this time?"

Cyn sat across from him on the bed. "This place keeps the demon at bay. The silver within the ground and walls is something it abhors. When I retrieved the portrait, I didn't share my body with the demon that inhabits me now. That came later.

"We wanted to study the demons to see what had happened to us. Ineth warned me against it, but I was too stubborn. He made a journey into the mountain and found the others of the order there. He told them what had happened to him, and they told him what had happened to them. They never mentioned you. They had taken control of their hunger and had a hierarchy set up by then. They gave us some of their ancient texts about summoning the old gods. They were mostly fairy tales at that point.

"I drew my own conclusions from the books and figured out how to summon one of the shadowed gods. An exchange was made. Knowledge of everything about them as long as it got to share my body. I jumped at the chance. I didn't realize what I was getting into, but neither did it. The demon was confined by all the silver in the area and it hates that. Plus, there's the silver in my blood. It gets harder to deal with at times."

"I am glad to see that you're well, considering the demon that's bound within you." Valik shook his head.

Cyn reached forward and laid her hand on his. Her flesh was warm. When he glanced at her in the low light, she resembled his wife.

"I am well. The distance of years has turned us into different beings. My childhood is a long past memory I can't even recall at times, but I have the portrait...so I can remember her face. Yours, too. It was a surprise when I felt you enter the forest. You might have sired me, but I don't think I'm your daughter any more than you're my father at this point. The person you remember was a child running around in short dresses and braids."

"You're right, but to see you—it brings back many feelings."

"I know, but you can't dwell on these feelings because you came here for answers on how to defeat the demon. If you succeed, it'll pull this thing out of me as well. I'll be glad to have it gone. Besides, you love the princess. Anyone could've seen it when you went to your knees before the whole order. That's the reason I told them to give you their blood. If you had not been truthful in this, then I would've had them take your head right then." Cyn's eyes grew cold. She *was* the leader here now, and what she said was law.

He understood that.

"I appreciate you sparing me. And yes, I do love Kaya. She showed me what it was like to have a heart once more. She enabled me to open up and see something else besides darkness. I can't kill her. I'd rip my heart out before I did any harm to her. I tried, but I couldn't. I have to save her, but I don't know where the demon spirited her away to."

Cyn withdrew her hand. "I'll have that answer for you in the morning. It means I must talk to the demon within me. Come. I'll show you to your own chamber for the night."

She led him out of the room and down the hall to a second room. Once he entered the guest room, the spells closed in around him. He might be a visitor in their space, but that didn't mean he wasn't closely watched.

"Thank you."

"Do you require more blood?" Cyn asked.

Valik took a moment and examined his hunger. It wasn't out of control the way it had been before. The magic and the amount of blood in the goblet had satiated that side of his nature.

"Not blood. Regular food." His stomach growled.

"You eat? The others don't."

"After sealing the node, I crave real food and water—at times more than I do blood. Something happened to me when I helped Kaya. I'm still adjusting to it."

Cyn placed a hand over his heart and closed her eyes.

She smiled. "Your heart beats. You never truly died and became one of them. I don't know why. You retained your ability to do magic and that's what made you different from all the others. I can see your soul. I've seen it in other Vyrkola. They do have them, but yours is not shrouded in the same darkness as most.

"It's almost like an eclipse. Dark and light with silver running through it. The darkness chokes off the magic in those who are turned. The illumination which allows us to do magic was gifted to us from the gods of light. I suspect if I were to see this princess, she'd have the same kind of effect as you, but more natural. You're still aligning. Sleep for tonight. I'll have food brought up to you. Ineth will come and get you when I have an answer for you."

Valik took her hand and brushed his lips across the back of it. She smiled. For a moment he saw his wife.

For another instant, he saw his little girl in Cyn's eyes. Her expression lightened.

She broke away from him. The door closed behind her and he was left staring at four walls with tapestries attached to them. Each wall hanging bore a different scene. He studied the scenes, and they seemed to be moving. He touched one and a spark of energy raced along his palm. Valik pulled his hand away and knew what Cyn had said was true. He couldn't think about the past and what could have been. She might have been his daughter once upon a time, but this woman was now a stranger.

Kaya was the most important thing to him. Staying cooped up here was not something he wanted, but it was the only way he could get the answers he needed. He would have them soon. He had to be patient. All the while, he knew Kaya was being tortured—but the demon wouldn't kill her.

He picked up the spell Cyn had translated and looked it over once more. It called for him to open himself up to the god. The name was one he remembered from long ago, but never put much stock in. He was an ancient god even when Valik was human.

If he was going to summon this being and let it into himself, he had to be prepared for the worst. Giving the blood and the permission was nothing. It was the ability to give himself over to it completely.

Whatever I have to do to save her.

Someone knocked on the door.

He opened it and found a servant with a tray of food. The stench of her fear turned his stomach a bit. She flashed him a troubled smile, handed him the tray, and rushed out of the room. He looked at the tray and saw two goblets—one of water and the other filled with blood. Valik grabbed the blood first but set it down again. He didn't need it. Instead, he drank the water as though he was a man who'd been lost in a desert. It tasted better than anything he'd ever had before. So did the food as he tore into the meat.

When he was done, he was full, but he wanted more. Instead, he lay on the bed and stretched out his senses to try again to find Kaya, but still there was nothing. Frustration built within him. He wasn't going to find her.

Instead, he focused on what he needed to know and as he did, he felt sleep overtake him.

———

Another knock on the door woke him sometime later. His sleep had been dreamless, which was one thing he was thankful for. He was ready to leave the room. They were keeping him prisoner—albeit in a comfortable cell.

Ineth stood on the other side with a grave look on his face.

"Cyn's in a trance and I can't get her out of it. I figured you might be the reason for it. Come."

Valik followed Ineth into another larger room reinforced with silver beams that ran along the ceiling and across the walls, creating some kind of cage. Cyn sat in the center of the room, where more lines of silver created a design underneath her.

"Why all the silver?"

The heat radiating from the silver made Valik wince.

"It's to contain the demon. This is where she comes when she wants to talk to it. We had this room built especially for her. Others have found it enhances magic-working as well. It focuses the power of the node that runs through the forest."

Valik understood why the room was so powerful.

Cyn sat cross-legged on the floor. Her eyes were closed. Dark veins lined her face, but they hadn't taken it over. It seemed as though she was in a state somewhere between herself and the demon. He touched her shoulder, but she didn't move. Valik sat down across from her.

Her eyes opened and her mouth turned up in a sneer. "Father," it was her voice and the demon's garbled together.

"You might be of my flesh, but I am not the one who raised you. We had this discussion last night."

"Ahh, but you're the father of an entire race. If it wasn't for you, then the Vyrkola wouldn't exist. My brother never would've gotten free. I would never have been freed. I like it here."

"You don't belong here. You need to bring Cyn back."

"She's already here. We've been talking. You want something from me. I know the location you're looking for. I know where the portal is, and where my brother has taken the one you love."

His fingers twitched. The demon was goading him. "Cyn, I need you to come back. I need you to take control."

Her fingers pressed into her palms. Some of the dark veins receded. Her eyes normalized. "It's hard to push it back sometimes. It was showing me the things you wanted to know." She reached into the folds of her robe, pulled out a map, and handed it to him.

It was a detailed drawing showing where they now were in the Silver Forest. The mountains were to the southwest. To the west was the land of the Thralls, and another extension of the Silver Forest winding into their territory and down to the other side of the kingdom. In the center of the forest the well was marked on the map, surrounded by other settlements. This was where he had to go.

"Thank you, Cyn."

"There's something you must know before you go. The demon is expecting you."

"I already knew that."

"No. He is expecting *you*." Her eyes narrowed, and Valik understood what she meant.

Cyn rose from her seat in the center of the room. As she did, her flesh returned to normal. She squeezed his shoulder. "It was good to see you. I don't know the consequences of what will happen. If you succeed in this, you'll save the woman you love."

"Cyn, we can't leave him here to perform the spell by himself," Ineth stammered.

"That's what we're going to do."

"It could mean the end of you," Ineth said to Valik.

"Then it's the end of me—or the end of all of this."

"The order has kept an eye on the darkness and the demons. We have to stay our course and if this is the way that happens, then so be it," Cyn said to Ineth.

She took Valik's face between her hands and brushed her lips across his. "Good luck, Father. May the gods watch over you."

Cyn and Ineth left the room and closed the door.

Valik took out the spell and stared at it. *Kaya, I love you.*

He stepped into the silver circle. The candles sputtered. He put the map safely inside his pocket.

Valik plunged his fangs into his own wrist. Blood dribbled onto the floor. It sizzled once it hit the silver and left scorch marks on the veins. The energy of the circle flared to life, locking him into place. He would have to complete the spell to get out. He closed his eyes and thought of Kaya. He would do anything to save her. The image he recalled was of him and Kaya holding their child. The feeling hitched in his throat. He needed to hold onto that picture.

Valik held the emotion and vision in his mind and read the spell.

"Leukos, god of light and brightest day I invoke you. Pull the darkness away and burn the shadows. By ancient bond and words to send evil back to its pit, I call you. By blood, I summon you. Shine upon this place and grace me with your presence."

A few of the candles flickered. He let out his pent-up breath and waited.

"Well that was a disappointment."

A dot of brightness appeared before him. It slowly grew until it was the size of a shield. The heat coming from it was cold and hot at the same time. As he stared into the center of it, he saw nothing but white.

"Who summons me?" The voice was an echo of someone calling to him over a long distance.

"I am called Valik."

"Why do you wake me from my slumbers?"

"You, or others of your kind—the old light gods—once helped the people here to put the shadowed gods back in their place and seal their portal. One of the dark gods has broken out and wishes to free his brethren. The people need your help. I need your help."

The brightness of the light dimmed for a few seconds.

Valik lowered his head. He could feel the god retreating. His hope went with it. Without the god, there was nothing. "Please," he whispered. "I don't call upon you for myself. I ask for your help because the demon has the woman I love. If you know anything of love, I beg you for her. I fear it is inhabiting her, using her as the key to unlock the gateway and free the others. If that happens, chaos will descend upon this land. You made a promise once to help drive the dark ones back if they ever got out again."

The light grew into the shape of person. "I know of love and of the promise. What kind of being are you? I sense the same darkness within you as in the shadowed ones."

"I was once a man, a *varaz*, and I became a creature—a mixture of man and demon—because I was trying to stop a shadow god. Many eons ago I was part of the order you formed to monitor the dark ones. I failed. Now the princess I love has been corrupted by that demon. You are the last hope we have."

The figure walked toward him and touched his forehead.

Valik screamed as it burned. He could feel the fire cut through his being, down to his nerves and his blood. He looked into the brightness and saw the face of the god. It was an outline with white eyes and locks of hair surrounding its face. Images of his life flowed out of him as though the god had plucked them from his mind. Valik didn't fight it. The power locked inside the god behind the brightness was more than he could fathom.

The silver lines in the floor ignited. Candles exploded.

Someone pounded on the door.

"To help you, I need a way into your realm. I can't exist outside of this circle. Many years have passed, and my foothold in this world is shaky. Most no longer believe in us. I need a vessel."

"Whatever you need."

"I need your body. To share my essence with yours. I can't say what will happen."

"I don't care. Kaya is the most important thing now. She's an innocent in this whole thing."

"From your memories, she's not an innocent. She's the key to unlocking the doorway. I didn't realize the dark ones were even capable of thinking so far ahead. They've learned much in the darkness. Your love for her is bright. It fights against the darkness I see within you."

"What do I need to do?"

Pain sliced down his arms. The sun god hovered over him. Valik saw his blood flowing over the floor and being absorbed by the silver and burning away the taint of darkness inside of him. Brightness engulfed his being.

The agony was bittersweet.

Valik embraced it, knowing that all he had done had led him to this moment. He felt the god enter his flesh. His last coherent thought was of Kaya.

CHAPTER TWENTY-FIVE

K aya lifted her head from the demon's constant barrage. It had been fighting with her for entrance into the mental dungeon it had locked her in. She didn't know how long she had been battling with the thing. It felt as though her head was going to split. Her body needed something. She could feel the urge for either blood or food. It didn't matter which it was...the demon was using up all of her strength—or she was by fighting it.

"Leave me alone. Get out of my body."

Kaya had to find a way to get him out of her body. Something within her was stronger than he was. He had invaded her body without her permission. She had a soul. It didn't.

"You're mine, little princess. I'll break into your room soon enough and find out what you don't want me to see. You and Valik won't defeat me. No one is alive anymore who knows what I truly am. You call me demon, but I'm something a lot more powerful than that." It peered into the window of the cell door.

"You're a god, from the beginning of this world, and you were driven out of it by the order."

"You know a bit about me but that doesn't mean you know everything."

She backed away from the door and settled on the floor. Kaya thought about her soul, and the power it brought to her. She could do magic because she was alive. She had closed the node of wild magic—with some help, yes—but that power was now all around her. She had to find a way to reconnect with her body and her spirit. The demon rattled the cage of her cell door again. Kaya covered her ears against its railing. She focused inward. Something the demon couldn't shut her off from.

It took a moment, but she felt the warmth fill her. She imagined sitting in front of the node and feeling the power of it flowing through her. It filled her body, and then it concentrated between her hands. When she opened her eyes, a bright ball of light balanced between her fingertips.

"What have you got there?" the demon crooned.

The floor shook underneath her. The quaking grew until the door rattled. The demon backed away from the window. She took that as a good sign. Kaya stood and stepped closer. The demon retreated further. The look in its eye was fear.

She dipped her hand into the middle of the sphere. A small piece of it broke off and she threw it at the demon. The magic caught it in the face. The demon clawed at its flesh. The door liquefied. The room around her began to crack. Small bits of light came through the fissures in the stone. She took another glob of the fire and threw it again. It hit the demon in the chest.

The walls around her burst apart entirely.

The demon's guise melted, and revealed nothing more than a dark, gaping shadow in the shape of a person. Its influence fell away.

It screamed.

Kaya released the globe until it encompassed the room and her. Heat washed over her, and she could feel the darkness within her fading away. The room shook around her until it shattered like glass.

The next time Kaya could see, she found herself encircled by woods. Her hands were bound. She tried to move them, but the binding was tight. It was dark and the feeling she got from her surroundings was gritty and evil. A screech from an owl, or something larger, sounded above her. The trees were blackened as though they had been burnt, but she could sense the life in them. They fed off of the evil fueling the land.

Before her was a large pool, clear as glass, but it didn't reflect anything. Instead, it gave off an eerie glow. Kaya looked around but didn't see the demon anywhere. She tried to access her magic but couldn't feel it inside of her. Something glimmered on the surface of the pond. Faces pressed up against the surface. They were a mixture of human and demonic. They pushed closer and closer trying to escape.

This is the portal I'm supposed to open.

This was what the demon wanted from her all along. It wanted to get her alone. Now it had her and no one knew where she was. Her thoughts turned to Stavros and Valik—the men she loved.

The demon had Stavros somewhere. Or at least that was what it wanted her to believe. She didn't know where Valik was. *I know he's searching for me. I should've listened to Thesia's warning about staying on the ground. It wanted me off the mountain away from the silver so it could grab me. And stupid me, the first thing I did was shift off the land.*

She closed her eyes and let her head drop back against a tree trunk. *I can't let that hinder me. I have to figure a way to get out of this. I won't let it free the rest of the demons. Valik will find me.*

She thought about the men she shared a bond with. As she opened her mind, she was hit with the brightest light she had ever seen. It burned to look at it. It shoved her back into herself. The after-burn left a ghost of heat along her body.

Kaya still couldn't sense Valik. Kaya gathered herself and reached along the bond she had forged with Stavros and felt it thrumming like a beating heart. His vibrancy throbbed against hers. He was alive. That gave her hope.

"Kaya?"

It sounded like Stavros, but she wasn't sure because of the demon. It could be playing another trick on her. Kaya examined the link between them and felt sure it was the king. His heartbeat was familiar. She could smell his scent, and his heartbeat calmed her.

"Are you all right?"

"For now."

"Where are you? The demon showed me you were bound on a cliff."

"I don't know where I am. It's dark. There's a faint light below me, but I can't get to it. I'm on some kind of ledge. It's hot. Thirsty. What about you? Have you succeeded? Is there a way to defeat the demon?"

She wanted to believe it was him. No. He's real. I know it's him. She sent a thought along the connection. "Valik and I were separated. The demon captured me. I don't know where I am either. I don't know where he is, but I know he's coming. Whatever happens, I love you, Stavros."

"We'll succeed. I know we wi—"

"Stavros!" Kaya called out to him, but their tie was severed. "No. No."

"Did you think it'd be that easy? I have to admit I underestimated your strength and your ability to form a bond with the human. I figured you would've punished him for all he did to you."

"That was all a misunderstanding. Once he realized who and what I was—"

"Tell that to yourself all you want—but he wanted you dead. The whole court saw it."

"How do you know that?" Kaya asked.

The demon's voice came from all around her, but it had a different tone to it. "Because the darkness has ears and helpers. Isn't that right, Petra?"

The king's sister stepped out of the darkness. Silver light emanated around her. Her aura was darker than it had been before. This was not the same woman Kaya had met at the castle.

"Why are you working with the demon?"

Petra smiled, showing the dark fangs that glistened in her mouth. "Isn't it obvious? It's given me everything I was promised. It's been a wondrous partnership. Some things didn't go as planned. I never figured my brother would fall in love with you. It all worked out in the end though. When this is over, all the blame will fall on you and what's left of your kind. Then I can rule it all."

Kaya tried to fit all the pieces together. She remembered Serena's warning about finding the one who killed her. "This was all about you being queen? But you ruled with Stavros. Why get him out of the way?"

Petra looked at her long talons in the moonlight. "You really should learn the laws and traditions of the people you're marrying into. I've learned many of *your* customs. Of course, that was to win the trust of my lover. He told me all about Queen Mila's big secret. I know Stavros told you there is an ancient law there must always be a queen to rule alongside the king. After Serena died, I was happy to take the throne."

"You didn't want to co-rule?"

"My dear departed sister-in-law was too good for my brother. She wanted peace. I had other ideas. Your land is rich with silver. Our kingdom is small. Kewskin had the idea of expanding. It was easy to twist him around my finger and use him to get in contact with the voice I'd been hearing since I was a child."

The demon stepped out of shadows. It had lost Kewskin's appearance and was now simply a dark twisted mass that grew and shimmered in the night. The evil and power coming off of it made her shiver. It slid its arm around Petra's waist and nuzzled her neck. It looked at Kaya with golden eyes that burned like coals.

Kaya could see the slit of its mouth, and its dark fangs —like the ones it sunk into Petra's throat. Petra's head fell back in ecstasy as the demon drew strength from her.

"Even as you want to kill our kind, you're seeking to become just like us," Kaya sneered.

"Oh no. I'm not going to be anything like you. I'm not going to be some base creature whose only desire is to feed like the last failed experiment the old ones tried."

"She's the perfection we've been looking for. I thought you might be it, but I can see you want nothing to do with me. Although, I might use you for breeding stock. That would make an interesting offspring. Part god, immune to silver and light—assuming they take after you," the demon purred.

The thought of having sex with that thing turned her stomach. "That's never going to happen."

"A lot of things are going to happen whether you want them to or not. You're ours. Once the gateway is opened, then you'll feel the wrath of the darkness envelope you. You'll crave it."

Kaya tried to access her magic, but when she studied the chains binding her hands, she realized they were the same silver ones Stavros had used to keep her magic controlled. Her heart sank. This was the spot she had never wanted to be in, but she didn't know how to get out of it.

"I think she sees the gravity of her situation, beloved. What do you think?" Petra asked the demon.

The demon walked away from the queen. "All of this talking has made me hungry. What about you?"

"I could use something to warm me up."

The demon muttered and Stavros appeared in the clearing across from Kaya, bound to a tree. He looked at her and then back at the demon. The surprise in his eyes when he saw his sister hurt Kaya even more.

"Petra, what are you doing here?" Stavros asked. "Did the demon capture you, too? The last time I saw you was at the wedding feast when Kewskin was wreaking havoc. I thought you were dead. I saw the chandelier fall on you. What happened?" Stavros struggled against his bonds.

Petra rushed over to Stavros and hugged him. "Brother forgive me. Forgive me."

"Stavros, no. Don't believe anything she says. She—" Kaya's mouth was covered in darkness and her words were cut off.

"Don't get ahead of yourself," the demon purred in her ear.

Kaya tried to bite down on the demon's hand, but her teeth sank through the shadow. The demon had her right where it wanted her. Its other hand slid over her body, and it kissed the side of her neck. She tried to tear herself away from it.

"Hush now. We're going to watch the show." It turned its attention to Petra. "Dearest, don't you think it'd be a good idea to keep your brother around for a little while? At least until we know the portal is open. The others will need living hosts."

Petra pouted. "I was hoping to take him and make him my slave. I could use him as a footstool."

The demon slithered away from Kaya, but the covering over her mouth remained.

"Do whatever you want to me, demon. Y-you won't get away with this," Stavros stammered.

"I already have. I have a better idea as to what to do with you, Your Majesty." It touched Petra's cheek. "Don't worry. You'll get him as your footstool, and the others will have him when the time comes—but for right now, we need to be sure he's with us."

The demon ripped into the king's flesh.

Stavros stared at Kaya. She saw the terror in his eyes.

"Stavros!" Kaya cried out to him, but no sound escaped her gag.

The demon giggled and looked at her as Stavros went limp.

His eyes, usually so vibrant with life, faded until they were filled with the darkness of the demon.

"Kaya!" he screamed, and then she felt the demon's evil taint engulf him entirely.

She felt a surge of something greater inside of her. All of her emotions flared together at once. Kaya rode the power, and the next thing she knew, she was free of her bonds. She spat out crystallized bits of darkness. When she looked at her hands, they were covered in a silver glow.

Stavros screamed again, so she didn't have time to marvel at what had just happened.

"I thought nothing could break out of those cuffs. They were supposed to cut off her magic," the demon growled.

"They should have. They did before. I don't under-stand it," Petra stammered as she glanced between Kaya and the demon.

Kaya smelled the scorched earth where the silver cuffs had hit the ground.

Something had changed in her.

Kaya thought about the ball of energy she had let loose in her mind, but she felt weak now she was free. Maybe she had used all of her energy. No matter what, she couldn't let the demon open the portal. Kaya gazed about for a way to escape, but she couldn't leave Stavros.

Stavros looked at her with dark eyes that didn't recognize her. He had become the thing the demon wanted, and there was nothing she could do to break him out of it.

"He's mine. Just like you're mine. No one is coming for you," the demon crooned.

"Valik will find me," Kaya told them.

She moved to rush past the demon, but it grabbed her. Kaya tried to fight it, but she felt weak. The entity thrust her at Petra. She grabbed Kaya's shoulders and held her with a strength she didn't have before. Kaya struggled again to get away but couldn't get free of her grasp.

The demon trailed its fingers down Kaya's face. "I think it's time. My brothers have waited so long, and they sense you are here. Don't you feel it?"

Stavros walked around her like a soulless wretch. The demon handed him a gold dagger it produced from nowhere.

Petra forced Kaya to her knees.

"You're the one I've waited for. When Eloise shared her soul with me, I could feel the magic that would make you. Petra's been calling out to me for a long time. No one could enter my prison, but sometimes things got out. Just like the little voice your father heard and so many other things. You should know, because I pulled you into the ruins."

"Enough pontificating. You've taken everything from me. You've killed my family. Taken away the men I love. Isn't that enough?"

"Darkness will spread across the land and those who are worthy will be given a new life. You don't now know how wondrous it will be."

Kaya glanced at the pool. Hands and arms pushed against the barrier. Dread filled her as the events of her life flashed before her. She thought of Valik. The feel of his arms around her, and how he made her feel. She had yearned to feel that intimacy with Stavros as well. All of the things she had learned over the last couple of months, coupled with the revelations of the last few days filled her mind.

"Did you really think I had to kill you to free the other gods? All that's needed is a few drops of your blood." The demon grabbed her and extended her hands over the barrier.

One of the creature's arms stretched out to brush her wrist.

She fought against it. It seemed all of Kaya's will was being leeched away.

Stavros watched and swayed.

The demon drew the blade along Kaya's wrist. A drop of her blood hit the demon's hand. It hissed and stepped back from her. She could smell its burnt flesh. The blood dripping from her wound fell toward the surface of the well. Before it hit the water, a bright light appeared over the portal. It started off as a mere pinpoint but grew brighter and brighter as if a star were exploding in slow motion.

The pressure on her shoulders eased. Kaya pressed her wrist to her chest to stop the bleeding. Within the center of the light, she saw a form. She recognized the form, but not the energy that came from it.

"Run, Kaya."

The words that came out of the center of the star were Valik's, even if it didn't feel like him. Kaya wasn't going to argue.

She tried to rush past Petra and the demon. Stavros grabbed her. He wrestled her with superhuman strength. Kaya elbowed him in the stomach, and he released her. She dashed away from the portal, but despite the brilliant light, she could see it was already too late.

CHAPTER TWENTY-SIX

Valik felt as though he were floating. The presence of the god sharing his body made him feel intoxicated. Its strength was beyond anything he had ever felt. It was as though he could see the entire universe, and feel the power of the stars, pressed inside of his body. The longer the god remained within him, the more it felt like he was burning out. He wasn't sure how long he was going to last, but he had to save Kaya. His love for her and the long-standing oath he had sworn so many years ago gave him the will to endure.

When they stepped between the worlds, he found himself staring into the edges of the twilight realm, with shimmering shades traversing into that other reality. He had never thought he would see it while he was alive. He had only felt it during his time on earth—in some of the haunted spaces where the rips between worlds were. Everything there was gray, with a silver tint to it. As it all began to make sense, they moved through the world and became something else.

His mind meshed with the god's, but if he focused too long on it, he would lose himself to the magnificence of the experience. He forced himself to think of Kaya. That was when he saw her standing in front of him. The demon had her. A dagger slid along her arm as the monster spilled her blood.

He tried to call out to her, but nothing came from his lips. He could see the scene but wasn't able to do anything about it.

"Patience," said the god in his thoughts. *"We are not yet in their world. It is harder to break through here because it is the seat of the shadowed one's power. It has been many years since I've walked on this plane and most do not know my name. You must let me mend that matter, so the people will understand what has become of the old gods."*

"Fine, but we have to stop them first," Valik answered.

"I will keep my part of the bargain and make sure my dark brothers are not freed. I will force them back into their darkness."

At that moment, Valik was able to feel Kaya. She screamed. Her distress was a beacon in his mind. It took all his strength, but he whispered to her, *"Run, Kaya."*

She tried to, but Stavros brought her back over to the portal and squeezed her wrist over the surface of the gateway. Valik smelled the blood as it fell through the air and landed on the portal. Screams erupted around him. A hole grew in the center as shadowy forms pushed through the opening. The demon and Petra scattered into the darkness to get away from him.

Once his feet landed on the ground, Valik felt the evil of the place. It smelled like death. He heard a rustling in the bushes and drew his sword. Flames flared from his fingers and stretched along the blade. The flame grew over the blade.

Petra rushed at him, but her features were a mixture of the demon and her own. Whatever had been left of the woman was now devoured and replaced by something else. He swung his weapon at her. The blade connected with her neck and severed her head. As he swung his weapon, small bits of flames dropped from it and crept along the forest floor. One of them glided across the surface of the pond. Petra's body burst into small pieces. Her head landed on the surface of the portal and rolled across it until it was consumed by the fire.

The glow around his body lit up the darkness of the forest. Shadows slunk away from the sun god's light. Valik didn't see Kaya, but the god was focused on the demon.

"Come out, Golge. I would know your handiwork anywhere," Valik said, but it wasn't his voice that came out.

"Leukos, did you really think I was going to stay in the dark forever? I thought you had turned your back on this world. The last thing you said to me was something about the humans not deserving to dwell in your greatness. Now it's my turn for greatness."

Valik ran his fingers along the flaming blade, but he didn't feel the heat. He gathered a ball of the fire and threw it at the demon. Golge dodged it easily. The demon collected a dark glob of shadow from the nearest tree and lobbed it at Valik.

The flames about him increased and the dark globule drifted to the ground as a blue flame.

"You were never meant to rule this world. Neither was I or my other brothers and sisters. I left this world behind with a promise to come back if you ever broke out."

"They need to be enlightened. They've had their chance. After the last time, I had to plan for the long term. See what I created. A whole race with my blood flowing through their veins and then the ultimate creation who could open the portal and still be my bride."

The demon's words raced through him. The anger built and Valik shoved the god aside. "She will never be your bride." The words spilled from him as the god took over once more.

The demon chuckled. "You have a feisty one. I'm surprised you lowered yourself to share the body of one of my children. My very first to be created in this new form. A combination of magic and me."

"*Let me deal with him,*" the god counseled Valik. "*Taking control of your body only makes it harder for me to orient. He is drawing this out so he can have more time to let the doorway open wider. Only a few drops of blood were spilled into the portal to open it. The others need to draw power from this side. Don't let him take any more time we already don't have.*"

Valik didn't answer the god, but he knew he was right.

"Enough of this, Golge. You could talk the ear off a sow. This is over now. You and the others are never coming back to this plane again."

Valik felt his body expand as the sun god settled completely into him. He was pushed into the back of his mind and became a spectator. The demon grew in size until it seemed they both stood ten feet tall and their heads brushed the tops of the foliage. He heard the blistering and the hissing of the branches as though the trees were alive.

He swung his sword at the demon.

It ducked.

The weapon hit the trunk of one of the trees. Black leaves rained down around them. Where they touched the aura of the sun god, they ignited into flame and lit up the darkness like quick paper that flashed around. The tree bled purple sap. Flames crawled up its trunk.

The demon swiped at him with its long talons. Valik felt the graze of them on his forearm and the sting of the darkness trying to take hold in his flesh. Fire seared it away from his body.

Kaya screamed. He needed to get to her.

The demon's claws dug into his stomach until he could feel the coldness of the evil spreading through him. He doubled over in pain as he felt the corruption within him. He grunted, but the heat of the god burned it away again.

"You won't be able to take over this host, Golge. Give in to the inevitable—that you'll be driven back into the pit."

"You're not strong enough to send me back, Leukos. You fight to remain in a body that is saturated with my darkness. Even you can't burn out the very nature of his soul."

"*He's right. I can burn away whatever new evil he pollutes your body with, but you have been changed down to the level of your spirit. For me to truly take over and be at full strength, you have to exit this vessel.*"

Valik knew it was the only way.

He wished he could hold Kaya one last time, but he would do whatever it took to defeat the demons. The time to pay the full price for his actions of so long ago had finally come due. He bowed his head.

"Do what you must do. I will go willingly. But—"

He felt a hand slip into his. When he looked up, Kaya was standing beside him.

"You're not alone," she said. "We can do it together."

He wanted to answer her.

"She is the one you wished to save?" the god asked him.

"Yes."

"She is a blend of darkness and pure magic. The two are in perfect harmony. She is the key that opened the portal. Why would she wish to send the demon back when he constructed her?"

"Because she's not in league with him and never has been. Look at her and tell me what you see. You say you see the darkness in my soul, but she is free of it," Valik told him.

Power moved from him and over to Kaya.

She cringed, but he didn't see any expression on her face except the hardness that had come from her own fight with the demon. She had aged in the months since this whole journey had begun when he first saw her in the castle being tortured. She was all the more beautiful battle-hardened, and his heart swelled with the knowledge she would come through this all stronger.

"There is no darkness within her, even though I can see it and feel it in her magic. An odd combination. We will work with her."

"She knows I am not me."

"Yes."

The god focused his attention back to Kaya and the demon. He smiled at Kaya, and Valik was there in the gesture. "Yes." He squeezed her hand. "Together."

The demon backed away and his form shrank.

Valik waved his hand and cast out a flaming rope that wrapped around the demon. It screamed and shrunk further, back down to normal size. Kaya let her magic flow through them both. It seemed they breathed together.

The demon shrieked under their combined magic.

Valik was able to lend his power as well and let it fill the sun god.

Golge struggled to get away.

"You won't get away with this," it bellowed.

"Can you hold the rope?" Valik asked Kaya.

She nodded as her face knotted in concentration.

He grabbed the demon around the neck and plunged his fist into the demon's mouth.

It thrashed harder.

Light flowed into the darkness as the god destroyed the creature so that none of it could escape and be reborn. The light grew so bright Valik had to look away, but he knew the god kept burning the demon until there was nothing left.

Valik turned to Kaya and found her leaning against a tree, trying to catch her breath.

"Are you strong enough to continue with the closing of the portal?"

She nodded. "Yes."

"I will need all your remaining strength for this. You

are the key to opening and closing it. You are the channel I will send my power along so it will scorch the doorway from this plane once and for all. Come. Too many have escaped."

He took Kaya's hand and they faced the gateway.

"Close your eyes and open your mind. Forgive me for this." He drew his finger over Kaya's wrist and reopened the wound so the blood once more flowed and hit the pond.

The surface glowed red.

Valik lent his magic to Kaya, and the god's power moved over them both. He could feel that power radiating between all of them. The faces and arms within the threshold melted away until only scorched earth remained.

"The corruption has sunk into the soil. The roots of the trees have been feeding on the evil for years. This entire forest has to be purged," the god told Kaya.

"I'm not sure I have enough magic for that," she whispered.

"You do not, but I do. Although, not while I share this body."

Her expression fell and Valik could feel the sorrow and realization in her. Kaya stared at the trees.

"Valik is with you."

"We share this vessel. He called me forth and I came because of his love for you and the oath he swore. It reminded me of the same promise I made long ago."

"*Can I say good-bye to her?*" Valik asked.

"*Of course.*"

The god stepped into the background of their shared mind.

Valik came forward and took Kaya's hands for the last time.

CHAPTER TWENTY-SEVEN

K aya gazed into the face of the man she loved. The glow around him had dimmed, but it didn't fade away completely. All of what they faced bombarded her. She should have felt victorious for killing the demon and wiping the gate off the face of this world, but some of the demons had escaped. They had to take care of them. The forest must be purged. All of it before the demons decided to find another home in the world.

"You're not going to survive this are you?" She tried to control the rising emotions caught within her throat.

"I've run my course. I've been on this earth for many years longer than I should've been. If not for my actions, none of this would have happened. *You* never would have happened. And I love you more than you know."

Stavros groaned across the clearing. Kaya looked at him and her concern for him was there as well. She'd have to knock him out so he wouldn't try and stop her from helping Valik defeat the remaining demons.

He opened his eyes, but they were still dark with the demon's corruption.

"You deserve to live a happy life with him. Give him the future you showed me," Valik told her.

Stavros rushed at him.

Valik caught him and wrapped his hand around the king's throat. Where his fingers touched the demon's bite wounds, smoke appeared, and Stavros screamed. He clawed at Valik's hand, but he wasn't about to get free. Flames appeared around Valik's fingers, and his eyes burned orange—but it was still Valik before her. He let the other man drop to the ground where Stavros sputtered and tried to pull in air.

"No darkness remains in him. You are what you are and there's nothing to burn out. You have many years ahead of you. I wish I could've spent them with you." Valik trailed his fingers down her face.

The soft caress of his fingers was not the farewell she wanted.

A tear slipped down her cheek.

Valik's lips curled into a sad smile.

"Valik," she whispered brokenly.

He brushed his lips across hers. "Kaya, you showed me how to love again and I thank you for that. You helped me find my magic and gave me a life I thought I'd lost." He touched her temple. "All my knowledge, I leave to you. Books and places in the mountain you'll need going forward. A little piece of me so you always have that."

A rush of memories flooded her mind. She could feel him within her.

She wanted to say something to him, but the light of

the man she loved went out in his eyes. His features shifted slightly, and his hair went from black to silver with red highlights.

"What happened?" Kaya asked the man with Valik's face.

"He gifted you a piece of his soul, so he'll always be with you before he went into the twilight. With his memories, you'll be able to rebuild all the demon has taken from you."

"Valik." Stavros stood up. His rubbed his throat and looked over at Kaya. He drew her into his arms with a quick kiss. Kaya melted under his lips and his touch. "I thought I'd lost you, Kaya. I saw everything that was going on, but I couldn't control it. Forgive me."

"There's nothing to forgive. It wasn't you."

"What happened to Valik?"

Kaya glanced at the man she had also loved, but it was true he was gone. His energy felt different to her. The light in his eyes was too bright to look at for too long. "He's gone."

"What of the demon?"

"The dark god has been vanquished," Leukos told them. "I must cleanse the forest of the corruption that's tainted it for so long. You shouldn't be here when the purging happens."

"What about all the other Vyrkola? Are you going to destroy them too?" Kaya asked the god. "What about the dark ones that escaped the portal? We have to find them. After I let them out...."

"I will find them. It shouldn't take long. When it comes to the race born from the magic that created you, I will have to see. Some may need to be sent into the twilight realm. I will find you once again if your help is needed. Step into the light with the thought of where you wish to go, and you will be there."

A large star appeared that nearly blinded her. Stavros clung to her.

Kaya held in her mind she wanted to go to his castle to find her mother. Many unanswered questions remained about what had happened. She pulled Stavros through the light and appeared in the castle. She took one final look back as the light died and saw Valik's face for the last time in the shadows.

Servants rushed around trying to get things back in order.

"What happened?" Kaya asked Stavros.

"After you and Valik left, Kewskin massed an attack on us and the Vyrks. I know he was killed before you left the castle, but the demon resurrected him. It used him. He had a few of them under his control, but what we didn't know was that he was in league with the Thralls all this time. He let them into the castle. We drove them back. The chandelier fell on Petra."

She laid a hand on his arm. "You know she—"

He looked up and the hurt was evident in his eyes. "I know. It's obvious now she was in the thick of it all along. I saw her when the demon pulled me out of the prison where I was kept. That wasn't my sister any longer."

"I'm sorry. She admitted she had planned this for years. She wanted to be queen all along and wipe out my people. The demon had been influencing her since she was a child. She and Kewskin must have planned this together."

"Kayanna!"

Kaya turned at the sound of her mother's voice and saw the queen running towards her. Her mother had her sleeves turned up. Her face and gown were dirty. Her hair hung in a simple braid. This was not the woman she was used to seeing. As Mila caught Kaya up in her arms, she hugged her fiercely.

"I thought I'd lost you."

"I'm okay, Mother." Kaya hugged her harder, feeling that she was real underneath the heavy cloak. She realized she hadn't thought she would ever see her mother again.

Her mother pulled back and touched her hair. Tears filled her eyes. "I thought I'd lost you. I felt all those in the mountain as they died. I thought you were among them because I couldn't sense you anymore—" Mila stopped abruptly as she realized Stavros stood beside her. "Your Majesty. Forgive me, for not seeing you sooner."

"You don't owe me an apology."

"After the attack, and your disappearance, I stepped in to be sure that things didn't descend into complete chaos."

"I'm sure you've done a fine job. Please don't let the others know that I'm back yet. I need some time. I think we both do."

Her mother looked between them. "Valik?"

Kaya shook her head and tried not to let sorrow overtake her. As she thought about him, his presence and memories warmed within her mind. "He sacrificed himself to free me and purge the dark gods from this plane. The demon used me to open the gateway. Some of his brethren escaped. He, or the god inhabiting him that is, is going to hunt them down."

"I'm sorry. I know you loved him. His sacrifice won't be forgotten. You need to rest. You're both tired. I can make sure you go unnoticed. I'll have food sent up to your room, Kaya."

"I'm going to be with Kaya." Stavros looped his arm around her waist.

Her mother smiled. She knew they wanted some time to be alone.

Kaya followed Stavros through a hallway she didn't recognize, underneath a ragged tapestry, and up some stairs. They wound up to the tower where she had read Alerik's journal. They also led to the chamber where she slept. "I didn't know there was another entrance to the staircase."

Stavros sighed and looked at Kaya.

She saw a weary man, and all he had been through. He took her hand and led her over to her bed and sat down. "I know how much you loved Valik. I don't...I can't think—"

She put a hand on his lips. "Before you say anything else, Valik is here." She put her other hand over her heart. "I have a piece of him with me. I don't expect you to be him. I know our relationship started off horribly. We still have some growing to do to get to know one another, but I love you."

His weary expression brightened. "I love you too, but this marriage—I don't know if it can work. We're just too different."

A shock went through her upon hearing those words. "I'm not going anywhere, Stavros."

She brushed her lips across his.

"Exactly. You're going to live forever. You and I...I'm human. I can't be as you are."

"If you wish to grow old, then I will be by your side. Our children will rule and so on. We can rebuild. Together, we can make your kingdom, and mine, stronger. The darkness is behind us. Can't we start fresh and see what time brings?"

Stavros touched her hand. "I don't want to hurt you again. I lost my sister. My first wife and child. I can't.... I can't lose you again. To time or anything else."

"You won't. I'm not going anywhere."

CHAPTER TWENTY-EIGHT

Six months later...

The battle with the Thralls had finally come to an end. Stavros, the Vyrk, Queen Mila, and the head of the Thralls were signing a treaty. Too many lives had been lost. The leader of the Thralls admitted he had been led to believe both kingdoms were out to kill him through the influence of the demon.

Queen Mila agreed to give the Thralls access to mine anything but the silver.

Stavros agreed to give them more fertile farmlands as long as they agreed to send tribute at harvest time. The leader didn't like that, but Stavros wasn't asking for a huge chunk of the harvest.

Kaya was glad the fighting had finally stopped. She had been at the battlefronts doing whatever she could to help the men with her magic, along with the other court *varaz.* Now, with the fighting done, Kaya stood at the top of the tower and gazed out over the land.

Something nagged her. Something she had to look into....

Snow blanketed the ground from a snowfall the night before. The sun shone off the frozen white and gleamed in the gray sky.

"Aren't you cold?"

She turned to find Stavros behind her. The war had taken a toll on him. The lines around his eyes had deepened. Some silver streaked the hair at his temples, but he was as handsome as ever.

She pressed her body to his warm one. "I'm not cold now."

A devilish smile teased his lips. "I guess I'll have to find other ways to warm you up."

She kissed him lightly. "Maybe later."

He stepped back, head cocked. "Maybe later? When have you ever told me no?"

"Many times."

She stepped away from him. She slid her hand along his toned body and held back the desire she had for him.

"What is it?"

"Something I have to do. Magic is stirring in the Bone Forest. I need to go check it out. I'll be back."

"Do you think it's him?"

She knew Stavros meant the one wearing Valik's face.

"I don't know. I have to find out."

"Be careful. I can ride with you, if you wish."

"You're needed here, and I won't be taking a horse. I'll be back soon." Kaya chose from the different forms she commanded and let herself shrink. Instead of the shapes she had always used in the past, she assumed the large one —the black eagle that used to be Valik's. Another gift from him, along with his knowledge.

She took to the sky and headed toward the magic she felt beating against her skin like a beacon in the night. She flew until she came to the source of the magic--the Bone Forest where the ruins used to be. Kaya transformed back to herself. Snow had formed around the trunks of the trees, but not where the magical well was hidden under all the rubble. The shadows of the bone trees loomed over everything.

Standing above the center of the node was the god who had taken Valik's face. His hair remained the same silver with streaks of red. He opened his eyes when she approached him.

"Hello, Kaya."

"Valik." The name slipped out before she realized it. "Sorry. I know you're not him. I never got *your* name."

"I have many. Golge called me Leukos. You may call me that if you wish."

"Leukos." She tested the name on her tongue.

"Why have you come here?"

"I felt stirrings of magic that pulled me this way. I wanted to be sure the node was still closed. Can't be too careful with things in these places of power."

He nodded. "This is very true. I came here myself to recharge and study the magic of this strange forest. It reminds me very much of the one I purged of the demon, but it's different. There's no corruption here, just change.

The trees aren't dead. They were just transformed long ago."

"Yes, after Valik did the spell on the node originally and the demon jumped into the stream, it changed them."

"Now that the channel is clear, and you have righted it with your magic, the trees are thriving again. The spirits only stay in the dark parts of the wood. Some of them I have freed from their grief."

"That's good. What about the demons who escaped?"

"I have found many of them hiding in dead flesh. Lurking behind faces that aren't quite right. The hunt continues. I'm not done with my journey yet."

She nodded. "Well, now I know the source of the magic, I guess there's nothing to worry about."

"There's always something to worry about. Someone needs to guard this spot. To watch the forest to be sure nothing corrupts it again."

"Is that what you wish me to do?" Kaya asked him.

He shook his head. "No. Your destiny is not to be the watcher in the woods. You were born for something greater than that."

"It's going to be mine. At least for now." Another woman stepped out from behind one of the trees.

Kaya didn't know her, but she recognized her from Valik's memories. "You're Valik's daughter—but the demon has gone from you."

She took Kaya's hands. The power in the woman surged through Kaya. She was immortal, like herself, but there was no darkness in the stranger, just silver. It was so bright she could see it working through her very being.

"Leukos was able to purge me of the demon I have lived with for so many eons."

"I'm glad to hear it."

"I can see my father in you. Thank you for restoring him to me. Even if it was only for a little while."

Kaya walked to the center of the node and looked into the alien eyes of the man she once knew. She hoped to see Valik there, but he was absent. Leukos alone stared back at her. He laid a hand on her heart, and heat shot through her until she cried out. He gripped her hand and his eyes glowed within their sockets until they filled her vision. The moment passed, and then he released her.

"What was that for?" Kaya stepped away, out of breath.

"A bit of me you can use to rebuild your fallen kingdom. You'll need the strength in the coming months. Things lurk in the darkness of the mountain, and you will need the sun. If the job proves too much, then you can also call upon me."

"Thank you."

"You should get home now."

Kaya took to her wings again, wondering what Leukos meant about the shadows. She would have to see when the time came. She felt the warmth within her. It had made her stronger. Seeing Valik's daughter had put something at ease within her. As she circled around the castle, she saw the mountains looming in the distance. Her mother had returned home earlier in the week.

Part of Kaya longed for the darkness and silence of the deep tunnels, but her home was here now. People ignored her, or mumbled under their breath, at times. However, they all accepted her as king's consort.

She flew back into the window and took human form once again. A dress was laid out for her. It was one of the most intricate gowns she had seen. She rang a bell in the corner and in a few minutes a servant entered.

She curtsied.

"Can you help me with this dress?"

"Yes, ma'am."

Kaya undressed and the maid helped her with the ties.

"Would you like me to do your hair?" asked the servant.

"Is there a reason why I should?"

"The king's been expecting you back and wishes for you to meet him in the throne room."

Kaya sighed. Stavros had something planned.

"Please, take the time to do my hair, but just something simple that keeps it off my face."

"As you wish." The girl took the brush to her hair.

Kaya closed her eyes and let the maid wind her hair up.

When she was done, Kaya went down to the throne room.

Before she entered, the guards pounded on the floor with their staffs. The great doors opened. All talking ceased as she entered the room. She felt as she had the first time she stepped into the throne room. Once more, she was under scrutiny.

Stavros sat on his throne. Kaya looked around as she slowly walked down the chamber between the rows of courtiers. They all looked at her. Some bowed. Others whispered as she neared the throne. Kaya curtsied before the king and looked up at him. His expression was serious.

"Princess Kayanna, you have been in the court for several months, and have helped deal with the troubles of the kingdom. When you first arrived, I believed you were evil, and displayed you as though you were a piece of meat. For this I extend my apologies. Many things were done to you that were unspeakable. I want to publicly announce that the feelings I've had toward the Vyrkola no longer influence me. All Vyrks are welcome in the kingdom unless, of course, they break the law." He stood, addressing the assembled court. "Also, I intend to finally make the princess my bride."

He escorted her over to the throne. A servant presented him with a circlet of gold that he placed upon her head. Applause broke out in the hall.

"May I present to you, your new queen."

Stavros's eyes lit up with love for her. It reminded her of the day, so many months ago now, when she had first seen him in the wood and his presence intrigued her. Little did she know then how her life would become entangled around the mortal who had pulled her away from her home, and how darkness would threaten their lives.

They had come through the shadows and into the light. The darkness might linger around the edges and in places away from the sun, but Kaya knew she could handle it. Their people were bound together. Peace had settled on the land and, within her heart, she knew it would last for a while.

Stavros led her out of the throne room and to his chambers.

"Are you going to claim me for your own now, my lord?" she teased.

He kissed her with a ferocity she hadn't felt in him before. "Only if it pleases you. Because I know now, I could never pin you down and say you are mine. I've learned my lesson on that front."

"I guess chaining me up again isn't going to happen?"

He trailed his finger down her cheek. "All those months ago, if I had known then what I know now, I never would've shackled you with those magical irons. I never would've paraded you in front of the court or had you whipped like I did. Forgive me. I'll keep saying I'm sorry until I draw my last breath."

She placed a finger on his lips. "Stop saying how sorry you are. Many things were done and said between us that are best forgotten. We're together now. We have until the end of time—and even beyond that."

"I say we stop wasting time and I finally bring you to my bed properly."

"Finally? The whole court thinks you've been bedding me every night."

"Ahh, but ask any of the servants and they know that's not true. I've kept your virtue intact."

She punched him on the arm and laughed. "I lost my virtue a long time ago. We might as well give the servants something to talk about, I suppose. I can be quite loud."

Stavros grinned. "I hope you scream so loud you wake the dead, my love. It's about time someone did."

"Hush, or it might happen. Magic can be unpredictable."

Those words were first uttered so very long ago by a

man that would also always be with her. Kaya still loved Valik, and—with his memories inside her—he was there with her. He would want her to be happy.

She giggled and drew Stavros down onto the bed. They were going to be together and nothing would separate them. Time would tell what other dangers might come but, for now, she was going to enjoy the gifts she had.

The End

ABOUT CRYMSYN HART

Crymsyn Hart is the author of over eighty paranormal romance and horror novels. Her experiences as a psychic have inspired many books. Vampires, grim reapers, and other paranormal creatures tend to end up in her books no matter how hard she tries to keep them away.

She currently resides in Charlotte, NC with her hubby and her two dogs. By day she is conquering the world of Commercial Insurance, but by night she gets to listen to the voice in her head telling her which rabbit hole to go down to find the perfect plot bunny.

Find Crymsyn Hart at:

Website: http://www.crymsynhart.com /
Blog: http://crymsynhart.blogspot.com
Facebook: https://www.facebook.com/crymsynhartauthor
Twitter: @crymsynhart
Goodreads: https://www.goodreads.com/CrymsynHart
Pinterest: https://www.pinterest.com/crymsynhart/
YouTube: https://www.youtube.com/user/Crymsynrhart
Instagram: https://www.instagram.com/crymsyn_hart/